MW01129585

Saints in the City

Andie Andrews

Outskirts Press, Inc.
Denver, Colorado

Visit my Web site at www.myspace.com/AndieAndrews

Saints in the City
All Rights Reserved.
Copyright © 2009 Andie Andrews
V2.0 R3.0

Outskirts Press, Inc.
http://www.outskirtspress.com

ISBN: 978-1-4327-1104-7

Library of Congress Control Number: 2008940978

Outskirts Press and the "OP" logo are trademarks belonging to Outskirts Press, Inc.

PRINTED IN THE UNITED STATES OF AMERICA

Dedication

ಜ
To Ed, whose love gives me wings…
To Jillian, who inspires me to dream…
To Jesus, my joy and my strength…

My eternal love and devotion.

November 1, 2008

Chapter 1
Saints in the City

I had been a beggar for over seven hundred years but no one would have taken me for a day past fifty. I was grateful for the spry manner in which I could still climb the polished granite steps that led to the massive, arched red door of St. Paul's Episcopal Church, despite the searing pain that occasionally pierced my ancient heart with the same speed and stealth as the vipers lurking in the grassy meadows outside of my homeland of Assisi. The air inside Epiphany Hall where I stumbled in for the third time that week was thick with an odious blend of sweat and meatloaf, and I took notice of the day laborers who huddled over a deck of cards, waiting for their table to be called to the midday feast. I gave the darkest boy with the bright green *fútbol* shirt a casual nod and he answered me with a slow, deliberate bow of his head.

He's got the goods, I thought to myself, the uncut stuff, I prayed, that would steady my hands which were shaking out of control. I stuffed them

1

into the pocket of my jeans as Helen drew near. God Almighty, I couldn't stand for Helen to see me that way.

"Frankie, you're looking awfully pale today," Helen said, her pretty green eyes traveling the surface of my long, narrow face, lingering over the stubble that had grown like a dark field of bad luck and sorrow.

"Nothing a cup of coffee and your southern charm can't cure," I replied, sorry I'd made her worry. She was a delicate girl with long wavy hair and an innocent smile that made most of the men in the soup kitchen think of their little sisters – except for the ones who saw her as easy prey for the desires of their flesh. I knew who they were, afflicted though I was by my own demons and a disease that marred my skin with dark purple lesions that made me an outcast in this distant American city that bore no resemblance to the leafy Italian countryside where I roamed in the days of my youth.

There, I had been a young man of privilege, the son of a wealthy merchant whose silken pleasures had made me soft and dispassionate. It was I who shunned the lepers with bent backs and mottled skin whose faces were shrouded in cheap white linen. Now, I recognized that same fear and loathing in the eyes of passersby who seemed to know at a glance that I was sick with the scourge of men who love other men, men transfused with tainted blood, and men like me who had needle tracks in their arms and toes and one foot in the grave and lived in a

halfway house for dying men behind the iron gates
of St. Paul's.

Yes, I knew who they were, the ones who would
do her harm, the ones like Mickey Lightfoot whose
keen blue eyes and shock of white hair earned him
the nickname "Hawk." For the last two months, I
have watched him hover over Helen in ever shrinking circles. I have seen her sit with him and his bat-
talion of homeless Vietnam vets like a dove in a
foxhole, radiating light and hope and making herself
an easy target. I have longed to tell her there is warfare in our midst, forces of darkness that masquer-
ade as feeble, old ladies with thick, crooked glasses,
as poor young men in green *fútbol* shirts who pre-
tend not to speak or understand English and peddle
death and self-destruction, as preachers of peace
and as veterans of war who are equally beholden to
the laws of darkness. But why should she heed the
warnings of an AIDS-stricken addict like me? I
wanted to tell her that I have been sent in this condition to test the hearts of men, but I am at the service
of my Master who, in His infinite wisdom, bids me
this silence and suffering – and I must obey.

"Frankie, come along with me to the head of the
line. We'll get you that coffee and set you right.
C'mon, Frankie, give me your hand."

I reluctantly took my hand from my pocket. Her
firm grasp eased its trembling and I was aware of
Hawk's eyes upon us as we wound through a path
littered with backpacks and bedrolls.

"Thank you, Helen," I managed to say as she

left me in the capable hands of the willowy, craggy-faced kitchen manager, Dorothy, who known to me alone has seen and ministered to me and to thousands of other poor, starving souls who gave rise to the Bowery's bread lines during the Great Depression in New York City. She gave me a comforting wink and a Styrofoam cup filled with the blackest coffee I'd ever seen.

"Peace to you, Brother Francis," she whispered.

"And to you, Dorothy," I whispered back as a surge of resentment sprang from the waves of hungry men and women who had given way for me. "Dorothy," I persisted, standing my ground for the moment. "Can this child be saved?"

"God only knows," Dorothy replied with a sigh that for a split second made her strong, square shoulders surrender their habitual stiffness. She paused to wipe her hands on her dark blue apron, then stood tall and cleared her throat like a drill sergeant preparing to lash into the newest recruit.

"Go on, Frankie, move along!" she roared to my surprise and to the satisfaction of the mob behind me. "We've got one hour to feed all these saints in waiting! What'll you have, Christine? You want milk and sugar with that?"

I sat at a table reserved for the residents of Damien House and watched the line of working poor and homeless people grow longer by the minute until it spilled out the tall red door and onto the street. I had no hunger or thirst that day, just a burning desire to rendezvous with my Costa Rican friend

4

whose fine white powder would bring powerful relief for the deep, cutting pains that wracked my
body and made me cry out in the street for mercy. I
knew the end was near for me, but I could not bear
to leave my dear Helen, this child who possessed
my heart in the same way that my beloved Clare
once cleaved unto it, this beautiful soul who teetered on the cusp of light and darkness.

I observed Helen across the room, vigilantly
scanning the crowd for anyone who might need
somebody to talk to. Employed by the county mental health department, she was paid by the hour to
do just that. If she found a soup kitchen guest in
need of special attention, she made sure the caseworkers back at the office got all the information
needed to intervene on that guest's behalf. Helen
didn't have any special training, just a heart for the
poor that attracted troubled souls to her like bums to
a bottle of Southern Comfort.

She was still as earnest in the discharge of her
duties as she was her very first day on the job
when she found herself paired with Tristan Bales
– a tall, blocky, buzz-cut gay man who once had a
weakness for good red wine, roughly a bottle a
night. He was put off by the notion that the mental
health department would hire a female outreach
worker who wasn't herself in the throes of recovery. How, he argued, could she get down in the
dirt with these poor, needy people and understand
their struggle to stay clean and sober? From what
little he knew, she was a cheerful, pretty girl who

had just recently relocated with her husband to New Jersey from the genteel suburbs of Richmond, Virginia. Nobody in Jersey was getting drunk on mint juleps while watching the Kentucky Derby and Tristan – accustomed to speaking his mind – made sure to tell the director of the mental health department just that.

Helen's anxiety that first day was palpable. I was among the first to meet her as she sat beside Tristan on the wide performance stage that flanked the rear of the hall. By contrast, his broad, six-foot frame made her look even smaller than she really was and her feet dangled capriciously, like those of a child on a swing. She smiled as Tristan introduced me as the troubadour of the soup kitchen. It was the force of habit that made me sing as I walked, a lightness of being that I had known from the days I had walked ten or even twenty miles a day to share the good news of Christ's salvation with men, women and children in little villages and big cities alike throughout the regions of Umbria and beyond. Now, afflicted as I was, it brought me peace and comfort to know that I continued to be a means of salvation to those who would offer me a hot meal or a cool cup of water. It was these hymns of remembrance that made my burden light.

"Frankie, sing a song for Helen," Tristan prodded with a slight twist of his lips.

"I'd be happy to, if the lady would indulge me."

"Indulge you? Why, I'd be delighted to hear your song," Helen said in soft southern drawl that filled the air with a haunting beauty reminiscent of the call of a mourning dove at the break of dawn.

"Your voice is as lovely as any song of mine," I said. "Where are you from, Helen?"

"I grew up in Dock Watch Hollow. It's a little bitty place in southwestern Virginia, in the hill country of Appalachia. I assure you, it's nothin' at all like this fine town. But there's so much natural beauty there in the narrow hollers and laurely hills," she said, her voice growing thinner as she traveled the distance toward home. "It's an old coal town, through and through, so it's seen its share of sickness and sorrow through the years. My momma and I moved to Richmond a few years after my father died. He's been gone twelve years now."

"I'm sorry, Helen."

"Thank you, Frankie. He was a miner," she said and shrugged, expecting that alone was sufficient explanation. "But we're so far off the track we might never get back! About that song of yours...."

I opened my mouth to sing a verse from a canticle I had often sung while traversing the long valleys between Tuscany and Perugia, but my breath caught in my throat as a jab at my back sent me reeling towards Tristan's broad chest.

"Hey Frankie, aren't you gonna introduce me to your friend?"

I had known the likes of that voice forever, echoes of the one who had goaded and taunted me in my youth into acts of depravity and surrender to the desires of my flesh. But it was not my mission to protect Helen from Hawk or the legions like him that roam with the fury of the fallen. I was but a witness as to what was to be chosen, permitted or ordained – and given the sweeping eyes of God with which to see and tell the story that began that early November day.

"Tristan, baby, you holding out on me too?"

Helen was fixated on the graffiti of tattoos etched into Hawk's neck. Most were not the work of a practiced hand, but rather the rough renderings of ballpoint ink furtively jabbed into raw, taut skin in the deep, long shadows and tedium of an eight-by-twelve prison cell.

"You like what you see, honey?"

Helen stammered and began to blush.

"I got this one when I got out of San Quentin," Hawk said, pointing to a colorful portrait of a hawk with a finger encased in a stack of silver rings. "That's me. Now I guarantee you'll never forget my name."

"Your name is Bird?" Helen said with a sly smile, and I realized she was much savvier than she looked. Tristan and I laughed loudly.

"Bird!" Tristan repeated, slapping his thigh. "Mickey the Birdman, that's funny, Helen! Jesus, I didn't know you were funny," he said, smiling for the first time that day.

Hawk's piercing blue eyes crinkled at the corners as he answered with a narrow gaze and a crooked grin. "All right, all right, the name is Mickey Lightfoot. Two parts Cherokee, one part

Dago, one part Irish. That's where this comes in," he said, reaching for a tarnished silver cross that hung from a long, thick chain and dwarfed a bronze-colored star pinned to his snug black tee shirt. "But you can call me *Hawk*."

"I'd rather call you Mickey," Helen said, "It's a right friendly name."

"No one calls me Mickey but my mother. I ain't seen her since I was twelve but I figure she's still got birthrights. It's Hawk or it's nothin'."

Helen nodded and thrust forward her delicate hand. "Nice to meet you, Hawk. My name is Helen."

"Helen. Is your last name Wheels? Miss Hell-on-Wheels?" Hawk was pleased with his play on words and laughed in a surprisingly boyish way.

"Hardly," Helen replied. "I'm gentle as a lamb, I can assure you of that."

"Yeah, that's what they all say, right, Frankie? These women act all soft and shit and then…BAM! You wouldn't know nothin' about that would you, Tristan?"

"Don't start." Tristan coolly raised his hand to deflect Hawk's attack, his eyes scanning the crowd for signs of trouble as a dull clamor arose from a table near the one occupied by the residents of Damien House.

"That's my boys," Hawk said, glancing toward the assembly of men who were predominately dressed in camouflage and dew rags perched atop graying ponytails. "Nice to meet you, Miss Wheels.

9

I'll be seeing you around. You gonna be around?"

"I'll be here every Monday, Wednesday and Friday, twelve to two."

"Me too, God willing and the creek don't rise."

"Well, all right then."

Helen wondered what this brazen, silver-studded man with a fierce-looking hawk and a faded pentagram tattooed on his neck knew about God or rising creeks. That was the stuff of coal country, where she was raised on the reality of rising water that swept away homes, property, and hillfolk with equal abandon. They, too, called it God's will, though Helen didn't believe it for a minute. Those were the things that happened when God turned his back, when He grew weary of watching his children run with the wind and give in to the urges that burned holes in their souls the same way that the drudgery of walking a beaten path to the coalfields wore holes in the soles of her father's boots and worse, made him a mean drunkard who spent his last breaths looking for one more covert fondle beneath her scratchy bed sheets.

"Don't let him get to you, Helen," Tristan said, his voice turning soft with concern. "If you've got a button, you can trust Hawk to find it. It's what he does. It's who he is. Don't get sucked in."

Helen swallowed hard and nodded. "Of course, I know better than that. Heck, where I come from there's fellows ten times more messed up than Mickey Lightfoot. I can take a little needling, Tristan, I'm tougher than I look."

"I'm beginning to see that," Tristan replied, "and it's a huge relief."

"What, you think I'm one of those helpless Southern belles raised on madeleines and sweet iced tea?"

"What's a madeleine?"

"Nothing you or I will ever sit on a wide porch and savor in our lifetimes, I guess," Helen quipped, the lightness returning to her voice and the fragrance of jasmine rising from the hollow of her throat where she absently rested the palm of her left hand. A simple gold wedding band encircled her ring finger and was the only trace of attachment that she wore. Even then, it seemed a size too small, the way it pinched the flesh of her finger, but she wore it proudly, the young wife of a preacher whose mission was to lead the strategic planting of a Baptist church in the foothills of this decidedly white Protestant stronghold. Surely the poor needed something more lively and hopeful than the Catholics or the Protestant orthodoxy could offer, the elders back home had reasoned. Her husband Todd's missionary zeal and gift for preaching had proven him a worthy candidate for the job. Together, they had been blessed and sent. And yet Helen couldn't help but feel that she'd been left behind almost from the moment they had arrived.

"You know you're allowed to eat lunch here if you want to," Tristan said.

"You mean with the guests?" It might be nice to have some mealtime companionship, Helen thought, having grown tired of dining alone while her husband worked late into the night.

"Yes, sometimes it helps if you break bread with them. Makes them feel less like it's *us* and *them*. But you can't sit just anywhere, with anyone. You have to be *invited*."

"But the director told me not to get too close, to keep proper boundaries."

"You mean Stuart? Stuart has never even stepped foot in this soup kitchen."

Helen rolled her eyes, having suspected all along that Stuart Lipsky had a little too much *book larnin'* for his own good!

"Listen up, people! This is the one and only call for seconds! You don't listen, you don't get 'em!" Dorothy's voice was deep with age and yet it had a soaring quality that made every guest pick up his or her head and take notice. "I want law and order, you hear?"

Team Costa Rica, as the local immigrants were known, snapped into action, dodging obstacles and leaping over benches until they dominated the head of the line. Other guests shuffled, the sound of their donated green, blue or black nylon jogging suits rising like a chorus of cicada wings. The poorest ones continued to sit, stunned like paralytics, knowing that the call for seconds was the last saving act before the red door opened and forced them back into the vast urban wilderness. Meanwhile, Hawk and his fellow veterans muscled their way anywhere they pleased, some with a smile, others with a strong and practiced arm.

It was almost too much for Helen, I could tell, by the way her eyes darted around the room, trying to absorb the shock and the sweat and the furies in the air. She fiddled a lot with her hair, twisting it around her slender fingers which had perfect, crescent-shaped nails coated in a glossy polish.

As for me, Tristan and Helen hadn't noticed that I had retreated to my designated table in the furthest corner of the soup kitchen where I would come each day to be the ruin of many and the salvation of some. I didn't know if Helen would be among those who would rise or those who would fall; I only knew that she had the heart of a dove, wounded though it was, and that I would be there to minister to her to the end.

In the meantime, I had my own demons to defeat.

Chapter 2
Brown River Rising

"Take your umbrella and stick it, lady. You don't know squat about what it feels like to be me!"

Helen flinched and let go of the black umbrella she'd thrust toward James. The nylon strap caught her wrist and the metal spokes flared to form a deep, black well that she wished to dive into and then disappear.

"I know a body with a blind eye to God's mercy when I see one," she might have chastised a local boy back home who didn't have the sense to come in from the rain. But this, she knew, was different. I was proud of Helen, who in just two short weeks was already gaining the grace to patiently love and indulge every one of us who stood in line with a shiny red plate and set of plastic flatware in hand. She knew that even James, the most belligerent sort of human being, whose shredded tennis shoes flapped on his size-ten feet, whose fat, muddy shoe-laces dragged behind him like entrails in the street,

was to be treated as a precious guest under the roof of this cavernous hall that sheltered hundreds like him for ninety minutes, five days a week.

"You're right, James, I don't know how it feels. I'm sorry I offended you." Helen looked down at her own muddy boots, resisting the urge to kick herself.

James' bloodshot eyes narrowed at Helen's quick apology. Was this some kind of head game the newbie was playing with him?

"But if you change your mind, I'll be sitting right over there on the stage." Helen pointed. "The umbrella's yours if you want it."

James didn't answer. He turned his back and shuffled through the lane created by long strips of yellow tape, careful to close the open space that had formed before anyone jumped the line. It was the same kind of tape one would see around building sites throughout the city, but in this case, Helen thought, it marked a path of deconstruction where people were dismantled, step by step, piece by piece, until there was just a red plate and a pair of needy hands and a thin voice that said, "No peas!" to the smartly dressed churchwoman at the head of the banquet table.

It was only her sixth lunch hour spent observing the local homeless men and women who filtered in and out of the city. Some of the faces were becoming familiar, faces that stared at her with unchecked curiosity accompanied by the occasional shy smile. Other faces reminded her of the famous Edvard

Munch painting, each contorted into its own silent scream with round, anguished eyes that shouted, "I can't believe this is happening to me!"

But Helen didn't belabor the difference. The friendly, smiling ones were as likely to be plumb crazy as the overmedicated zombies who marched past her perch on the wide open stage. It didn't matter what the diagnosis would ultimately be after she linked them to a caseworker, as long as they were both homeless and mentally ill. They just couldn't be exclusively "down on their luck." That category didn't get a body anywhere.

Clearly, that's where James fell. All she could offer him was a flimsy umbrella on this particularly foul November day, an offer preceded by an innocent, *"My, we're really getting rained on today, aren't we?"*

She hoped James would change his mind. In the meantime, she had her sights set on bigger targets – like Rhonda. She hadn't liked it much when Tristan used Rhonda to set her up for failure her first week on the job, though to his credit, he had since shown slight signs of remorse.

"See that woman over there?" Tristan had pointed to a table near the window where a thin, blond woman dressed in black slumped over her plate and gripped her sandwich in two hands like a starving chipmunk.

"What about her?"

"She's been coming here almost every day for the last eight months. I've tried to reach out to her. I don't think she likes men. Go on, Helen," he smiled encouragingly. "Her name is Rhonda. See if you can make a connection with her. Hell, I couldn't."

"But what should I say?"

"Here," he said, thrusting a roll of toilet paper into her hands. "Give her this. It's a pretty hot commodity around here."

Helen thought it was bizarre to offer a perfect stranger something with which to wipe her behind. But she trusted Tristan, who made it clear he had an insider's knowledge of what street people liked and wanted.

Helen sidled off the edge of the stage and walked towards Rhonda, making a large half-circle to avoid approaching her from behind. She'd already learned the hard way: never approach a mentally ill person from behind.

"Rhonda?"

Helen hovered on one foot, ready to take a giant step backward if needed.

"Can I sit down?"

Rhonda's pale blue eyes inched from the table to Helen's face. She slowly put down the turkey sandwich she had chosen over a plate of lasagna and stared. Helen was equally mesmerized by the way in which Rhonda had meticulously nibbled off the crust of her sandwich, leaving the bread as ragged as the bitten nails on her long, bony fingers and the meat inside untouched. The next thing Helen noticed was the tension that flattened Rhonda's frosted pink lips and her failure to blink, even when the metal chair made an unpleasant shriek across the linoleum floor as Helen pulled it out to sit beside her. She had never actually seen Rhonda up-close, skilled as she was at sneaking into the soup kitchen and strategically darting past the outreach workers to anchor the top of the line.

Her fair, rosy complexion, golden blond hair, and mouth iced with some version of *Stardust Wonder* were a striking rarity in these wan surroundings, and rarer still, it looked as though Rhonda had found a place to take routine baths and change her clothes, even if it was from one floppy black sweater to another. Whether or not she was truly homeless and mentally ill remained to be seen, and that was the purpose for which Helen had come to court her with toilet paper in hand like a springtime bouquet.

"I thought you could use this. I mean, I thought you might *want* this," Helen said, aware that her voice sounded awkward and small. A nervous giggle bubbled up from her belly.

"You think that's funny? Ha. Put it in there," Rhonda said dully, gesturing to the floor and the weather-beaten black canvas tote emblazoned with a bright purple logo from a local pharmaceutical company. Helen was aware of Tristan's eyes monitoring their interaction.

"My name is Helen."

Rhonda returned her gaze to the sandwich on her plate.

"Rhonda. That's a pretty name. Did your mother

name you after that song? You know, that old Beach Boys song...*Help me, Rhonda?*"

Helen thought she saw the corners of Rhonda's lips curl into a weak grin.

"How's the sandwich?"

"It's got pepperoni in it."

"I thought it was turkey. It looks like turkey."

"It's pepperoni, goddammit."

"Okay."

"They always give me pepperoni on days when they're out to get me. That's why I won't eat it. If I eat it, they'll get me. They give me poison apples, too."

Rhonda ran her hands through the hair at the crown of her head and then slammed them on the table, her delicate palms slapping against the cold steel.

"You did this?"

Helen slowly pushed her chair backward, poised to flee.

"Did what?"

"You told them to give me pepperoni?"

Helen stood and spoke in a low, soothing tone. "No, I didn't, but I'm glad you saw it was pepperoni before you ate it. I do beg your pardon, but I've got to go talk to Tristan about this...this...*conspiracy*...." She noticed the table of Costa Rican laborers had begun to gesture and laugh, and spin their pointer fingers in little round circles aimed at their temples. She was going to have a talk with Tristan, all right! Surely he knew that Rhonda was a raging paranoid-schizophrenic and he'd deliberately failed to warn her!

"Don't come back here. You're one of *them,* I know it!" Rhonda shrieked, grabbing her tote and holding it protectively across her flat chest. Helen didn't look back as she zigzagged through the tables and chairs that were now filled to capacity. She forced herself to keep her chin level and her stride long, even as she passed by Hawk and felt the heat of his gaze boring into her back.

"Secooooonds!" Dorothy shouted.

Helen was relieved at the sound which brought several dozen people to their feet, each scrambling for a share of leftover lasagna and toasted garlic bread. She winced as she took jab in the ribs from the one called Big Steve. He was big, all right. His head was huge and balding, and his neck thick with lumpy folds, culminating in a pendulant, baggy chin that gave him the look of an enormous pelican. He was all arms and legs besides, a sweeping, black hulk of a man who didn't seem to know how large he really was.

Ignoring the pain, Helen continued to smile and greet various guests, weaving between metal chairs as she made her way back to the stage where Tristan sat with Marcy, a gap-toothed redhead with a horrible speech impediment that made every third word unintelligible. Helen learned her first week on the job that Marcy was the soup kitchen prostitute, the one all the boys laughed at and wanted and stole extra cupcakes for in the hope of getting a freebie or two. This was no time to get stuck talking to Marcy, Helen groaned. It would be another fifteen minutes before she'd take a breath.

She never did get to tell Tristan exactly what she thought of his cruel methods of initiation. By the time Marcy finished her treatise on the broken down washers at the Laundromat, her anger and humiliation had lost their heat and momentum. Tristan stood and stretched his long arms and legs and proclaimed it a helluva first week. Helen agreed, and turned her thoughts toward going home to her husband and what movie they would rent and what kind of late-night pizza they would order. Any kind, she thought, but pepperoni….

She longed to tell Todd about the victories and defeats of life in St. Paul's Soup Kitchen as she experienced them day by day, about the people she'd met and the hardships they endured; the way she loved them but loathed the smell of them; the way they were smart and savvy and primitive all at the same time; the curious way they made her cringe, and weep, and laugh at odd turns; of her desire to be accepted by them and yet never to be one with them. After all, they were transients, criminals, and addicts and all those things she always feared she might become if left to languish in the hills of Dock Watch Hollow, trapped for years in her narrow bed under sooty hands and liquored breath.

But Todd rarely made it home much before midnight. His tender, apologetic kisses and promises of better days to come made it easy to forgive his prolonged absences. She had only to look into his eyes, which were the warm color of toasted pecans, and to hear him speak in soft, excited whispers of the movement of the Spirit in his fledgling church, to humbly remember the higher purpose to which they had been called. By the following Monday morning, her sense of peace had returned and she ventured calmly into the storm.

She had hoped it would be an easy commute; it wasn't. The heavy rains lashed against the windshield making it almost impossible to see, while canals of water overran gutters clogged with dead leaves, flooding the city streets. But she didn't begrudge any of it. All she could think about were the unsheltered guests, guests like Rhonda who were getting rained on without mercy and were too hopeless or crazy to care. She'd brought an extra umbrella with her. It wasn't much, just a little travel-sized model, but she hoped to give it to the first person who needed it.

As it happened, James was the first person to slog through the door. She'd studied him a couple of times before and thought he seemed like the kind who would be grateful for the gift. He didn't sit at the table of "woodsies," the ones who lived in makeshift tents in the woods near the landfill and spurned the company of domesticated folk. Nor did he seem particularly afflicted in one way or another. He was just poor. And hungry. And God-awfully pissed off about it, too.

Helen drummed her fingers on the stage, waiting

for the regulars to wander in. She wanted another crack at Rhonda. She wanted to see if Marcy had been beaten up again over the weekend by her Puerto Rican "boyfriend," whom Helen suspected was little more than her pimp. She wanted to see the happy hippie with his saggy jeans and purple bedroll, and Hawk and his friends, especially the shy, wooly-faced Vietnam vet with the dented aluminum cane who wore camouflage cargo pants and carried a grungy backpack that was plastered with POW stickers and seemed weighted with a thousand stones.

Tristan arrived just a few minutes after her and gaily shouted greetings to every person who walked in the door. Helen knew she was in a slump, that she'd have to do something stellar pretty quickly if she was going to win Tristan's respect and the confidence of the guests. She dangled her feet and kicked her heels against the stage; she glanced down the food line, searching for familiar faces, trying to remember people's names. Dang it, why couldn't she remember people's names?

"Frankie!" Helen smiled and reached for my hand, despite the fact that it was plastered with bandages to hide the sores that plagued me.

"How was your weekend, Helen?"

"It was okay, I watched a couple of old movies and went to church, you know…."

"Oh? What church?"

"Well, momma raised me Catholic, even though my daddy didn't approve. Never did get my

confirmation, though. Daddy found out we were going to the mission church on the hill while he was
working overtime Sundays and made us quit. Said
there weren't going to be any flesh-eaters in his
family. So we went to the Baptist church house after
that. My husband's planting a Baptist church just
down the road from here."

"That's a beautiful thing, Helen."

"I suppose it is, Frankie. Now, what about
you?"

"Avowed flesh-eater," I confessed, and made
her laugh.

"Ma'am?"

Helen and I were interrupted by a petite, dark-
haired woman who had just come in from the rain.
A raindrop clung to her slightly hooked nose and
Helen tried not to be distracted by it.

"You work for the mental health department,
right?"

"Yes, I do."

"I have a terrible problem, a female problem.
Can I talk to you in private?"

"Of course, honey. What's your name?"

Helen had to document every interaction she
had during the course of the day. *"A missed name is
a missed connection,"* the lead caseworker explained to Helen her first day on the job. *"If you
can't be bothered to remember their names, they
sure as heck won't bother to remember yours."*

"Susan."

"It's a pleasure to meet you, Susan. I'm Helen.

So – how can I help you?" she asked, ushering her toward a pocket of empty space near the front door while keeping her back to Tristan's watchful eye.

"Man, I haven't gone to the bathroom in three days," she said with an appropriately pained look on her face.

Helen tilted her head, evaluating the impact of Susan's confession. She stared at her blankly. First it was the toilet paper fiasco. Then she'd been told by James to shut up and stick it. Now, it was all about this poor woman's bowel movements. By jinks, she thought, this was shaping up to be the crappiest job ever!

"Look, I just need a little help. Can you give me some money so I can go to the drugstore and get something to…to move things along?"

Helen quickly assessed the middle-aged woman standing before her. She was dressed in high-waisted, straight leg jeans that had gone out of style in the eighties along with spandex leggings and Madonna's lacy accoutrements. Her thin brown hair hung in strings over her bony shoulders and her skinny face was furrowed with deep, serrated lines where she imagined sorrow after sorrow had been planted through the years. Helen had been warned against falling for every cockamamie story, against indiscriminately handing out the petty cash and the coveted laundry vouchers the agency had given her. But the rules allowed her to make small purchases as needed for soup kitchen guests at her own discretion.

"C'mon," Helen said. "I'll walk you to the drug-store and get something for you."

"Thank you, Helen," Susan said with a sigh of relief. "You know, I can't get shit from anybody else. They say I got to go to the hospital emergency room if I have any kind of medical problem."

"Well, I'm no expert but don't think this quali-fies as a medical emergency."

Susan laughed. "Me neither."

"Hang on, let me grab my umbrella."

Helen was glad that Big Steve was standing in the gap, blocking her from Tristan's view. She grabbed her umbrella and met Susan at the door.

The two women laughed and yelped as they ran through the rain. It was only a block to the phar-macy and upon arriving, Helen took care to read the packaging on each box that hailed itself a *gentle remedy* for a *woman's occasional needs*. She finally decided on a familiar, trusted brand of little pink pills, thrusting the white paper bag into Susan's hand as they left the store.

"I can't tell you how grateful I am," she said.

"No problem, I'm happy to help."

"I guess I'll be seeing you around."

"You're not coming back to the soup kitchen? You should eat something."

"Nah," Susan said. "No appetite. Got to set things right, then we'll see…."

Helen nodded. "Feel better."

Susan waved as they parted ways. Tristan raised his eyebrows as Helen walked through the door with a satisfied smile. She casually leaned against the stage and folded her arms across her chest. "So what's up? What'd I miss?"

"Where did you go?" Tristan asked.

"Oh, that woman, Susan, had a little problem. She was constipated and just needed a little over-the-counter fix. So I took her to the drugstore."

"I see," Tristan said. Helen didn't like the way he said it.

"See what?"

"You should've told me."

"I didn't realize that I had to."

"Susan is an addict."

"I didn't give her any money."

"Yeah, you did."

"I gave her a box of little pink pills to relieve her constipation."

"Jesus, you gave her the whole box?" Tristan echoed loudly, this time attracting the attention of several guests seated at a nearby table.

"Yes," Helen whispered back. "What the devil is your problem?"

"So let me get this straight," Tristan drawled. "You gave a drug addict a box of, let's say, twenty-four little pink pills that she can scrape the writing off of and then deal to homeless drunks looking score a cheap high for two bucks a pop. So that's close to fifty bucks in a heroin addict's pocket – enough to do some real damage – and on top of it, now we've got two dozen *homeless* men running around town with diarrhea. Is that everything?"

27

Helen gasped and pressed her palms to her cheeks.

"Oh, Tristan!"

"You said it, Helen. You are standing in some deep shhhh…."

She heard a man chuckle. It was James, who had been hovering behind them, carefully picking through the pile of charity clothing strewn across the stage in search of a hat to cover his shiny brown head. Helen pretended not to notice he'd overheard everything she and Tristan had said. For now, losing face was the least of her worries; Lord, she hoped she wouldn't lose her job!

"So what do I do now?" Helen asked. Tristan refused to answer.

"Let it rain, baby. Just let it rain," James said softly, revealing the quiet resignation that girds the poor and makes their suffering bearable.

Helen glanced up at James, who smiled kindly and nodded. She smiled weakly and nodded back. In an instant, and if only for a moment, they were kinfolk, for she had been baptized into the bowels of a wretched new world; in solidarity, she paddled madly in a brown river rising, no longer aware of any gap between herself and these children of want, temptation, poverty, and shame.

"Well if it isn't Miss Hell-on-Wheels. What's up, doll?" The wholesome scent of baby powder dusted the air, which had the odd effect of making Helen flinch and raise her guard. Still, she was glad for the diversion.

"Hawk, I was just about to mark you absent," Helen teased. "Truly, I was getting worried about you."

"Aw, you're making me blush," Hawk said, though it would have been impossible to tell given the black streaks he had painted across his cheeks with the burnt end of a cork, giving him the look of an exiled jungle warrior. "So what gives with Susan? She makin' trouble for you? If she's makin' trouble just say so and I'll take care of it for you. Nobody messes with my girl Helen."

"Everything's fine, Hawk. She and I had a lovely chat." Helen wondered how he even knew about her encounter with Susan.

"She playin' you for a fool?"

"Not without my cooperation." Helen winked and forced a smile. Hawk stepped closer to whisper in her ear. He smelled of talc and leather and autumn leaves, combined with a hint of minted mouthwash.

"It's all right, Helen. The people here think you're okay. They're happy they have someone besides that tight-ass Tristan to talk to."

"Yes, but I made a big mistake," Helen whispered back, surprised at the tears that flooded her eyes.

"Jesus, Helen, knock it off. If you let them see they're getting to you, game over. Listen, I'm a Marine. I know what I'm talkin' about."

"You're a Marine?" Helen was surprised that the United States Marine Corps would accept a drifter with a criminal past into their hallowed ranks, so surprised that she stopped crying on the spot.

"Vietnam. Three tours through Hell and back – including Tet. I was Special Ops. You name it. I got the job done."

"I thought you were in San Quentin."

"Hell, that's where the military did their best recruiting. Guys like me were...*expendable*, you know what I'm saying?"

"So you were in prison before you went into the Marines?"

"And after," Hawk admitted. "But what the hell, it's only time and a change of scenery. I got good friends on the inside and out. I got friends everywhere. That's why you need anything done, you just let me know. I take care of my friends, you know what I mean?"

Helen twisted a strand of hair around her finger and shrugged.

"You got friends, Helen?"

"I'm a married woman, Hawk. My husband is my best friend."

"I asked if you got friends, not a husband."

"I had a lot of friends back in Virginia. Not so many here. I don't have the time and my husband, Todd, he expects me to be there for him when he gets home at night."

Helen thought of her best friend, Joan, whom she'd left behind in Dock Watch Hollow after her father died. She was the one to whom she whispered

shame-filled confessions the mornings after her father took to her bed; the one who helped her patch
her bicycle tire so she could run away for the fif-
teenth time in her fourteenth year; the one who convinced her that she was still beautiful and worthy to
marry a handsome flatlander someday. That flatlander turned out to be the son of a celebrated
preacher, a tall, handsome, God-fearing man fresh
out of seminary school who knew nothing of her
haunting past and loved her in a righteous way that
made up for in sincerity what it lacked in attentive-
ness.

"I'll be your friend, Helen. You can come and
sit at our table any time. Not Tristan or any of those
other stiffs from your office. Just you."

"Why, thank you Hawk. I appreciate that."

"Don't give me lip service, girl. I expect to see
you at our table. Soon."

"Your friends," Helen gestured to the table of
Vietnam vets who occasionally nudged one another
and laughed and whistled while pointing in her direction. "They won't mind?" Helen was excited by
the prospect of making inroads where no other outreach worker had gone before. Stuart had been
quick to inform her that most of the vets suffered
from post-traumatic stress disorder, choosing booze
or street drugs to dull their senses and to help them
cope with haunting flashbacks that spawned epi-
sodes of violence, guilt, and self-loathing underscored by psychotic breaks with reality. It was hard
for her to imagine any one of them in such dire

straits. They seemed to be a high-spirited bunch and Hawk was no exception. He had a quick wit that belied his stern demeanor and made Helen doubt he was nearly as menacing as he looked.

"You leave my boys to me," Hawk replied, running his fingers through the blunt mohawk that crested slightly above his military-style crew cut. "Look at you, you're beautiful. Who wouldn't want a gorgeous girl like you sitting at their lunch table, huh? Inside we're all still just a bunch of twelve year olds who want the pretty girl to show them a little love."

Helen laughed loudly, then pressed her hand to her mouth to silence the sound. It was unprofessional to fraternize with the guests in such a way, she chastised herself, knowing Tristan was watching her every move. But he wasn't the only one. I was watching Helen too, silently urging her to exercise caution and heed her inner voices, the ones that appealed to her higher nature and implored her to be as wise as a serpent and as innocent as a dove. But it was out of my hands. I could only intercede for her with my penance and prayers, as any good friend would do. The rest? Well, the rest was a matter of spiritual warfare that would see her rescued from that brown river rising – or send her far into the deep.

In the end, it would be Helen's choice.

Chapter 3

Chasing Ashes

That night, Helen curled up next to Winchester on the sofa, the brown and white field setter she'd rescued while living in Dock Watch Hollow. He'd appeared on the front stoop with a soft, limp-eyed expression and barely enough energy to wag his tale, which was fluffy and grand despite the neglect revealed by his bony body. He came with a bad case of heartworms and a choke chain one size too small that dug into his neck for months – maybe longer – causing raw, painful blisters that oozed and smelled like rotting flesh. He was skittish at the least sound and movement, identifying him as the worst kind of dog in those parts – the kind that wouldn't hunt, despite the name etched into his cheap metal tag. The bit of broken chain that trailed behind him identified him as a captive who had reached his limit and made one last bid for freedom. It had landed him squarely in Helen's lap, where she'd cradled his head and cried at the sight of him. Despite her mother's protest that Chester was too big and too sick to handle, Helen begged for a chance to save his life and offered up her pitiful savings from working at the corner store to pay for the gas to take him to the veterinary clinic thirty miles away.

Doc Forester was sympathetic to Chester's case and offered Helen a six-month payment plan to clean the wounds and purge the parasites from his heart, but gave her no guarantee that he would live out the week. But Chester surprised them all, his strong will and endurance gradually turning his dull matted coat to glossy silk, and his limp eyes into shiny brown orbs of vitality and joy. In gratitude, he became Helen's guardian against all sorts of real and imaginary evils, for he sometimes stared into the empty space before them, sniffing the air and curling his floppy lips menacingly to ward off an impending threat.

"What is it, Chester, who's there?" Helen asked as Chester stiffened beside her, then hopped off the sofa and took several slow, deliberate steps towards the door.

"Silly boy," Helen said, glancing at her watch. "It's just your daddy. Daddy's home." Helen smoothed her hair as she stood and tied her flannel robe around her slender waist.

"Hi sugar," Todd said as he stepped into the flickering light of the television. "I'm sorry I'm so late. Those architects can make a simple church project seem like the rebuilding of Solomon's Temple."

Helen pressed against her husband's chest and wrapped her arms around his broad shoulders. She kissed him lightly on his mouth and lingered in the warmth of his breath. "I know, darlin', I'm just happy you're home. Can I fix you something to eat?"

Chester circled around their feet and nudged the space between their knees. "Hey Chester, you been lookin' out for the Missus? That's a good ol' boy." Todd laughed as Chester gave a low, happy woof in reply.

"How about a sandwich? I got a half pound of ham from the deli today. It's got that maple sugar crust, just the way you like it."

"No thanks, Helen, I've got some work to do before I hit the sack."

"More work, Todd?" Helen asked, taking a step backward to examine her husband's face. "You've already got three nights worth of dark circles under your eyes. Surely you can take one night off."

Todd softened at the hurt in Helen's moss green eyes, knowing he had neglected her in every way over the past several weeks. She turned her shoulder, prepared to walk back to the sofa and settle in for the ninth *Seinfeld* episode in a row. She didn't get that show anyway, all that fuss about a lot of nothin'. The folks in Dock Watch Hollow never did take to it the way the rest of the country did – at least those who had a television and a satellite dish to watch it with.

Todd grasped Helen's hand and pulled her close

to him again. "I said I have work to do. I didn't say I was going to do it." He kissed Helen on the lips, then in the arch of her neck, followed by a trail of kisses over her shoulders that lay bare beneath her robe.

"You should come 'round more often, Pastor Todd," Helen sighed, her hands weaving into his dark mop of curls and pressing closer to meet his surge of energy and strength.

"I reckon so," Todd whispered as they drifted in unison toward the sofa where they made love until they were breathless, then blissfully at rest.

"I've missed you," Helen murmured, trying not to sound like she was complaining.

"I've missed you too," Todd replied, kissing her on the forehead. "I know this has been hard on you, but it won't be like this forever."

Helen nodded, burrowing into the comforting dent of Todd's shoulder. "There's just so much I want to share with you at the end of the day. We never really get to talk much anymore."

"Well, I'm here now. Tell me, how are things at the soup kitchen?"

Helen propped herself up on one elbow and grinned. "I think I made it to the big league, Todd. It's all very exciting."

"What are you talking about?"

"The Vietnam vets. I got invited to sit at their table today."

"You have to be invited?"

"Why, yes, of course you do. The soup kitchen's

not some kind of backyard picnic where you can just sit wherever you please. There are certain protocols that must be respected. It's like a little society of its own," she explained with authority.

"And so you're in with the crème de la crème?"

"The what?" Helen replied, her eyebrows furrowing. "I've told you times on top of times your fancy talk is wasted on me." Helen felt herself growing surly.

"I'm sorry," Todd offered, hiding his own displeasure at Helen's lapse into mountain slang. "Please, finish your story."

"Tristan, he's been looking for a way to get closer to these guys since he started working at the kitchen three years ago. He's never had a chance to sit with them. Most of them won't even talk to him. And they're the ones who decide whether or not you get to be first or last in line, or if you get a hard time or a free pass, or any kind of protection at all when you're in harm's way."

"So they're kind of like guardian angels?" Todd said, his expression growing doubtful.

"Yes and no. I mean, if you're on their good side, by all means, they surely are your guardian angels – especially their leader."

"Oh? They have a leader? You mean he's like the archangel?"

"Don't poke fun, Todd. There's a lot of good work to be done if I can just get close enough to know what they lack."

"How about morals? Do they have any of those?"

37

"Please, don't get all righteous on me."

"Helen, did it ever occur to you that you might be playing with fire? What do you know about Vietnam? Heck, you weren't even born yet."

"Well, my momma used to wear one of those POW-MIA bracelets. She got it from a lady in the Peace Corps who was passing through Dock Watch Hollow and promised to send word if the boy was ever found. She wore it for a long, long time before she gave up the ghost on that young man's return. I grew up praying for his soul every day. Sometimes I still do…" Helen said, tendering a wistful smile.

"So you know the name of one Vietnam soldier."

"I do. I'll never forget it either. His name was Michael L. McMahon." She thought back to the simple steel band stamped with the name, rank, and date of disappearance of the young man who had captured her imagination until one day, twenty-five years after the war had ended, her mother wept and finally buried the old bracelet beneath the golden dome of the willow tree that dominated their back-yard.

"So what's your plan, Helen?"

"I'm not entirely sure. But I do know Mr. Lightfoot will be terribly offended if I don't take him up on his offer."

"Mr. Lightfoot?"

"Yes, he's two parts Cherokee."

"Gee, that makes me feel better."

"Are you worried about me, Todd? Why, you

know I can handle myself. I don't exactly come from the right side of the tracks myself, or have you forgotten?"

Helen had always feared that Todd's genteel upbringing would come between them someday. He was ever the good Christian soldier, planting churches and preaching truth and justice and forbearance, but at the same time, she secretly wondered if he'd ever known a moment of suffering or want in his time. If he had, it wasn't something he'd shared with her in their short time together. Nor did she speak much or often of her own shameful past, for in remembering it, it sprouted arms and legs and chased her in her dreams until she would wake soaked in a pool of cold sweat and fear.

A long moment of silence settled over them, making them shift uncomfortably. Helen reached out and grasped her robe from the hardwood floor where it had settled in a crumpled heap. She disentangled herself from her husband's arms and stood over him in quiet wonder.

She'd always thought he was a beautiful man. He had inherited the fine features of a family line that traced it roots back to the Englishmen that had settled in the Richmond area centuries before the rebel Scotch-Irish came to the land in a wave of tartan plaid and inhabited the mountains, bringing with them their peculiar dialect that had since evolved into a language of its own – one that only her own people, the ones with roughed-up faces and calloused hands, could speak and understand.

Her mother had taken great care to see that Helen had developed a tongue that was simple yet refined, often warning Helen against sounding like a common hillbilly. Once they arrived in Richmond she had been merciless, broaching not a single lapse in Helen's grammar and elocution.

"You goin' to git to work?" she would have said at one time. Now, she gazed into her husbands eyes which were already clouded with thoughts that didn't include her, and formed her words carefully.

"I suppose you're going to get back to work now."

"Just for an hour or two," Todd conceded, "but I sure would like a little bit of that maple sugar ham you talked about earlier. I believe I've worked up an appetite." He smiled and thanked God for his dutiful wife, that rare, true-blue Proverbs 31 woman who understood the importance of supporting her husband's needs and desires, in every biblical way. She had been good for his ministry, a faithful, quiet girl with the simplest needs and desires of her own.

Still, he knew there were sides to Helen that he'd yet to fully know or understand. The way, for instance, that she would sometimes startle and pull away when he reached for her in the dark, or those times when he would catch her staring blankly into a mirror, as though she hardly recognized the person looking back at her. His family had warned him against marrying a girl from the coal country, from those far-off counties in the arrowhead of Virginia that might as well be another nation for all they had in common. But he had fallen for Helen the day that he saw her in a cubicle at the Richmond Public Library, absently twirling a strand of glossy brown hair around her fingers and displaying a knitted brow as she labored over a book on modern social etiquette.

She'd seemed embarrassed when he asked for the privilege of buying her a cup of coffee at the quaint café around the corner. He would normally not have acted in such a forward manner himself, except that in addition to her physical beauty, she emanated a certain grace and lively spirit that could never be found in any such book. It was evident in the way she would glance up and smile sweetly at anyone who caught her eye, as though she really didn't know or understand the social constraints that kept people at arm's length, and often for good reason. Every now and then, she would sit back in her chair and doodle in her notebook in wide sweeping circles. On approach, he was able to decipher not circles, but hearts, drawn on the page. Empty hearts. He could not resist.

"Excuse me, Miss, I couldn't help but notice that every heart you draw is empty. Shouldn't there be some initials inside or something like that?" he'd said with a smile that he desperately hoped she would not find creepy.

Helen laughed and he found himself captivated by the sound. It was not some coy or delicate giggle, but a joyful ripple that seemed to purify the very air he breathed with its innocence.

41

Emboldened and hopeful, he motioned to a chair beside her.

"May I sit down?"

Helen studied his face for a long moment. He shuffled his feet like a shy school boy at a dance.

"I'm sorry…" she finally said.

Todd stiffened at the rejection, and then raised one hand as though to offer both an apology and a farewell.

"I mean I'm sorry, I haven't read that chapter yet, so I don't know a fittin' way to reply." Helen smiled playfully and pulled out the chair beside her. "So feel free to set a spell."

They became inseparable from that moment on. Several months later, Todd asked Helen to be his bride. She responded by falling into his arms weeping, saying she was unworthy to marry a man of God. She urged him to find an upright woman, one with his refined upbringing who would make his momma and daddy proud. While it was true, his parents had been less than receptive, they had to admit that Helen was one of the most wholesome and good-natured young women they had ever known, and so had not withheld their blessing.

With no father to walk her down the aisle, Helen had insisted that her best friend – Chester – be allowed to accompany her. It was the first and last time his father allowed a dog in the church house. The way that Chester careened his long neck and howled every time the choir broke into song was more than he had bargained for, though the memory still made everyone laugh. With few exceptions, it had been a blissful three years; now, for the first time, there was a fracture forming as wide and long as the seams of coal on the side of the mountain where Helen had been born.

"You go on ahead and get started while I fix you that sandwich. You want a glass of sweet milk with that, too?"

"Helen," Todd said gently.

"I know, I'm a saint. I can't help myself," Helen replied as she headed for the kitchen with Chester happily trotting behind her.

"No, Helen, that's not what I was going to say."

Helen turned to face her husband, surprised by the tension in his eyes.

"I want you to quit working at the soup kitchen."

"What?"

"I want you to quit working at the soup kitchen. It's too dangerous."

"Oh please," Helen smiled indulgently. "You're teasing me, right?"

"It's not like we need the money – and there are other ways to help the poor. In fact, I was going to ask if you might be interested in leading our church's foreign missions program."

"Why would I want to take on foreign missions when there's a mission field in my own backyard?" Helen protested. Her cheeks burned and she felt her fingers curling into a tight fist. "Laws a mercy, Todd, you make about as much sense as a turtle on a fencepost!" Helen shook her head at the sound of Grannie Hick's words flying out of her mouth, uncomfortably aware that her hillbilly roots were always lurking just below the surface of her practiced manner of speech. Humiliation mingled with her indignation and deepened the color pooling in her cheeks from pink to crimson. She glanced down at her bare feet, which Chester had begun to lick in consolation.

"*Ahainna quittin' the soup kitchen, Todd*," she said, no longer caring how she sounded.

"There's no shame in leaving a job that's just too complicated for a simple girl like you."

Helen inhaled deeply and lifted her chin from her chest. "So I'm simple, huh? You talkin' to me like the tall people now?" Helen said, choosing the expression of her kinfolk for the well bred, citified men and women who walked around with their noses in the air.

"Aw, Helen, I mean that it's too complicated for *most* people. Those Vietnam vets have some really serious issues."

"I believe I can help them."

"Helen, I know you too well. You don't just think you can help them, you think you can save them. Just like you think you can save every stray cat or sickly dog that lands on your doorstep." Todd glanced at Chester, who rested his chin on Helen's foot. "There's only one Savior, do you understand that?"

"So now this is about religion?"

"No, it's about how much I love you. I just want you to be safe."

Helen nodded. "I believe that, Todd. But I'm not quitting the soup kitchen," she said softly, taming her native tongue. "I'll be careful, I promise."

Todd knew that Helen's promises were true, and settled for the compromise with a thoughtful nod. At least he'd raised her guard, he thought to himself, hoping that would be sufficient for her needs.

"I'm sorry I made you fret," Helen said, then roused Chester with a low whistle that brought him scrambling to his feet. "Come on, Chester, momma's got a little special treat for you in the kitchen. Don't have to ask a dog twice if he wants something to eat," she said, "not like some men I know."

Todd smiled as Helen's slender silhouette slipped from the living room and into the stark light of the kitchen where she began to hum softly, though Todd couldn't make out the tune. But it was sweet and soothing and brought peace into his troubled soul. He didn't like keeping secrets from Helen – especially the kind that would brand him as the worst kind of sinner in the eyes of God. He consoled himself by remembering that he had rescued Helen from her lowly heritage and raised her up to a new and respectable life as the wife of a minister of God. He had hoped she would take kindly to the idea of working beside him at the glassy storefront church where they temporarily held Sunday services until construction of the Little Flock Baptist Church was complete.

It was only fitting that a preacher's wife would participate in the outreach and evangelization of their new community by joining the local women's clubs and making their presence known. But Helen had balked at the very idea, preferring the company of vagrants, prostitutes, and the chronically mentally ill. He hoped this fascination would soon run its course and she would settle in as his helpmate in winning souls for Christ instead of chasing ashes. After all, he had aspirations of rising through the ranks of the Regular Order Baptists and developing a far-reaching ministry like the great televangelists of his father's time, and now, the 24/7 Internet preachers who used every medium to get across the message of Christ's salvation. He wouldn't be a church-planter forever. Someday, he would be a household name. And he needed Helen beside him, standing tall, when that happened.

"Here you go, darlin'," Helen said, setting a plated ham and cheese sandwich and a glass of milk on the desktop beside his computer.

"Thank you, sugar," Todd replied, fixated on the words running across the screen, his finger poised on the delete key.

"You writin' your sermon for Sunday?"

Todd nodded, setting his chin in the palm of his hand.

"I can't hardly wait to hear it," Helen said, watching for a moment as the cursor blinked impatiently and the silence grew long. "Well, g'night then."

"Good night, Helen."

She could hear the miles between them, the distance of a dozen generations and thousands of manicured hills and acres that stood between Richmond and the wilderness of the Blue Ridge Mountains.

"Keep him off the bed, will you?" Todd called out absently.

"Who? Chester?"

"I'm tired of having to fight him for my fair share."

"Of course, I'm sorry." Helen lingered to see if Todd would say anything more. But she could tell by the way he began to rub his forehead and pull at his chin that he was preoccupied with crafting a sermon that would make the assembly raise their hands and shout spirited *hallelujahs* and great *amens* loudly enough to peak the curiosity of anyone passing by the plate glass window on Sunday morning.

Helen often spent the whole of Sunday mornings staring out that plate glass window, hoping to catch a glimpse of Rhonda, Marcy, or Hawk – or even of me, though my shame and my sickness often confined me to my bed at Damien House. One cold Sunday morning, two weeks after the feast day of Saint Valentine, I did stumble into the city square for a cup of coffee and a little "horse" to shoot, just enough to ease my gripping pain. I saw Helen before she saw me, waving her arms overhead in a slow rocking motion as a small choir in crimson and

47

white robes sang *Nothing but the Blood of Jesus* in beautiful harmonies and riffs that brought tears to my eyes. I thought Helen looked like an angel with her eyes closed tightly and her face upturned, her expression soft and blissful. I don't know why, but she opened her eyes just as I was about to continue on my way. She smiled and motioned for me to come inside, but I was on a mission of my own that day. I stepped away from my sickly reflection and quickly retreated down the street with the sound of the good news resounding in my ears: *Oh! precious is the flow that makes me white as snow; no other fount I know, nothing but the blood of Jesus...*

Then without warning, another verse sprang into my mind from an ancient letter written by my good brethren, Paul, a verse that seemed to me to have an ominous double meaning and I asked my Lord for whom the message was intended. *"Without the shedding of blood, there is no remission of sin."* Whose blood, Lord? I cried out from the depths of my soul. Whose blood besides yours would be shed as a sin offering in the days to come, for your sacrifice is perfect in every generation! I wanted to fall to my knees right there in the street and beg for the whisper of my Master in my ear. But I was bereft of any such revelation, hearing only the hollow sound of a mighty wind that made me pull my brown hood closer around my face and gasp for air as I quickened my pace. I hoped my natural end would come soon for I longed to be reunited with my Lord in the glory of His kingdom. As I turned the corner, I sunk into a low crouch and closed my eyes, comforted by the vision of Helen's radiant countenance that made me feel loved with an age old love that was familiar and strong. When at last my breath returned to me and I opened my eyes, it pained me to see the sorrow I had caused my dear friend in God.

"Frankie, didn't you hear me calling out to you?" Helen said breathlessly as she hovered over me with a grave expression. "Why, you'd think you were runnin' from the devil himself!"

Helen sunk down to the pavement beside me and wordlessly uncoiled her bright red cashmere scarf from around her neck. Then, in slow, tender circles, she wrapped the fabric around my neck and tied the loose ends into a half knot. I did not thank her aloud, for I somehow knew she was only doing what her heart commanded, that my thanks and praise would only serve to diminish the purity of her intention.

"I was wishin' you'd come and set beside me in church. I know it's not a Catholic church, but there's good fellowship inside," she said softly.

"Helen," I faltered, knowing that I looked sick and disheveled. "I'm not fit for Sunday services."

"Me neither." Helen shrugged. "Aren't we all just a sorry sight in the eyes of the Lord!" she said, following up with a low, sorrowful whistle and a thoughtful pause. "I would've liked for you to meet my husband, Todd. You'd take a shine to him, I think."

I smiled and nodded.

"Come back with me, Frankie. There's coffee and doughnuts for everybody afterwards and it looks like you could use some warming up."

I found it hard to deny Helen's earnest green eyes as they skipped over my face, taking notice of my sunken cheeks and pale, cracked lips. "All right, Helen."

We stood and she tightly locked her arm with mine, as though fearing I might change my mind and bolt in the opposite direction. I almost did, but I couldn't bear to disappoint her. We walked in silence until we reached the canopied entrance to the temporary home of the Little Flock Baptist Church. Helen tugged at me gently, wordlessly pulling me inside. The congregation had already begun to disperse, moving toward the back of the room where a tall silver coffee urn and several plates of pastries were arranged among pots of bright yellow mums with dark brown centers. For a moment, my mind wandered to the tall yellow sunflowers that swayed like a sea of gold on the Umbrian plains. I could see the rosy peak of my beloved Monte Subasio in the distance where I had often found refuge and solace in its secret caves, safe from the judgments of man – especially those of my father who despised my new life as a beggar for Christ.

"Todd?" Helen waved her hand overhead. "Todd, over here, there's someone I'd like you to meet."

A tall, curly-haired young man in a dark blue suit and yellow tie moved through the crimson sea of choir gowns and flinched at the sight of me. But he quickly recovered and had already extended his hand towards me by the time he reached Helen's side.

"Todd, this is my good friend, Frankie."

"Pleasure to meet you," Todd said as we shook hands, then glanced at Helen with the obvious question in his eyes.

"I know Helen from the soup kitchen," I said, sparing Helen the awkward moment.

Todd nodded, taking note of Helen's scarf around my neck. He pulled at his chin and surveyed my frail physique. "Yes, I believe I've heard Helen mention your name before. She says you're quite the singer, is that so?"

"I fear your wife is being much too kind."

"Might I interest you in joining our choir, Frankie? It surely could use a tenor or two."

I laughed and shook my head. "Thanks for the offer, but I'm not sure how much longer I'll be staying in the city. I was thinking a change of scenery might do me some good."

Helen startled. "Well, that's news to me, Frankie. When were you intending to tell me? Where will you go?" She looked genuinely hurt and I placed my hand on her shoulder reassuringly.

"Well, I was thinking of going home," I said, and it was true. I prayed the Lord would somehow enable me to return to the rolling hills of Assisi, to die at home in the Church of the Angels where the Cross of San Damiano – the one from which the corpse of Christ had once come alive and commanded me to rebuild his Church – still received the veneration of scores of pilgrims more than seven centuries later.

"Home?" Helen prodded, her voice small with bewilderment. "Frankie, you're sick. You need to stay at Damien House."

"Damien House?" Todd echoed, his eyes narrowing.

Neither Helen nor I answered, though I saw Helen stiffen at her husband's austere tone.

"Helen, I'm parched from all that preaching. Would you mind getting me a cup of cold water?"

"I'd be glad to," Helen replied, her eyes meeting mine in silent apology. "Coffee, Frankie?"

"That would be nice, Helen, thank you," I said, determined to sound cheerful. As she slowly drifted from my side, I sensed her powerful desire to shelter me – from what, I did not know.

"So, Frankie, where is Damien House?"

"It's just around the corner, behind St. Paul's Episcopal Church."

"Helen says you're sick, is Damien House a hospital of some sort?"

"It's for poor people who are dying of AIDS."

Todd nodded and pulled at his chin again. "I'm sorry, Frankie. Is there anything Little Flock can do to help?" His voice sounded practiced and overly polite.

"I wish there was," I said truthfully, "but this will run its natural course." I didn't have the courage to speak of the powerful addiction that only deepened my love for suffering humanity. Todd was already keenly disturbed and I felt his judgment settle over me like a black cloud of condemnation and shame.

"You know, I just remembered," I said, glancing at my watch. "I have an appointment I have to keep. Please, apologize to Helen for me...." I hoped I could flee before she returned.

"I'm sure she'll understand," Todd replied flatly.

"It was nice to meet you," I said, gunning for the sidewalk. I didn't want Helen to see the anguish I felt at being a poor, sick man who was despised by her husband for reasons that would surely shatter her heart. I was glad for the clear path to the door that made my exit swift and certain.

"Where's Frankie?" Helen stood with a Styrofoam cup in each hand, her eyes scanning the room for a flash of bright red.

"He forgot he had another commitment. He asked me to apologize to you."

"Oh," Helen said, cocking her head in confusion. She glanced at Todd suspiciously. "Did you say something to hurt his feelings, Todd?"

"Helen, you know me better than that." He leaned into her and lowered his voice to a whisper. "But you know that homosexuality is an abomination in the eyes of the Lord. You shouldn't have brought him here."

"What are you talking about?"

"He's got AIDS, Helen."

"He's an addict, Todd. He got stuck with a dirty needle." Helen's eyes darkened with fury as she thrust her arms forward, forcing Todd to accept both cups from her hands.

"Where are you going?"

"I'm going to find Frankie."

"Let it be, Helen."

Helen paused, thinking how many times in her life she'd heard those cautionary words from her mother and others who knew that things were wrong, dreadfully, horribly wrong in Dock Watch Hollow, where husbands hit their wives and kicked their dogs till they curled up in tiny, tearless balls of submission and shame; where fathers visited their daughters' beds and mothers turned their backs in silent complicity for fear that a confrontation might give rise to more beatings or worse, the loss of food on the table and a tin roof overhead; where cheap whiskey was king, and the coal mines gave rise to black lungs, black hands, and black hearts.

She didn't care that the slam of the door behind her might set tongues wagging inside the Little Flock Baptist Church. It felt good and right to slam the door. And so she did with reckless abandon, taking care not to look behind her lest her heart of flesh should turn to stone.

Chapter 4

Love is Kind

"Well if it ain't Miss Hell-on-Wheels!"

Helen stopped short in her tracks, just in time to avoid careening into Hawk's chest as he anchored the corner of Market Street and Main. The neon light radiating from the window of the Pour Man's Pub cast a blue halo around his head and she quickly stepped backward to create a respectable distance between them.

"Hawk, have you seen Frankie?"

"Nope, not since Friday. What's the matter, doll?"

Helen was determined not to cry in front of Hawk again. She knew he expected her to toughen up and for some odd reason, she didn't want to disappoint him. Yet she could feel the frigid air converging with the hot tears that welled in her eyes as she scanned the city square, praying that her red scarf would flag my whereabouts.

"Is he in trouble, Helen?"

"No, it's not like that. He's just…he's hurt."

"Some kind of accident? Jeez, he didn't try to off himself, did he?" Hawk sounded genuinely concerned and Helen struggled with what to say. There were clear boundaries she knew she must not ever cross if she was to keep her job and her personal life separate; and yet there were words in her throat that she longed to speak, words that would make her sorrow real – and perhaps bearable – if only she could share it with another living being.

The past two months with Todd had been like watching a *Seinfeld* marathon, with nothing of substance ever happening to change the rhythm of their daily lives. She hated that she was beginning to understand this insipid show about everything and nothing in particular and how it had even begun to make her laugh every now and then. Her laughter was once reserved for private jokes that Todd whispered in her ear, for late night reruns of *I Love Lucy* they watched while holding hands and sharing a pint of butter pecan ice cream, for silly faces he made at her across the room when he thought no one in the congregation was watching. Every now and then he would still cozy up behind her as she stirred a pot of soup on the stovetop, murmur something funny and endearing as he kissed the back of her neck, and remind her that she was a wonderful wife, a blessing from a mighty and merciful God. And she, in turn, would pat his hands as they wrapped her narrow waist and utter a demure word of thanks.

Despite those occasional romantic interludes, it had been several weeks since they last made love and longer still since they had spent any real time together, except for the New Year's Eve potluck supper at the storefront church. It had been a beautiful, starry night; one she hoped would see them reunited in faith and intimacy as Todd whisked her away shortly before midnight to the threshold of the newly constructed Little Flock Baptist Church several blocks away. The interior was almost complete, lacking only the installation of the oak pews that were being handmade by craftsmen in Virginia. If all went well, they would be celebrating Easter in their new space with a congregation that had already grown to be a hundred strong.

"Todd, you keep promising to introduce me to your lovely wife. Perhaps now it's inevitable."

Helen and Todd startled at the deep voice that bounced across the stucco walls of the church. A tall, hulk of a man emerged from the shadows cast by stately white pillars and Helen thought he looked like a modern-day Samson, such was the breadth of his chest and the muscular arcs of his arms and shoulders. All that was missing was hair.

"Jonathan! Happy New Year, buddy! What are you doing here?"

"I could ask you the same thing. Aren't you supposed to be celebrating with your people?" Jonathan said, marching forward with outstretched arms. When he reached Todd and Helen, he clutched them in a bear hug and patted Todd heartily on the back.

"I thought I'd sneak away and surprise Helen with our progress. Helen, this is our architect, Jonathan Miller."

"Pleased to meet you, Jonathan," Helen said, glad to have a face to go with the name that had monopolized her husband's time for far too long! "So what's your excuse for being here at quarter to midnight, Mr. Miller?"

"I didn't have any plans for tonight." Jonathan shrugged and smiled.

The absence of friends and family with whom to ring in the New Year struck Helen as grounds for pity and she instantly regretted the hardness of her heart.

"Aw, don't feel bad for me, Helen; I'm a workaholic, down to the bone. I figured this is as good a time as any to get some work done without a thousand distractions. Todd, I've been rethinking the configuration of the daycare center downstairs. If we bump the kitchenette down the hall by about eight feet, we could probably pick up just enough space for that conference room we've been talking about."

"But we've already got the kitchen plumbed out."

"Yeah, I thought about that…" Jonathan said, taking a small spiral notepad from the back pocket of his smartly pressed jeans. He patted himself down in search of a pen, then glanced into Helen's rounded eyes.

"Heck, Todd, it's New Year's Eve. This can wait

until Monday," he said.

Todd looked at Helen, who arched a dark brow and waited for Todd's reply. His searing gaze made her realize he expected her to respond like any good preacher's wife should.

"Oh! It's fine, Jonathan – *really*," she said, trying to sound convincing. "Todd, why don't you drive me home, then you can come back here and talk about plumbing and drywall all night long if you want to."

"You wouldn't mind, Helen?" Todd said.

"Helen, please, I don't want to spoil your celebration," Jonathan added, his mouth sagging in a wordless apology.

"Well, truth be told, I'd rather spend the first night of the New Year with my husband, but I'm willin' to sacrifice for a worthy cause." Helen smiled graciously, knowing that if Todd came home with her, he would only lament the lack of progress that might have been made.

"You sure, Helen?"

"Of course, I'm sure."

Todd took Helen's hand and kissed it. "She's a keeper, isn't she?" he said to Jonathan with a nod and a wink. "I'll be back in twenty minutes."

"Never mind that, just give me the keys. Jonathan, would you kindly see to it that my dear husband comes home before daylight?"

"Of course, Helen." Jonathan smiled sheepishly. "Happy New Year," he added, skimming his hand over the top of his bald head.

"Happy New Year, boys," Helen replied. She kissed her husband sweetly on the cheek, waiting until she was curled up beside Chester on the sofa to weep the first of many tears that would fall that year.

"Jesus, Helen, you're not gonna cry again, are you?" Hawk winced as he peered into Helen's eyes. She flicked away her tears with a sweep of her hand. "No, Hawk, I'm not going to cry. I'm just worried about Frankie. I'm afraid my husband might have said something...unkind."

"Ain't he a man of God?"

"I thought so."

"You want to talk about it, Helen? Come on, I'll buy you a cup of hot chocolate and we'll talk."

"I have to find Frankie."

"Helen. Stop. Frankie's a survivor, hell, we all are. You think a few hard words are gonna make any of us curl up and die?"

Helen surveyed the city square, this time more calmly. "I guess not," she conceded.

"You got somewhere to be?"

Helen paused and glanced behind her, tracing the city blocks back to Little Flock's front door. At that moment, it was the last place on earth she wished to be.

"No, I don't."

"Good, then you have no excuses. Follow me."

"Where?

"You'll see," Hawk said, motioning for her to make up the paces he'd already put between them.

Helen quickened her steps until she met and matched Hawk's brisk, long-legged stride toward a more deserted place. Helen sensed this was no time for small talk; Hawk walked tall and straight like a man on a mission. All she'd signed up for was a cup of hot chocolate and a sympathetic ear, she reassured herself. Still, it confused her when they passed the last café in town.

"Hawk, where the blazes are you takin' me?" Helen said lightly, although she felt more than a bit of trepidation. After all, what did she really know about Mickey "The Hawk" Lightfoot? Sure, she had spent a couple dozen lunch hours sitting at his table over the course of the last few months, but that hardly made them intimate friends. The first time she approached the disheveled band of brothers they had given her a good going over, with the one they called Butch leading the charge. Hawk had simply leaned back in his chair and folded his arms across his chest, waiting to see what Helen's tolerance was for pain and insult.

"So Helen, you married?"

"Yes I am, Butch."

"She's married to a preacher," Hawk chimed in. Helen wondered how he'd managed to breach her private life so quickly.

"Yeah? Well, fuck that," Butch said, with a dot of spittle clinging to his wooly gray beard. "God is dead."

"Really?" Helen said. "That's funny because I just talked to him this morning." She hadn't intended

61

to make his tablemates laugh but they did, in loud guffaws that broke the tension that had been slowly building between them. Hawk grinned approvingly.

"So what can I do for y'all? Everybody here got shelter?" Helen ventured to ask, knowing that she could wheedle a couple of hotel room vouchers from the caseworkers if one or more of the vets were in need. They were considered the brass ring in the social work arena, wily and elusive, haunting and haunted, fierce and yet fearful of anyone who had not themselves endured the bloodbath that was Vietnam.

"We take care of our own," Norman said, peering at Helen through perfectly round wire-rimmed glasses from the seventies. Norman was one of many vets who walked with a limp, but he was the only one at the soup kitchen who relied on a cane to keep him upright. It wasn't until Helen happened to glance below the table that she saw the steel bar that joined his prosthetic left foot to the stump beneath his pant leg. She was embarrassed to discover that Norman had followed the direction of her gaze.

"Goddamn gooks."

"I'm sorry, Norman," Helen said.

"I don't need your friggin' sympathy."

"I know," Helen said, standing her ground. "But I'm still sorry that happened to you. Shame on you for not allowing me to say so."

Hawk lifted a wary eyebrow and pressed his palms to the table, ready to leap to Helen's defense. Helen leveled her eyes to meet Norman's stare. For a moment she wondered if she had indeed over-stepped her bounds, but she was not about to be told what she could or could not grieve!

"I'm sorry, Helen."

Helen nodded and Hawk relaxed.

"I guess you could say I got a complex of sorts," Norman continued, his gravelly voice softening to a sandpapered hush. "You would too if people spat on you and called you a baby-killer."

Helen dropped her jaw in disbelief as several others nodded in agreement and grunted bitterly.

"Here I come back from Da Nang just in time for Christmas with my family. Mind you, I ain't seen a civilian for over two years. So I step proud off that military plane, my head held high, my uniform fresh and stiff, you know? But the people in the airport, they don't salute me or shake my hand like I expect. You know what they did Helen? They hissed and spat at me, and called me a baby-killer. They screamed at me and my buddies that we were cold-blooded murderers and a disgrace to our country. Jesus, my ma and pa were there. My kid brother, too...man, that was so fucked up," he finished in a coarse whisper.

"Oh, my God!" Helen replied, unable to say more.

"God is dead," Butch repeated dully. This time Helen didn't argue.

"Goodness, Hawk, are we almost there?" Helen said, her question floating in frosty puffs between them.

"Just a little farther," Hawk said, slowing enough to allow Helen to catch her breath. The dense but leafless woods were straight ahead and Helen flinched at the sight. In just a few feet, the sidewalk disappeared. She continued walking in silence across a broad, open field, then hovered at the woodland's edge.

"I'm not an axe-murderer, Helen," Hawk said sternly.

Helen twirled a strand of hair that had escaped the ponytail peeking out from under her red cashmere beret. "Of course you're not," she replied, but she considered casually dropping her hat on the frozen ground behind her as a clue for anyone who might come looking for her just the same. She had to admit, she was already teetering on the edge of regret for having agreed to follow Mickey Lightfoot anywhere. All of her soup kitchen training had warned against this moment. And yet, she felt oddly safe in his hands.

She followed his lean, agile body as he wove between spindles of trees and cagey thickets, traveling a path of pressed down leaves that was barely perceptible. Soon, the sound of running water trickled into Helen's ears. She knew there was a river on the outskirts of the city where the woodsies made camp with tarps fashioned from old bed linens and oversize plastic garbage bags. But it was not the woodsies who greeted her on the muddy banks of the Passaic River.

"Good morning, Miss Helen," shouted Henry,

the only black soldier who routinely sat at the soup kitchen table with the other Vietnam vets. Helen thought he had the saddest brown eyes she'd ever seen, though he was given to fits of excitement that made him hoot and holler and dance a frenzied jig like a drunken hillbilly. Some simply took him for a dumb and happy fellow, but Helen thought he seemed more like a man too tormented and troubled to sit still with his own thoughts.

"Good morning, Henry," Helen said, noticing a crooked, hand-carved sign that had been fashioned from a piece of plywood and nailed to a nearby tree. *China Beach West. No Gooks Allowed!*

"What's she doing here, Hawk?" Butch's coarse voice called from somewhere above. Helen turned her face toward the dappled, gray sky and saw Butch perched in a rickety tree blind thirty feet off the ground. His camouflage clothing made him nearly invisible; he would have been so had he not also sported an orange knit cap that made him look like one of the colorful orioles that nested and sang in the treetops back home.

"She's come for a visit," Hawk replied, "what's it to you?" Helen had never heard Hawk sound so menacing. After a flurry of rustling leaves, clumsy footfalls, and whispered profanities that made Helen cringe, the campsite known as China Beach West fell silent. Helen knew that she and Hawk were alone in what might as well have been the far side of another world. She sighed and stared into a nearby fire pit littered with budget beer cans that were crushed and singed around the edges. A respectable fire burned in the middle of the circle and Helen found herself gravitating toward its warmth.

"Have a seat, Helen," Hawk said, motioning to a chunky log beside the fire pit.

"Thank you," Helen said, vaguely aware that that she had more or less entered someone's home. Hawk walked over to an old, rusty footlocker and flipped open the lid. When he turned around, he held two dented tin cups in one hand, a plastic jug of spring water in the other, and a canister of powdered cocoa under his arm. He grinned and held the cups up high.

"Military issue, built to last hellfire and damnation."

Helen laughed. "You're full of surprises, Hawk, I will say that much."

"Hey, I said I wanted to buy you a cup of hot chocolate, didn't I?"

"You surely did."

"Helen," Hawk said, squatting down to look into Helen's eyes. She felt the cool, blue intensity of his gaze dominate her senses and she fought the urge to look away. "If nothing else, I'm a man of my word. You can count on that."

She exhaled slowly as he stood and turned his back to her to stoke the fire. She was mesmerized by the pulsating embers that flashed orange like a thousand danger signs that she was determined to ignore for just this once. Before long, Hawk produced a steaming mug of hot chocolate, which

Helen gratefully accepted with half-frozen fingers. How, she wondered, could anyone make their home in the woods for months or years on end? Why didn't they demand hotel vouchers, or Section 8 housing, or help from the Department of Veterans Affairs? Surely they knew such options existed, and yet their preference was clear.

"Hawk, do you live here all the time?"

"Nah," Hawk said, wrapping his hands around his own tin mug. He wore black, fingerless gloves and a black leather jacket that made him look like one of Hells Angels, but Helen thought his manner thus far had been nothing short of chivalrous.

"I got an apartment, but I don't stay there much. I'd rather be out here with my brothers from 'Nam, you know what I mean?"

Helen nodded, although she herself had grown up without brothers or sisters; her mother, who had given birth to Helen when she was just a teen herself, had been as much a sister as a mother to her. It devastated her to bury Mary Elizabeth Hicks in the faraway city of Richmond, sick as she'd been with the kind of cancer that was rampant in coal country, the kind more than one city folk had warned was the result of once-pristine streams now polluted with heavy metals from sheared mountaintops and broken pond slurries that leached toxins no body could stand up to for long. Her mother was only forty-three when she died – just two months after the wedding and one month shy of Helen's twenty-sixth birthday. Helen always supposed that seeing her daughter marry into a family of some means gave her mother the freedom to die in peace. For that much, she was grateful.

Hawk sat directly across from Helen on a tree stump worn smooth over time. The amber flames throbbed between them as the wind picked up speed and made the barren trees clatter overhead. "So, you want to tell me about it?"

"There's nothing to tell, really," Helen said, beginning to think that perhaps she had blown things out of proportion. Maybe Todd was right, maybe she was making a lot of fuss about nothing these days. But it was hard not to have a friend to confide in, a friend who would tell her when she was acting plumb crazy or simply remind her of the perils of PMS. Lord, how she missed Joan, the one friend back in Dock Watch Hollow she could always count on to tell her the cold, hard truth when she needed it most. Right about now, she was certain Joan would tell her she'd already been gone too long, that she ought to leave this strange, deserted place and get straight home to her husband.

"So you were crying over nothing?"

"I guess I was cryin' over Frankie."

"But it was your husband who made you cry."

"Well, I guess, indirectly."

"Does he make you cry a lot, Helen?"

Helen hated the way Hawk's pointed questions always made her feel bare-naked as a jaybird. "Not a lot – just sometimes."

"Over what?"

"I don't know, we just have our differences, that's all."

"What's he like?"

"Todd?"

Hawk nodded, and Helen began to search for the words that would best describe the man who was her husband – and yet still a stranger in so many ways. "He's a preacher, but you already knew that…he's very refined, very intelligent, a man of great moral character," Helen mused, glancing skyward and noticing the dark underbellies of converging, low-flying clouds. "He's also very handsome…and funny, too…but not so much these days," Helen conceded.

"Is he good to you, Helen?"

"What kind of question is that? Of course he's good to me."

"Well, he makes you cry."

"I guess that's just the darker side of love. We can't expect somebody to make us happy all the time," Helen reasoned.

"First Corinthians, 13."

"What?"

"First Corinthians, 13. You know, Helen: *Love is patient, love is kind. It is not jealous, it is not pompous, it is not inflated, it is not rude*, blah, blah, blah."

"Why, Mr. Lightfoot, you quotin' Scripture to me?" Helen laughed, the sound of which made Hawk laugh too.

"What, you think I'm a heathen? I'll have you

know I'm an ordained minister."

"Really?" Helen replied, intrigued by Hawk's claim.

"I walked into Cook County Prison on felony charges in 1978 and walked out the Right Reverend Lightfoot in 1984."

"So you're a mail-order minister?"

"I am."

Helen giggled. "And what is your denomination?"

"I represent the Church of Hard Knocks," Hawk said wryly, drawing a long, noisy sip of hot chocolate from his tin cup. "We're based in Ireland."

"I see," Helen said, "and what is your theology?"

"Do not mistake my kindness as a sign of weakness."

Helen raised a thin, dark eyebrow. "That's it?"

"Yeah, that's it." Hawk's manner took a sudden and somber turn. Helen stiffened at the difference.

"Seriously, Hawk," Helen proceeded cautiously, "how is it that you know that chapter and verse so well?"

Hawk glanced sharply around and beyond the clearing, then spoke in a guarded whisper. "I could tell you, Helen, but then I'd have to kill you."

Helen's eyes widened and Hawk laughed at the sight.

"I was an altar boy for five years at St. Virgil's Catholic Church in Brooklyn. I paid attention." Hawk shrugged. "Okay, that's my secret. Now tell me one of yours."

Helen placed her tin cup at her feet and rested her chin on the fist of her hand. Sure, she had secrets; secret dreams, secret thoughts, a secret past that she kept buried so deep that she was just this side of denial that anything bad had ever happened to her. But it did, she made herself remember. It did happen, and if she didn't periodically purge herself, she thought she might burst like the side of a mountain and rain her secret blackness all over her tidy new life.

"I was molested by my father from the day I turned twelve till he got too sick to lay on me anymore."

Hawk didn't flinch. He simply set his tin cup down on the ground and slowly rose to his feet as Helen gazed into the fire, expressionless and calm.

"Christ, Helen. I was expecting something more along the lines of 'I dye my hair' or 'I'm afraid of clowns,'" Hawk said quietly, wishing that Helen would look into his eyes. Somehow he would've felt better if she was crying, but all she did was stare down the flames and fiddle with her wedding band for the longest time.

"I'm sorry to disappoint you then," she finally said, her voice small but peaceful. "But I'm not sorry I said it." It felt good to speak the truth, one she'd hidden from everyone but her best friend, Joan, who herself had been at the mercy of a father who beat her senseless on more than one occasion. Together, they had commiserated over their hard luck, but never once did Helen ever share her secret with anyone outside of Dock Watch Hollow who might actually grasp the true horror of it all.

Hawk stooped next to Helen and rested his hand on her forearm. She startled at his touch but didn't shrink from it. "Fuck him, Helen," Hawk said with a tenderness that made the words sound like a soft summer rain. But it wasn't rain that was falling now; the silver sky spit cold, jagged pieces of ice that pelted their faces and bounced off their empty tin cups with sharp, indiscriminate clinks. Hawk turned up the collar of Helen's coat and she thanked him with her eyes.

"You're not at all like you seem in the soup kitchen," Helen said softly. She leisurely examined Hawk's face, realizing that despite his unconventional appearance he was still a very handsome man – not in the classical sense, but in a rugged and enigmatic way that was pleasing just the same.

"You don't know shit about me." Hawk stood abruptly and began to poke the embers in the fire pit with the pointed end of a long stick.

"I know what I see," she said, watching him masterfully stoke the glowing coals back into flame.

"What do you see, Helen?" Hawk challenged.

"I reckon I see a sheep in wolf's clothing."

"Then you better get your eyes checked, sweetie. I ain't no sheep; you know what happens to sheep, don't you?"

Helen shrugged.

"C'mon, Helen, you know your Bible, right?"

Hawk raised his fist and made a slow, slicing motion across his tattooed neck. The gesture sent a chill down Helen's spine. She glanced over her shoulder, suddenly wishing Henry or Butch would reappear.

"I should go," she said abruptly, hoping she'd remember the way back into town. "I'm sure Todd is already frettin' my whereabouts." She stood and vigorously brushed off the seat of her pants.

"I'll walk you back."

"No need, Hawk, I can find my way. I'm a country girl, remember? Only city folk get turned around and lose their bearings." She hoped to restore some measure of levity to their conversation and was relieved to see Hawk smile.

"Thanks for the hot chocolate."

"You're welcome, Helen."

"And for letting me bend your ear awhile."

"Anytime, now you know where to find me," Hawk said, pointing to the welcome sign that was already glazed in a thin layer of ice.

"Hawk, if you see Frankie…."

"I'll tell him, Helen, I'll tell him your husband meant no harm, is that what you want me to say?"

Helen nodded and pulled her hat low on her forehead. Just then, the sleet began to turn into supple white flakes that seemed to soften and purify the air between them. Helen tilted her face skyward and closed her eyes, thinking just for a moment of the white-capped peaks where as a child, she'd lain on the snowy carpet and flapped her arms slowly, boring angels into the mountain-side. As I watched her from afar, her red scarf tucked securely in my backpack, I prayed God's angels would stand in the breach that opened in her heart that day.

"I'll see you tomorrow," Helen called out behind her with a casual wave of her hand.

"God willin' and the creek don't rise," Hawk replied, his lighthearted words annulled by his steely delivery. Helen wrapped her coat tightly around her body, aware without a backward glance that Hawk's eyes were locked on her with the cold precision of a veteran sharpshooter. And yet he had revealed to her a certain tenderness that belied his icy blue stare and the military sharpness that underscored his movements.

She absently caressed the spot where Hawk's hand had rested on her arm, the guilt of savoring his comforting touch causing her to flush with shame. As she neared the clearing, she turned back to see a distant orange glow and a flurry of stick figures that seemed to have suddenly appeared from the leafless woods to form a company of men who were mere shadows themselves, stripped of their verdancy and frozen in time. It might well have still been 1968 for all they knew or cared, and Helen wondered if she, or anyone else, could ever bring them back to life.

In one small, determined step, Helen emerged from the woods and then, as if carried on the wings of angels, found herself racing towards home.

Chapter 5

Semper Fi

Helen gingerly closed the front door behind her, then lifted and shook each foot in mid-air to loosen the snow from her boots. Normally, she would have stomped on the doormat and aimlessly tossed her jacket onto the tip of the overburdened coat tree in the center hall that tumbled to the floor at the slightest imbalance. She wished to make a quiet entrance, knowing Todd liked to take a long nap after teaching and preaching all morning long. Besides, she wasn't prepared to face Todd's questions regarding her hasty departure and prolonged disappearance. She didn't want to lie to him – she never had before – and yet she feared the recriminations that would surely come if he knew where she'd been. If he'd wanted her to quit the soup kitchen before, surely he would demand it now!

She cautiously hung her coat and hat on the sparse side of the coat tree and took a deep breath. She was relieved that Chester hadn't met her at the door. His prancing feet and thumping tail had a way of announcing her arrival home. She thought perhaps Todd had confined him to the kitchen or the guestroom to keep him from pawing at their bedroom door, which she could see from where she stood was shut tight. But then again, as Chester grew older, he sometimes slept through the same sounds that used to make him scramble to his feet. She whistled soft and low and then walked into the living room, expecting to find him curled into a tidy ball on the sofa.

"Where have you been?" Todd said. She could see that he was clutching Chester by the collar, holding him hostage on the sofa in an effort to retain the element of surprise. A fire burning in the brick hearth cast frenzied, orange shadows that bounced off the walls and illuminated Chester's misery-infused face.

"Let him go, Todd."

"What?"

"For heaven's sake, let the dog go." Helen almost laughed aloud at the absurdity of Todd's strategy and the words coming out of her mouth, but she was reluctant to make a bad situation worse.

As Todd unclenched his fist, Chester leaped from the couch in one fluid motion, landing inches from Helen's feet. She pointed to the ground beside her where he instantly settled on cue.

"Where have you been?" Todd repeated. He stared into the fire, refusing to look in Helen's direction.

"I went for a walk."

"In a snowstorm?"

"It wasn't snowing when I started out."

"My point, exactly. You've been gone for hours."

"I'm glad you noticed," Helen parried. She wasn't going to lie, but perhaps she could redirect his line of questioning.

"What's that supposed to mean?" Todd's eyes darted to Helen's face, squinting at her as though trying to discern if she was angry or hurt.

"I just find it interesting that you can go for weeks hardly aware that I exist and then get all riled up when I'm not at your beck and call."

Todd looked genuinely confused by what was clearly Helen's ire. It was unlike Helen to speak to him that way and he wondered what had gotten into her. Helen pressed on, surprised by her own momentum.

"I know you need a wife who will submit to you as the head of the household but sometimes I have needs of my own, Todd. And today I just needed a little time for myself, is that such a terrible sin?"

"Of course not," Todd sputtered, "but you were upset with me when you left Little Flock this morning, you can't deny that. I got worried when you didn't come back."

"I always come back, Todd. You know that," Helen said softly, and it was true. The few times there were bitter words between them, Helen was always the first to smooth things over, even if she had to eat a whopping slice of humble pie, as her momma used to say. That was her mother's abiding philosophy: don't upset your man any more than is necessary to get by, lest he find himself a younger, prettier woman who hasn't yet developed a mind of her own. And yet Helen recalled her mother as an exceptionally beautiful woman with strong, glamorous cheekbones and an even stronger back. Despite the fact that she was barely five foot five, Mary Hicks was no hundred-twenty-pound weakling, daily carrying two five-gallon pails filled with water a quarter mile from the mountain stream to the horse barn, pitching hay by the baleful, and shoring up the dilapidated stalls with ten penny nails and a rusty claw hammer that she swung high and wide like it was therapy. No, Mary Hicks didn't need any man, and yet she never failed to bend to Horace Hick's will, especially on Friday nights when he arrived home from the mines two hours past quitting time with a coal dusted face and whisky breath, demanding that she fetch him this or that from the Wal-Mart thirty miles away. Why hadn't she seen through his ploys to send her away, too far away to hear her daughter's muffled cries that lasted only as long as Horace's heavy panting and feeble masculinity allowed? Afterwards, there would be milk and cookies set out for her and sometimes even a few silver coins to seal her pretty pink lips, which despite the years of abuse had at least never suffered a single sloppy, sordid kiss. She wondered how her mother stood it, those clumsy, wet encounters with Horace's mouth that she'd seen her mother wipe from her lips with the back of her hand when she thought no one was looking.

For a long time, that had been Helen's consolation; that her first real kiss had been given to the man she would eventually marry. It wasn't much but it was something, and even still, whenever Todd kissed her she felt pure and innocent, glad there had been at least one small part of her being that was incorrupt and exclusively his. She found his kisses sweet and gentle and always mannerly, never so forcefully delivered so as to leave the kind of telltale whisker burns that perpetually branded the tender skin around her mother's mouth.

Oh, Helen wished she had gotten off so easily, for it was her very soul that was branded, stamped with the "O" of Oreo cookies that had leveraged her silence, abetted by a few shiny nickels and dimes. Later, she thought she was protecting her mother, whom she adored, from the horrifying truth about her husband by keeping the shame-filled silence. Now, she wondered if Mary Hicks had gone to her grave truly without one iota of knowledge regarding Horace Hick's perverse and abusive nature – or if she had simply spent years downing a whopping slice of humble pie.

"I'm sorry I upset you, Helen," Todd said, his heart turning soft at the sight of Helen's bright red cheeks and damp, flattened hat-hair that made her look like a pathetic, windswept orphan.

Helen sensed his apology was sincere but remained bothered that Todd missed the point; that he was still oblivious to the fact that it was his disdain for the local poor – and Frankie in particular – that had riled her in the first place. "I'm sorry I made you worry," she replied.

The sudden crackle and whoosh of toppled burning wood broke the silence between them and startled Chester out of his obedient sprawl. He stood and shook his body vigorously, his collar jangling much the same way that Hawk's silver cross and battle-scarred dog tags collided and clanked around his neck. Helen flinched at the sound and the memory it provoked.

"So where did you walk?" she vaguely heard Todd ask.

"All over," Helen replied. "I stopped and had a cup of hot chocolate…did a little window shopping…the city is so much prettier dressed in white, don't you think?"

Todd smiled. Helen had a naturally poetic point of view that he admired and often used as inspiration for his sermons. He thought for a moment about his sermon that morning; how Helen's recent rant on the modern practice of surface mining in Appalachia – that is, the blasting off of mountaintops to exploit the valuable seams of coal hidden within – berated the way a small squadron of yellow bulldozers chips away at an ancient stone mountain day by day, week by week, year by year, layer by layer, until one day, everybody suddenly looks up and realizes that their glorious, life-sustaining mountain has been reduced to a useless, stumpy plateau. *Now how do you suppose that happened?* Helen mimicked...*oh, just ten yellow bulldozers creeping along a hillside one day....*

Her passion inspired Todd to compose that Sunday's treatise on *The Ten Bulldozers of Sin*, which brought his congregation to their feet with shouts of affirmation and a few repentant tears. Helen was a good muse, a righteous and good wife, he reminded himself. It was in his best interest to keep the peace between them.

"You look like a little red ice pop, Helen. Maybe a cup of tea will help you defrost," Todd said, rising to his feet and motioning for Helen to sit in his place. "C'mere, sugar. Put your momma's quilt around you while I put up some hot water. Chester, here boy, keep my girl warm for me till I get back."

Helen obediently sat on the sofa and drew her knees up to her chin, staring into a rousing fire for the second time that day. Todd called out to her from the kitchen.

"Earl Grey – or green tea with honey and ginseng?"

"Honey and ginseng," Helen replied, recalling the patches of wild ginseng that grew on the sides of the mountains back home and how as cash-poor teenagers, she and Joan spent hundreds of hours hunting and harvesting the precious aromatic roots to peddle at the farmer's market on Sundays. There were professional wild crafters who had far less luck than they did locating and digging up the fabled aphrodisiac amid the tangles of mountain laurel and rhododendron. For years, they had pooled their proceeds into a special fund earmarked for their escape from Dock Watch Hollow. Last she heard, Joan was still living in her parents' old single-pen house and waitressing from four to midnight at the Daisy Mae Diner. Though it was never discussed, she hoped Joan had made good use of their sizeable freedom fund to see to her own needs, whatever they might be. Even then, it hardly assuaged the guilt she felt at leaving her best friend behind.

Helen's long, slender fingers caressed the patchwork quilt Todd had slung over her lap. There were bits and pieces of fabric from childhood dresses and bedcovers, potholders and aprons, tablecloths and handkerchiefs, and a hundred other things, all stitched together to form a vivid manifesto of Helen's life. She couldn't forget a snippet of it, even if she wanted to. Somehow, it was all there in riotous living color, a wedding gift from her mother, who despite her failing strength and eyesight never abided as much as a single crooked stitch. She closed her eyes in ten second interludes, remembering the bitter or sweet memory evoked by each swatch of fabric….

Todd set the fragrant cup of tea on the end table and adjusted the quilted coverlet over Helen's shoulders as she lay sleeping. There was something decidedly different about his young wife these days; something restless and rebellious had rooted in her though he couldn't name it and he sure didn't like it. Her door-slamming departure from the church that morning had done its share of damage and set tongues wagging as to Helen's fitness to be a pastor's wife and helpmate. He didn't like to see her maligned by the other women in the congregation, but between her increasingly defiant behavior and her deepening attachment to the soup kitchen's scandalous ilk, she had left him without a reasonable defense. He'd had no choice but to ask one of Little Flock's elders, Betsy Whitmore, who also happened to sit on the governing board of the city's Department of Mental Health, to initiate creative cuts in staffing at St. Paul's Soup Kitchen. Perhaps that would set Helen back on her heels and give his wayward wife the push she needed to return to the fold!

Chester lifted his speckled head and blinked at Todd serenely before settling into Helen with a long, contented sigh. In my communion with wild birds and beasts of every kind throughout the ages, I have learned, for instance, that there are many things a dog can comprehend, but bitterness is not among them, for it is contrary not only to his nature, but to his very soul. Not so with human flesh and blood; long ago Saint Paul had admonished our Hebrew brethren to *see to that no bitter root spring up and cause trouble, through which many may become defiled.* I feared the bitter root that might have already embedded in Helen's heart and the trouble it would cause should its twisted vines rise up and run rampant under a steady rain of resentment and reck-less desires.

Todd surveyed the tranquil scene, made all the more so by the bronze glow of firelight and the low, steady murmur of the wind outside. He was heartened by the sight of Helen's peaceful slumber, confident that she would soon return to her senses. As for me, I was not so sure, for Helen's last waking thought had not been of her childhood or of her wedding day, of her mother's lovely handiwork or of harvesting ginseng root in the deep green forests of Appalachia, but of keen blue eyes staring back at her through a thin wall of yellow flame….

***

Helen awoke the next morning just moments before her eight o'clock alarm screamed the official time. She threw her arm overhead and batted at the snooze button, making contact on the third try. As she stared at the ceiling, she vaguely recalled waking on the sofa around midnight, seeing the amber coals in the fireplace blinking in the night, and then stumbling to her bed without so much as a change of clothes.

Now she was sorry. As she sat up and raked her fingers through her long wavy hair, she could feel the tangles and the funny ridge where her ponytail had been locked into place for far too long. She had done a long, slow defrost all right, to the point where she felt soft and soggy all over. She peeled back the covers and stood, noticing that Todd had already made up his half of the bed. She wondered if they would be able to start the day afresh, or if there would be an emotional hangover from the day before that would hover between them like fog and reduce their relationship to muffled pleasantries. She had drifted off to sleep hoping that all would be well. She hadn't meant to behave badly, she chastised herself, only to seek out the lonely and the lost, just as the Bible exhorted her to do. There had been no real harm, no foul committed, she reasoned. So why did she feel all aflutter about going to the soup kitchen today – or filled with dread at the thought of her next encounter with Todd?

Helen wavered in front of the clothes rack in her closet, anxiously picking at the different fabrics and unable to commit to any one of them. She threw off her stale clothes, put on her bathrobe, and marched down the hallway, gunning for a bowl of cornflakes that she hoped would set her morning right. She missed her morning grits with sweet butter and a dash of salt. They didn't have grits in the North, she'd soon learned, only fifteen kinds of instant oatmeal and featherweight granola bars that tasted like the kind of stuff they set out as squirrel bait back home.

"Good morning, sugar," Todd said, glancing up from the stovetop where he was just about to pour a mixture of diced tomatoes, onions, and mushrooms into a frying pan. "In less than five minutes you'll be enjoying the finest three-egg omelet this side of the Mason-Dixon line."

Helen smiled, relieved by Todd's cheerful disposition. Maybe she had it all wrong. Maybe he was just as eager to please her as she was to please him; maybe he had been equally neglected these past few months, preoccupied as she was by her job at the soup kitchen. Maybe today was a fresh start for them, as new and unsullied as the five-inch snowfall outside their front door. "No matter how those eggs turn out, I think I might well be the luckiest girl this side of the line, just the same."

She liked that funny, reserved grin, the one Todd sported whenever she complimented him. She thought he was exceedingly humble at heart, even though he had enough charisma and good looks to make a she-devil swoon.

"Let me get you some juice. Orange? Cranberry?"

"I can get it myself, you've got you're hands full right where you are," Helen said, arching onto her tiptoes to kiss Todd on the cheek. Todd lightly grasped her by the chin and redirected her lips to his.

"We're good?" Helen asked shyly. Over the years, it had become their code for gauging the health of their relationship.

"We're good," Todd replied.

Helen nodded and smiled, savoring the peace between them.

"So, what do you have planned for today?" Helen asked, striding toward the refrigerator.

"I'm meeting with Jonathan at nine."

"Shouldn't the architectural work be over by now?"

"Almost," Todd conceded. "But the truth is, I've asked Jonathan to direct our foreign mission program. He's traveled around the world, Helen. He has a lot of good ideas about where we should focus our efforts, and I think the congregation is ready to hear them."

"He's not even a Baptist. What are you thinking?"

"I'm thinking good help is hard to find. I made you the first offer, remember? Besides, he's considering joining our church. He was raised a Methodist, but that's no impediment. It's not like he was a Catholic or some other poor soul who might take some real time and effort to save."

Helen winced at Todd's obvious bias which hit closer to home than he knew. She never did tell him that her mother had her baptized in the Catholic Church and that she'd even received the sacraments of First Holy Communion and Penance. Her father's disdain for the Catholic faith had made an impression on her soul that even now made her feel like she'd somehow been marked with an indelible seal of shame instead of sanctifying grace. And yet, she recalled the mystical beauty of The Church of the Little Flower, a cozy Catholic chapel set on a hillside the next town over where she and her mother worshipped whenever the opportunity would arise. She recalled the large crucifix that was suspended behind the bluestone altar and the lifelike corpse of Christ that was fastened to a rugged cross made of rough, local timber. The sight of it always reminded her that Christ Crucified was not some distant historical event, but something that took place every day right there in the dark hills and hearts of Dock Watch Hollow. It was fearsome and awful to go to Mass, she recalled, and yet the reception of the soft, tender flesh of Christ pressed into her palm and melding with her tongue was a truth and a promise she could neither forsake nor forget.

"Point well taken," Helen replied.

Todd tossed the omelet in the pan once more for good measure and then set it on a plate alongside a crescent of honeydew melon. "Here you go," he said proudly.

"Where's yours? Aren't you having anything?"

"I've got to run," Todd said, picking up his briefcase. "I'm supposed to meet Jonathan at his office downtown...rush hour in the snow, could be slow going."

"Thanks for breakfast," Helen said, her mouth half-full. "It's delicious!"

"You're welcome, Helen. I just wanted to make sure you knew –"

"I do know. I love you, too."

"Have a good day at the soup kitchen, sugar. Be safe, ya hear?"

"I will be," Helen called out as Todd left the kitchen. She heard him whistle his way down the hall and close the front door behind him. Then she glanced at her watch and pushed back her chair, scraping the remains of her breakfast into Chester's bowl. He'd waited patiently at her feet for a morsel or two and she wasn't about to disappoint him. He wagged his tail as he ate without the fear and frenzy he demonstrated when she'd first taken him in. It was likely he'd gone for days at a time without nourishment, and Helen vowed to make up for it by never making a distinction between what was good enough for either of them. She despised the mentality that assumed man's superiority over the animals, preferring to interpret the idea of dominion over the earth as a God-given stewardship and a sacred trust. There was always food enough for the three of them, she asserted, even when Todd balked at the sight of anything but kibble in Chester's bowl.

In the same way, she never felt above the men and women in the soup kitchen, knowing all too well that she might have shared their destiny under only slightly different circumstances. She, however, had borne the sorrows of poverty without ever realizing she was poor until the day the strip mine company took over her town and built fancy living quarters for their managers and their families with broad, white wraparound porches and tall peaks that stood in stark contrast to their tin can trailers. Nor did she know that her clothes were anything less than fine, starched and pressed as they always were, until the day she noticed that the clothing worn by the flatlanders – the children of privilege – were not only starched and pressed, but made of far gentler, prettier fabric than her roughshod white cotton blouses and threadbare jeans. She remembered the day that William Martin, the son of one of the coalfield managers, stuck his hand up her shirt at Joan's thirteenth birthday party, and when she objected, spat on her and called her white hillbilly trash. It seemed like a double pejorative, twice as harsh as was necessary to make his point for she was equally horrified to learn she was either.

From that day forward she lived in a state of disgrace, like a naked, hillbilly Eve whose Paradise had been wheedled from her by a cold-blooded fourteen year old boy with slippery hands and a venomous tongue. There was still a part of her that felt like a phony in her designer brand shoes and long sweaters made of soft Marino wool, like the sapphire-colored one she put on that morning over a pair of fashionably faded jeans. Todd had insisted she buy herself a new wardrobe once they got married; her castoffs had been bundled and brought to the local Goodwill mission in Richmond to be shipped right back to the poor in Dock Watch Hollow and other dwindling coal towns that formed a sooty trail of poverty that pockmarked the emerald hills and valleys of the Blue Ridge Mountains. More often than not, her citified ways and means made her feel more like a traitor than a trendsetter. She grimaced at the thought, then hastily fixed her mind on the midday hours that lay ahead.

She didn't know what she was going to say when she saw Hawk. It was the better part of wisdom to chalk up their encounter to mere serendipity. And yet, she couldn't help but feel there had been a wind at her back that propelled her towards that moment in time, that exhilarating moment when she felt unmasked by clever eyes that knew and accepted her impersonation of Helen, the good preacher's wife. It was a relief, if only a fleeting one, to feel the pulse of her own restlessness and pain. Still, she worried that she had irreparably breached the cardinal rule of outreach that forbade such mixing of the personal with the professional rules of engagement. And yet, she realized, it was all personal, every last bit of it, from the liquid pain in the eyes of the homeless and the sick and the needy, to the way they reached out to her for affirmation that they were not as hopeless and invisible as they felt, to the ache they created in the deep of her chest to ease their pain and give them shelter, not in the form of a paper voucher that was good for a night or two at the local economy hotel, but real flesh and blood shelter in the land of the living. But mostly, it was the kindredness she felt with them that moved her, the reflection they threw back at her as though she labored in a house of mirrors she could not escape until she assimilated all the pieces that stared back at her.

Helen pulled her hair into a loose bun with wayward tendrils that cascaded down the sides of her narrow face and made her look even more delicate than usual. Then, with a tender pat atop Chester's head where it rested on her pillow, Helen strode to the front hall and grabbed her coat and hat. She briefly hunted for her matching cashmere scarf before remembering she'd given it away, much to Todd's consternation. Granted, it had been a gift to her from his sister, Jane, an authentic Southern belle who was just slightly older in years but far more worldly than Helen could ever hope to be. When Jane sent the hat and scarf ensemble to Helen the previous Christmas, she'd written a note on magnolia-scented paper that she thought red suited Helen's vibrant personality; at the time she thought it was a compliment but had since come to wonder if it wasn't Jane's way of saying that Helen just didn't fit into her genteel, pastel-colored world. As a result, Helen hadn't thought even once about the sacrifice or twice about Todd's disapproval – until then. She decided it would be a good idea to purchase a replacement by the time Jane came to visit in less than three weeks.

The drive to the soup kitchen was as slow and arduous as Todd had predicted. She wished she'd followed his example and left a few minutes earlier than normal. If there was one thing Dorothy frowned on, it was when the outreach workers showed up late. While Helen didn't report to Dorothy directly, she withered under her scrutiny just the same, knowing that her opinions were highly valued and solicited by her supervisors.

"Nice of you to show up, Ms. Baldwin." The displeasure in Dorothy's faded blue eyes was magnified by thick corrective lenses in fat, black-rimmed eyeglasses that covered her face like a pair of goggles. Her long white hair was pinned into a high, tight bun that made her look even more severe than her sharply angled face suggested. And yet Helen knew that Dorothy had a genuine soft spot for the poor that made her position of authority at the soup kitchen less of a job than a full-time ministry. She wore a simple wooden cross that dangled from a braided brown cord and on more than one occasion, Helen had seen her grasp it tightly, her thin lips moving in a whispered recitation of prayer at the sight of a particularly pathetic looking soul or the makings of a brawl in the bread line.

"I'm so sorry, Dorothy, the traffic was horrendous." She was glad to see that Tristan was running late as well.

"Never mind that, Helen. There's someone who's been waiting to see you. It's not right to keep our guests waiting, like they haven't done enough waiting in their lifetimes. Waiting for food, waiting for their welfare check, now they're waiting on you," she finished gruffly, gesturing to a doe-eyed girl who sat in a metal chair and stared out the window with her chin in the small cup of her hand. On her lap, nestled in the folds of a chocolate-colored coat that was clearly meant for a man, was a bouquet of long-stemmed pink and red roses. Helen thought she was beautiful; too beautiful to be lacking, for the world always paved a way for pretty girls with the kind of sweet, childlike smile this young woman flashed as Helen approached.

"Hello," Helen said cautiously, testing the temperament beneath the docile expression.

"Hello," the girl answered. "My name is Tess. Are you Helen?"

Helen nodded, captivated by a clear, melodic voice that sounded like wind chimes skipping in a summer breeze. She wondered why she had never seen Tess before, then guessed she must have just arrived by way of a New York City train.

"Are you new in town, Tess? And where did you get those lovely roses this time of year?"

"Oh, they're easy to come by in the flower district," Tess answered. "I get them for a dollar a stem and then sell them 'round here for three dollars apiece. But sometimes I just give them all away if it feels right...depends on the day."

Helen decided that Tess was indeed a transient from New York City, likely one with some form of mental illness if she regularly parted with her livelihood on a whim!

"So what can I do for you? What do you need?"

"What do I need?" Tess repeated with a giggle. "Why, I'm here to give something to you, Helen."

Helen grew suspicious at the sight of Tess' enigmatic smile. She watched as Tess lifted a pale pink rose to the tip of her delicate nose and inhaled deeply, closing her eyes to savor the fragrance. She rolled the thornless stem in her fingertips, then opened her eyes to gaze at the blossom lovingly – almost reverently – before handing it to Helen.

"You came out in this weather to give me a

rose?" Helen said, as she accepted the flower from Tess' outstretched hand. She couldn't help but take a long, deep breath of it herself, for a soothing, mystical fragrance wafted from its creamy center and commanded her senses.

"I had to. I was asked to deliver it here to you."

"By whom?" Helen asked, pleased with herself that she'd remembered to use proper grammar.

"Can't say," Tess replied, turning her gaze to the window once more. She seemed to detach herself from the present moment – to hover somewhere mysterious and distant – then abruptly turned her attention back to Helen. "But it's yourn just the same."

Helen flinched at Tess' lapse into a mountain slang that only Helen would recognize in these parts. The Appalachian hills were thick with such local vernaculars: *hisn* for his, *hern* for hers, *ourn* of ours, *theirn* for theirs…and *yourn* for yours….

"Tess, where did you say you were from?" Helen asked as Tess gathered the eleven remaining roses into a tidy bouquet. She tied their stems together with a wispy yellow ribbon and then tucked the flowers deep into a makeshift holster she wore around her hips.

"I came in on the 7:10 Midtown Express," Tess answered, smiling as she carefully tightened the belt of her overcoat which hung like a long, brown robe. "It was lovely to meet you, Helen," she said as she prepared to leave. Her little round face radiated joy as she clearly considered her mission complete.

"Enjoy your flower," she said as she headed for the door, "somebody's got an eye on you!"

"Thank you," Helen called out weakly. She glanced around the soup kitchen, wondering who else had witnessed their exchange. Oddly, it seemed as though no one was paying any mind at all; she was glad for the evidence of the rose in her hand lest she conclude she'd just met a ghost who had strayed too far from the coalfields!

"Nice flower, Helen. You got a secret admirer or what?"

So Hawk had noticed her encounter with Tess, Helen thought, debating if it was mere coincidence or something more. Helen rattled the thought from her head. But who else knew where to find her on any given Monday, except for Todd? Surely that was it, she decided; Todd had run into Tess on his way downtown and sent her a rose to confirm that all was well between them. How utterly sweet and thoughtful! Helen smiled and took another deep breath from petals that had splayed even wider in the few moments since Tess' departure.

"It's from my husband," Helen replied as she turned around to face Hawk, her nose still buried in the fragrant petals. She didn't realize how feminine and beautiful she appeared at that moment; Jesus, Hawk thought, she looked like something out of a dream, the kind of dream he used to have before the war turned beauty to ashes and his body into a slave to slanty-eyed boom boom girls who sold themselves to lonely GIs for a pack of menthol cigarettes. Hawk looked away, suddenly at a loss for words.

"What's the matter, Hawk?" Helen said. "Why, you look as restless as the tip of a bullock's tail," Helen teased.

"What the hell does that mean?"

"Why, you're all bumfuzzled! You know, out of sorts." Helen laughed at Hawk's pained expression. "What's gotten into you?"

"Look, I just came over to see how you're doing. I see you got home okay…that's good," Hawk stammered, cussing softly as he realized how lame he sounded.

"I told you I'd manage," Helen replied absentmindedly, noticing that Tristan had arrived at the soup kitchen and was observing her intently. "I think I was just feeling a mite sorry for myself, that's all. But I'm fine now, really, I am." The last thing she needed was a dressing down from Tristan for fraternizing too closely with the guests again. She'd already gotten her day's fill from Dorothy!

"Sure you are, Helen," Hawk pronounced, turning on the heels of his boots and taking a long stride in the opposite direction.

"Hawk — "

Hawk stopped walking but refused to turn around. He suspected Helen was messing with his head, a dangerous thing to do to a Vietnam vet, he thought to remind her. The last thing he needed was a woman getting under his skin, even if she did make him feel like he was something better than a half-crazed leatherneck who had 93 confirmed kills to his credit and a dog-eared copy of his DD214 in his pocket that more or less said he was FUBAR – *F'd Up Beyond All Repair* – courtesy of the Viet Cong.

"I just wanted to thank you again for being a right good friend to me. I appreciate the kindness."

Hawk slowly careened his neck around and gazed at Helen with narrowed eyes. "Don't mistake my kindness as a sign of weakness," he reminded her.

Helen stiffened at the hardness of his tone. She nodded and offered an uneasy smile, then returned her focus to the flower in her hand. As quickly as it had opened, its blossom had begun to droop and fade. She feared it was a harbinger of things to come as the lightness in her heart threatened to give way to the anxious roll in the pit of her stomach. Why, she wondered, did Hawk have this uncanny shock-and-awe effect on her that made her want to bare her soul and run for cover all at the same time? She caressed a scalloped rose petal between her fingertips and glanced nervously around the room. Her eyes circled back to Hawk, who had turned to face her once more.

"I meant it when I said you can stop by China Beach anytime." Hawk's face was set like flint and Helen marveled at the rugged dents and chiseled angles that made it appear like the forbidden side of a mountain. She dared to look more deeply into his eyes in the hope that she would rediscover the keen interest he'd shown in her the day before, but there were only cool, dark vaults of blue looking back at her.

"You're a good man, Hawk," was all she could think of to say.

"Semper Fi, baby," Hawk replied, then he shrugged and walked away. Helen followed him with her eyes to the far side of the room where he stopped to chat with the pretty interns from Legal Aid. He made the blond one giggle and blush. Helen bristled and clenched her withering rose.

"Helen!"

The voice that shouted into the soup kitchen was shrill and unfamiliar. Helen startled at its urgency and whirled about, searching for its source.

"Helen, come quick!"

Helen saw a teenage boy waving from the front door. She watched Tristan rise from his customary seat on the stage to intervene. She arrived at the doorway just seconds after him.

"What's the matter, Randy?" Tristan said.

"It's Frankie, he's really sick and he wants to see Helen."

"Where is he?" Helen replied with a dead calm that belied the panic in her chest.

"He's on the back steps, behind Damien House. I think maybe he overdosed or something. Jesus, I think he's dying."

"For God's sake, call an ambulance," Tristan demanded, shoving his cell phone into Randy's hand. "Helen, come back! It's not our job to get involved in things outside of the soup kitchen!"

Helen bolted out the door and down the stairs, running full tilt through icy slush in the direction of Damien House. It took her less than a minute to arrive; when she did, she stooped in the snow, her frosted breath forming a protective shroud around me. I smiled at her weakly. I wished I could do more.

"Frankie! Good Lord, Frankie, you're bleeding, what happened?"

Helen heard the voices shouting at her back, voices warning her not to touch me without latex gloves and a mask. She sat behind me and gently raised my bloody head from the crusty ridge of hard-packed snow onto the pillow of her thigh. She stroked my hair and pressed the red scarf I wore over the deep wounds on my forehead, speaking in soothing whispers and assuring me that help was on the way.

The sight of me brought tears to Helen's eyes and it made me wince to see them.

"Are you in much pain, Frankie? How did this happen, can you tell me?" Helen begged. I could tell she thought I'd been felled by too much Costa Rican *tecata* tunneling through my veins. I didn't have the strength or the will to refute it.

The wail of police and ambulance sirens bounced off the low-slung clouds and drew closer by the second.

"Frankie, would you like to pray? I can pray for both of us, okay?"

I blinked, hoping she would understand my heart's desire.

"Our Father, who art in Heaven..." Helen began, just as the ambulance arrived.

"Step back, Miss. What? Does she know? Miss, did you know this man has AIDS? You're putting yourself at a terrible risk...."

"Hallowed be thy name..."

"What's her name? Helen? Helen, we're going to need you to come along with us to the hospital. We'd like to check you over for possible exposure to the virus that causes AIDS...."

"Thy Kingdom come. Thy will be done on earth as it is in Heaven..."

"Helen, do you have any open cuts or scratches? Did Frankie spit at you or bite you?"

"Give us this day our daily bread and forgive us our trespasses, as we forgive those who trespass against us..."

"Please, Helen, let go of his hand. We've got the situation under control."

"And lead us not into temptation, but deliver us from evil..."

As I was taken away, I mustered all my strength to silently mouth my soul's agreement. *"Amen,"* I heard her speak for me.

Heavenly Father, have mercy on Helen, I implored before I closed my eyes and drifted toward the Light, deeply grieved by the sight of Helen kneeling and weeping among a shower of fleshy rose petals scattered upon the crimson snow.

Chapter 6
Gift and Mystery

"I suppose you're wondering why Stuart asked you to report to the office today instead of the soup kitchen."

"Yes, Ma'am, I was wondering about that," Helen replied. The truth was, she'd been worried sick about whether Dorothy had given her a bad report for being late to work on Monday – or if there was something more to the cryptic phone message Stuart had left for her yesterday morning. He had simply instructed her to come directly to his office for a meeting at noon on Wednesday. Even then, he'd sounded ill at ease, barely murmuring a proper goodbye before hanging up the phone. Now, he looked downright fretful.

"Helen, we understand there was an – *incident* – at the soup kitchen on Monday."

Betsy Whitmore seated herself at the head of the dark walnut conference table. She was a tall, fashionably thin woman with ash blond hair that flipped girlishly at the ends and made her appear far less threatening than she actually was. Helen found herself fixated on Betsy's carefully drawn eyebrows which accented pretty blue eyes that crinkled at the edges when she smiled – a smile that made Helen think of those silly toothpaste commercials that were all teeth and no substance. Or all vine and no 'taters, as the folk back home would say.

"I suppose you could call it that," Helen said, glancing at Stuart for moral support. He smiled wanly from across the table but offered little more.

"Can you be more specific?" Besty asked, tilting forward in her high-backed, polished leather chair, prepared to note Helen's reply on a legal-sized yellow notepad.

"Well, if you're referring to what happened to Frankie, it wasn't really at the soup kitchen," Helen said carefully. "It happened on the steps of Damien House."

"But you were there?"

"I was summoned," Helen replied.

"By whom?"

"I think his name is Randy, but I'm not sure. My friend, Frankie, asked him to find me."

"Your friend, Frankie? You mean Frankie Bernadone, the soup kitchen client."

"Yes," Helen replied, wondering why she was making such a fuss.

"You are aware, Helen, that the parameters of your job call for you to be an objective observer and source of referral on behalf of the Department of Mental Health."

"Yes," Helen replied.

Betsy leaned into her seat and clicked the top of her ballpoint pen several times in a slow, pensive manner. She rifled through a short stack of paper in front of her, selecting one sheet in particular from the middle of the pile.

"I trust you've seen this?" she said, holding up a thin paper that was rife with black boxes and ink. Helen tried to read what was written at the top of the page but couldn't quite discern the words.

"No, Ma'am, I don't believe I have. What is it?"

"It's the police report detailing what happened on Monday. It says here, Helen, that you put yourself in a position to be exposed to the virus that causes AIDS. Were you aware that Frankie B. had AIDS?"

"Yes, I know he has AIDS," Helen replied, refusing to think or speak of me in the past tense. "They checked me out at the hospital pretty good. From what they told me, I shouldn't fret about being infected. They said to come back for a blood test in six months, just to be sure."

"I also understand you were expressly informed prior to leaving the soup kitchen that it was not within the scope of your duties to intervene."

"Yes, I believe Tristan said something like that, but —"

"But you were too emotionally involved to follow the protocol for handling a crisis situation."

"I wouldn't say that," Helen replied, unsettled by the emptiness of Betsy Whitmore's gaze.

"Frankie is a friend; wouldn't you want to help a friend?"

"Frankie was a guest who needed medical intervention from first responders and other qualified personnel."

"Well, until they got there, there was me," Helen said. "I believe I was of some comfort to Frankie, surely that counts for something."

"That makes you an awfully nice person, Helen, but not a very effective outreach worker. What do you think the other guests in the soup kitchen thought when they saw your emotional breakdown outside of Damien House?"

"I suppose they thought I was upset about my friend," Helen said, recalling her resistance to being separated from me and the heavy sobs that overcame her when the ambulance workers wrenched her hand from mine.

"More likely they saw someone who was emotionally unstable and in no position to help them deal with their own distress. Certainly, I would have to second the motion," Betsy finished sternly.

"I'm sorry," Helen said, "I guess I didn't think it all the way through. Everything happened so fast...."

"It always does," Betsy said. Stuart nodded in agreement.

"Look, Helen – "

"Please," Helen said, tipped off by the sappy looks she was receiving from the two of them. "I love my job. I'll do anything to set things right, I know I can."

"The truth is," Betsy said haltingly, "Stuart and I have been going over the agency's budget. It doesn't look like the federal funding we were counting on is going to come through for us this year. I'm afraid we're headed for some staff reductions anyway."

"What are you saying?"

Betsy looked at Stuart, prodding him with her eyes.

"I think what Betsy is saying is that we're going to have to let you go, Helen. I'd really like to give you another chance, but the numbers – well, they just don't support having two outreach workers at St. Paul's right now. For the good of the guests, we'll allow you to bring proper closure to your relationships there – but this Friday will be your last day on the job."

Helen grasped a thread of hope in Stuart's carefully chosen words. "So, is this a temporary thing? I mean, is there a chance I could get my job back?"

Betsy smiled kindly. "Why of course, Helen. There's always that possibility. After all, I know you have only the best intentions. There's something to be said for that."

Helen nodded, determined to retain her composure despite feeling stung by Betsy Whitmore's poor excuse for a compliment.

"Will you call me?" Helen inquired softly, forcing Stuart to meet her gaze. She trusted he wouldn't lie to someone who looked him straight in the eye.

"If something opens up, we'll call you," Stuart replied as Betsy gathered the papers in front of her and stiffly set them on edge, signaling that their meeting was over.

"Then I can't ask for anything more. I'm awfully sorry I disappointed you," Helen said, rising from the deep cushion of her chair and extending her hand across the table. "Truly, it was a pleasure working with you."

Helen thought Stuart seemed as discomfited as a bullfrog in a hailstorm, but she didn't pay it any mind. She was too preoccupied with what she was going to tell Todd and how the guests at the soup kitchen would react to the news. She was grateful they were at least giving her a chance to say a proper goodbye, though one day hardly seemed like time enough. There were people whom she might never see again, given their sporadic visits to St. Paul's. The very thought of missing the chance to see them and explain her hasty departure made her misty-eyed and fearful they would think of her as a traitor, just another hired hand who abandoned them without a backward glance. They were used to a revolving door of do-gooders. She swore she would never be one of them, that she would stand in the breach for them as long as she had the power and breath to do so. As she veered from the conference room, she felt that she had been robbed of both, for she felt helpless and faint in the wake of her dismissal. She had expected a reprimand and a warning – but she had not expected this!

Helen stepped onto a sidewalk scattered with leftover crumbs of ice. The temperature had begun to rise, turning the once-pristine landscape into a shrinking vista of soot-smeared snow banks and piles of inky slush that reminded her of the slurry ponds formed from the coalfield's toxic run off. It was half past noon; she imagined Todd would be in the middle of his meeting with the building and grounds committee, discussing plans for landscaping around the new church house come the first sign of spring. Besides, she wasn't quite ready to face him with the news that she'd been…laid off? Fired? She wasn't sure herself what had just happened! All it really meant was that she was out of job – but not just a job. Working at the soup kitchen had become her passion and her joy for when she was with her friends – *the guests* – in the soup kitchen, she felt as though she was among family: a great, big, hungry, dysfunctional family that asked nothing from her but to simply be who she was. She had only begun to discover what that meant.

She stood still for a moment in the middle of the sidewalk and forced herself to breathe slowly and deeply, feeling the cool rush of air pierce her lungs and spur them back into a rhythmic rise and fall. The pressure of unspent tears gathered below her eyes and she blinked once, long and hard, in an effort to banish them.

By the time Helen crossed the parking lot and reached her car, she had already decided where she would go next. No longer bound by restrictions or propriety, she headed straight for the hospital's east ward, the one reserved for the poor and uninsured. They were relegated to the windowless rooms on the third floor, in a wing that had been converted from storage space and still had the cold, steel pillars and beams to prove it. She would have come sooner, but Todd had advised her not to do anything that could further impact her health or jeopardize her job at the soup kitchen. He'd held her in his arms that night as she cried about "the incident" as Betsy Whitmore called it – urging her to give things a few days to work themselves out. He had even called the hospital on Helen's behalf, using his influence as a minister to gain access to privileged patient information. Then again, it didn't seem like the poor really had any privileges at all, for the hospital seemed more than willing to part with details to anyone who might actually have the resources to pick up the tab for an indigent's care.

"Looks like Frankie's going to make it," Todd had assured her, stroking the crown of Helen's head and placing a box of tissue within reach. "He's going to be in the hospital for a few more days. He has a concussion and a broken rib, but he's stable for now."

"For now?"

"For now," Todd repeated. "Given his – *affliction* – he's always going to be in a vulnerable condition. You do know that sooner or later, Frankie is going to die from AIDS – if his habit doesn't kill him first."

"Yes, Todd, I know that."

"What were you thinking, Helen? You put your-self in a perilous position today." Todd was reluctant to further upset her but unwilling to let her poor judgment slide.

"I was only thinking that I didn't want him to die alone. He was bleeding everywhere – his hands, his head, his side – I thought he was dying, Todd. Surely you can imagine what a terrible thing it would be to die alone with no one to comfort you or to hold your hand or to pray with you."

"Is that what you did? You prayed with him?"

"Yes."

Todd nodded, stroking his chin thoughtfully. "Then you did a merciful thing, Helen. I can't fault you for that. I only hope that you stay as healthy as the hospital says you are. In the meantime you must never speak a word of this to anyone," Todd warned, knowing he could count on Betsy's cooperation and discretion.

"I'll be fine, Todd. I just know I will be," Helen said with quiet conviction.

"I guess we'll just have to wait and see," Todd replied. As far as he was concerned, the question of Helen's health would be handy justification for the lack of intimacy between them, knowing he couldn't continue to dodge the issue much longer. He didn't rebuke Helen anymore that night. Instead, he allowed Chester to curl up beside her in their bed and relegated himself to the living room sofa where he'd grown accustomed to sleeping whenever his conscious got the better of him.

Helen's heels clicked across the checkerboard brown and white tiles that stretched from the elevator to the swinging double doors that marked the entrance to the hospital's east wing. Unlike other areas of the hospital that bustled with noisy visitors and an ever-changing landscape of blue and white uniforms in diligent motion, the east ward was steeped in the hush of ennui and abandonment. There were no gaily painted murals on the walls or chatty messages and smiley faces scrawled on dry-erase boards outside the patients' doors; no floral bouquets or boxes of unfinished chocolates left at the nurse's station by patients who were discharged into the care of their happy families; no comfy couches in little niches where people could gather for cheer or consolation. Here, there was only the white glare of fluorescent light bouncing off shiny floors that never scuffed for lack of traffic and a broad green chalkboard that announced the name and room number of each patient sequestered within.

Helen proceeded to room number 307 and peeked through the narrow panel of glass that ran down one side. Unable to find a reason not to enter, she knocked lightly, then opened the door and stepped into a room with blue concrete walls.

"Frankie?" she called softly. "Frankie, it's Helen – from the soup kitchen."

I would have known who had come through the door had she only said my name and nothing more, for her voice was like that of a meadowlark, full of sweetness and sunlight. And had she said nothing at all, I still would have known she was there, for whether she knew it or not, a faint but ever-present fragrance of roses announced her comings and goings and infused the air with the eternal breath of summer. I felt my heart leap with joy in my chest, which was still heavily bandaged from my fall.

"Helen," I whispered back, my voice hoarse from lack of use, for no one had come to call on me that day except for a strapping male nurse who peeked his head in the doorway every couple of hours, and whose manner was both solicitous and foreboding: he would not tolerate any bad behavior from the indigents! For the last few days, I had been sweating and shaking profusely as my body fought the painful withdrawal of opiates from my daily routine. The hospital staff could only do so much to ameliorate my misery and promised that the worst would soon be over – though it hardly felt that way. I was embarrassed by the tangle of sheets on the floor and the way my paper-thin hospital gown clung to my bony frame and outlined my nakedness beneath.

Helen walked past the empty bed from which my roommate had been evicted that morning. The notorious five-days-and-out policy was strictly enforced by the hospital's administration lest the street people start to think of the east ward as the local flophouse. Only those with potentially life threatening illnesses or injuries received extended stays and I hoped I would qualify, not knowing if Damien

House would allow me to return. After all, I had promised to kick the habit….but….

"Stuff happens," Helen said, looking down at me with a sympathetic shrug as she pulled a chair to my bedside.

"Thank you for coming," was all I could manage to say, but with a bit of effort, I was able to stretch out my hand to this precious child who had risked all to be my consolation in my hour of need.

"Aren't you a sight for sore eyes," Helen continued, grasping my hand and gazing curiously at the smooth unblemished flesh of my palm. Her expression was apprehensive and I didn't have to ask what it was that troubled her. I had suffered the stigmata – the five wounds of Christ – since mid-September of my forty-second year. Back then, in 1224 when it first appeared, it was not the fabrication of magicians or hysterics as it was so often today, but a supernatural mark of grace and the most intimate union with Christ Crucified. But how could I explain the nature of such things? Even if I'd had the words, I did not have the will, for it was contrary to God's plan that I should reveal my true identity.

"I thought…" Helen started, then stopped. "Your hands…your head…." Helen replayed her mind's own version of the events of that day, sure of what she'd seen and felt: a warm crimson tide pressed between our palms as she held on tightly.

"Yes, I banged my head pretty good," I interrupted, recalling the excruciating, supernatural pain that had sent me reeling. "They tell me I have a concussion. Maybe even some memory loss."

"But you're going to be all right," Helen asserted, and I could tell that she was desperately hoping I would agree. The truth was, I was weary of the confines and weakness of my flesh and longed to return to the radiant light and peace of my homeland. But the look in Helen's face – the way she fluttered her eyelashes to disburse the tears before they brimmed – made me choose my words more carefully.

"So they say," I replied, suspecting otherwise.

"Frankie, I was thinking," Helen said, and for a moment it seemed as though she'd been given the ability to discern my thoughts as well. "Remember that Sunday when you came to Little Flock with me?"

I paused, wishing it was among the things erased from my memory.

"And you said you were thinking about going back home?"

"Ah, yes, I remember saying that."

"Well, maybe this is a good time to go home, Frankie. Maybe I can help you get there."

I smiled and felt my heart swell with love for Helen, who knew nothing of what she was saying but still believed it with all her might.

"Not that I want to see you go, mind you," she continued, scrutinizing me with a sharp, steady gaze. "So – where is home?" she prodded.

"My dear Helen," I began softly. "That was

merely the ramblings of a sick and tired old soul. You shouldn't have taken it to heart."

"But where will you go when you're discharged?"

"I'll go back to Damien House if they'll have me. If not...."

"If not, then you'll come home with me," Helen finished. She arched her eyebrows expectantly, prepared to fend off any objections I might have.

"I can't imagine your husband would approve," I said, not wanting to offend her but loathe that she should suffer any illusions. My presence in Helen's life had already caused its share of trouble and I wished to spare her further heartache, though I knew it was a futile hope. "I'm pretty sure your boss at the mental health department wouldn't like it much either."

Helen released my hand and leaned back in the chair she had shimmied to my bedside. For a moment, she buried her face in her palms, then slowly let her hands slide down her face, revealing dewy green eyes that quickly looked away.

"No sense troubling yourself about that. I've been – *let go*. They said they ran out of funding. That's how they put it to me anyhow."

"When did that happen?" I asked calmly, hoping to defuse Helen's distress.

Helen glanced at her watch. "Oh, about an hour ago," she said, mustering a brave smile. "Congratulations, you're the first to know. Well, misery loves company, isn't that what they say?"

"I'm not miserable, Helen," I said gently; at least I didn't feel that way in my soul. "But I can see that you are, and I'm sorry for that. I'm sorry you got hurt."

I wanted her to cry, to plunge herself into the pain and humiliation the world had just heaped upon her so that she could pass through it and rise above it like Noah's dove over the waters of the flood. Otherwise, I feared she would sink into the confusion and despair that threatened to engulf her these past few months and sweep her away to a place that was too wild and deep for her redemption or return. "Besides, I'm pretty sure this is entirely my fault," I added.

"They're just being biggity, that's all," Helen said, her soft southern drawl in full effect. She straightened her back and flattened her lips into a tight line of self-defense.

"Biggity?"

"Uh huh. That's what we call them folks who think they're better than everybody else. I've a mind to ask 'em how we're ever s'posed to *outreach* anybody if we're not allowed to get close enough to touch 'em. It just doesn't make a speck of sense to me." Helen shook her head ruefully, well aware that her perfect syntax was slipping faster than a muddy pig on the butcher's block.

"I do know that if it wasn't for your prayers and consolation, I wouldn't have made it through," I said, certain that it was true. I could remember the feel of Helen's hand in my own, connecting me to this world in a way that made it unbearable to leave, at least until I'd had a chance to say a proper good-bye.

"You remember that?" Helen said.

"I'll never forget it, Helen. Nor will our Lord forget the mercy you showed me that day."

"You sound pretty sure of that, Frankie. You got an inside line? 'Cause if you do, I sure could use a little help. I don't know what I'm going to tell Todd when I see him."

"What are you afraid of?"

"Oh, I don't know," Helen sighed. "Maybe I just don't want to hear him jawin' at me, sayin' it's all for the best – or that God works in mysterious ways – or some other hokum that will make it sound like this is anything less than the whopping cow pile that it is!"

I tried not to laugh but Helen's no-nonsense mountain slang caught me off guard. I held my wounded side protectively as I laughed long and heartily. At first, she looked at me perplexed; then she realized that I couldn't stop even if I wanted to and followed my lead so that we were both crying and laughing and laughing and crying until we both heaved and hawed and finally caught our breath.

"That felt good," Helen finally managed to say.

I could do little more than nod and wipe the tears from my eyes. Just then, Carl, the head nurse, poked his head in the room and glared at us suspiciously.

"What's going on in here?"

"We're just catching up," Helen said sweetly. "Everything's fine."

"He's not supposed to get himself worked up, Miss..."

"Helen. Helen Baldwin."

"It's not good for his vitals."

"I beg to disagree – *Carl*," said Helen, squinting at the badge he wore around his neck on a strand of yellow lanyard. "I reckon his vitals are more vital than ever." She winked at me and smiled broadly as Carl approached.

I shrugged and feigned innocence. Carl lifted my wrist and timed the beats of my heart, commanding silence from the both of us. When he was done, he gently laid my arm at my side and imparted one last warning shot with his eyes.

"Easy does it, Frankie. Doctor's orders," he growled unconvincingly as he passed through the doorway. In fact, I thought I saw him stand a little taller and stifle a satisfied grin that all was exceedingly well on his watch.

"I guess you checked out all right," Helen said, feeling relieved.

"Lucky for you," I replied.

Helen laughed softly.

"Tell me why, Frankie, every time I have a mind to comfort you, I'm the one who walks away feeling better just for being with you."

"Maybe you just feel free to be yourself, Helen. Maybe it's easier when you don't have to worry about being the perfect wife or outreach worker or

Bible-belt Baptist. Maybe you already are."

"What?"

"Perfect."

Helen cocked her head as though flummoxed by the notion that she didn't have to change a single thing about herself. Not for Todd, not for God, and certainly not for Betsy Whitmore! She twirled a corkscrew of hair around her pointer finger until she spiraled through to the end, thinking the whole time about Betsy's impeccable steel gray suit and matching gray pumps, her classically squared shoulders, her smooth blond hair, and her flawless, porcelain complexion, all of which converged with a host of other attributes to form the epitome of perfection. But there was one thing Helen hadn't seen peering out of Betsy's crystalline blue eyes, and that was *soul*. The woman lacked soul and it pleased Helen to put her finger on the abstract thing that had bothered her so.

"Thank you, Frankie," she murmured.

"You're welcome, Helen," I replied, my voice getting thinner as my strength began to fade. The excitement of Helen's visit had taken its toll, but I was happy to pay the price of her nearness. My eyelids started to droop beyond my control and I felt her reach for my hand once more.

"Frankie, I'll be checking up on you. I'm going to leave my phone number on your bedside table. You make sure to call me if there's anything you need. I won't see you put out on the street, you hear?"

I could sense Helen hovering over me and below the sweeping blackness of my eyelids I constructed the earnest expression of her face, its utter beauty and its soulful quality that both uplifted and broke my heart in swift and unexpected turns. I felt her squeeze my fingers before letting go of my hand, and then this – what was this? – a tender kiss on my forehead where the sensation of long slender barbs had pierced the skin and left me dazed and breathless on the steps of Damien House. How strangely beautiful that Love comes as softly as a brush of the lips and as brutally as thorns pressed into flesh. That it is one and the same Love is gift and mystery to me.

***

Helen didn't go straight home that day. She wandered the streets and narrows that bordered the city square, hoping to run into guests from the soup kitchen whose attendance was too sporadic to assure she would see them on her last day of work. There had been a recent spate of cloudy days that made the city look even colder than the north wind that bit her cheeks and ears and made her stop in the middle of the sidewalk from time to time to brace herself against its powerful gusts. She wasn't used to the ferocity of the wind. Dock Watch Hollow was tucked into the mountainside and sheltered from all but the wiliest of winds that managed to wend their way through the mountain passes and shake the trees silly every now and then. No, it wasn't ever the wind that she feared; it was the cool muddy water, the torrents that churned and gushed through the foothills and valleys on the heels of a crushing summer storm that were altogether another matter. Whole towns such as hers collapsed like a big box of matchsticks turned loose on the ground and carried downstream until they came to rest at some crazy bend in the river, a million pieces of kindling and a kitchen sink or two up for grabs. There'd always been at least one bloated body of a man, woman or child found by some passerby along the wooded banks once the water receded; Helen was grateful she'd been spared any such horror on her long hikes into the woods where she often hid from the sooty cloud that started its descent upon her own little house when the five o'clock whistle blew, a shrill and sure signal that her father would be home in an hour – more or less – depending on which tavern lured him and for how long. People liked Horace Hicks and his broad, easy smile and lively green eyes that were mirrors of her own. He had a way of making every man feel like he was his best friend, the way he'd sneak up behind a fellow on his barstool and jostle his shoulders in a warm, familiar greeting that would elicit a cheerful exchange and a round of scotch on Fridays or cheap local beer on Wednesdays when money got scarce. He'd make his way down the bar until he told every new joke he'd heard on his prized, long-wave transistor radio that picked up stations as far north as Philadelphia, the ones with the shock jocks who said things no one in Dock Watch Hollow would dare to say – except for Horace, who often repeated what he'd heard with a schoolboy's innocent glee that made everything forgivable after a respectably long shake of the head.

Helen understood what her mother saw in him, at least insofar as his tall, muscular build and energetic manner. Those were highly valued traits in coal country, where the bend of a strong man's back put food on the table and a smile on a woman's face. All in all, Horace was a handsome fellow who never wanted for much of anything but an education, but it was want enough to keep him from ever being more than the black-and-blue collar grunt that he was from seven to five, Monday through Saturday, and even some Sundays, too.

On his odd day off, Horace would take *the wife,* as he called her, into Grundy to buy her a new dress or some other object of her desire, which Mary Hicks hinted at by leaving raggedly coupons and glossy newspaper ads on the kitchen table next to his gunmetal lunchbox. On rare occasions he even invited Helen to come along, but she always declined his offers, unable to abide the sight of her father holding her mother's hand so tenderly as though she were the only woman in the world – despite the fact that he pinned another young woman to a mattress every third night or so under the same tin roof. It just didn't square with Helen and she would've said something...something as hard and mean and wild as the eyeteeth of a junkyard dog...if only...if only her mother didn't look so Godawfully happy in her father's arms.

Helen stopped walking when she reached the end of the sidewalk that pointed to China Beach West. The trees swayed rowdily overhead, flailing their limbs as though to grab her attention and warn her against taking another step. Nevertheless, the crepe soles of her black boots inched toward the visible line where the dun-colored concrete came to an abrupt end and a matted trail of wintering grass began. She lingered there for a long time, searching for a flicker of firelight or a sign of life in the trees where Butch and the others stretched makeshift hammocks from branch to branch to avoid the chill of the frozen earth. The stillness of the woods disappointed her, but she knew the stealth and cunning of the Vietnam vets was reason enough not to trust her senses alone.

"Helen? Helen!"

She stiffened at the distant calling of her name – then slowly turned her head toward the city block behind her and the familiar voice that drifted into her frostbitten ears. She lamented that she'd mistakenly left her red beret in the car, which was parked a mile away in the commuter lot at the train station. She'd been all too eager – desperate even – to connect with soup kitchen guests before they disappeared down the fox and rabbit holes that were scattered throughout the city.

Todd's strong, broad shoulders rolled back as he

broke into a controlled sprint to close the distance between them. When he reached Helen's side, he exhaled heavily and examined her closely from her head to her toehold at the end of the sidewalk.

"Jeez, Helen, I've got half the congregation out looking for you. Where have you been? What are you doing here?" Todd searched the vista before him, the same one he'd seen Helen searching from afar, but saw nothing that gave him cause for concern. Helen struggled for a credible reply.

"You're just out walking again, is that it? Is this some crazy new habit of yours designed to make all of us worry ourselves sick over you?"

"Of course not," Helen murmured, prepared for the chastisement she knew would come. "As you can see, I ran out of sidewalk...so I stopped," she said with a hopeless shrug that Todd found both maddening and poignant at the same time.

"I know what happened today," Todd said softly as his anger began to fade.

"You do?"

"Betsy Whitmore stopped by my office early this afternoon. She wanted to make sure that there'd be no hard feelings on account of their decision to let you go, her being a trustee and elder at Little Flock and all."

"Oh," Helen replied, secretly glad she'd been spared the burden of breaking the news. "But why all the fuss? What did you think I was going to do, throw myself under a train? It's just a job," Helen scoffed, wincing as she said it.

"I don't know, maybe I did think that," Todd replied, "especially when Jonathan came back from a meeting in New York this afternoon and spotted our car in the parking lot at the station. He said he found a red hat lying on the pavement next to it. That's when I started to worry that maybe you'd panicked and hopped on a train, or were taken by force, or I don't know, maybe one of those homeless guys – "

"Don't say that, Todd," Helen admonished, looking him squarely in the eye and daring him to finish his sentence.

"You've been missing for hours. What was I supposed to think? Where's your cell phone, anyway?"

"In the car, I guess," Helen said, patting down her pockets.

"A lot of good that does," Todd said, taking his own phone from the inside pocket of his trench coat and dialing furiously. *"Yeah, this is Todd...I found her...yeah, she's okay...call the others, will you? Tell them I said thank you. I'll do that. Goodbye."*

"You'll do what?" Helen asked.

"Go easy on you," Todd replied. He sighed and reached for Helen's hand. "I know how much that job meant to you, Helen, no matter what you say. I'm sorry it turned out this way, but you know that in the end, things always happen for the best."

Helen smiled vacantly and nodded. She thought she saw the slightest movement in the woods ahead

– or perhaps it was simply the encroaching shadows of dusk that played tricks on her eyes and made her heart skip with hope and wonder.

"Come on, sugar, let's go home."

Helen nodded and leaned into Todd's sturdy frame, grateful for the warmth of his arm around her waist as he steered her away from the sidewalk's end. Two hundred yards away, Hawk arose from the stillness of his sniper's crouch on the cold, hard ground, a position he had learned to assume for hours – even days – on end in tall patches of exotic elephant grass that barely stirred under the scorching heat of an Asian sun. His life depended on his ability to lay motionless, waiting for his target to come into view. And when it did, he had but one straight shot to the head or the heart before his cover was blown for good. Only this time, his target wasn't a wily gook in the grass…his sights were set on a beautiful southern girl who made him forget he was *FUBAR*, who made him believe in second chances, whose heart he wanted for his own, given of her own free will. It would do him no good to seize by force what was too fragile to grasp, lest it fall to pieces in his hand. If nothing else, he was a patient man. He would wait for time and circumstance to make the first move, and when they did – he would be ready.

Despite the preacher's untimely interruption, he was heartened by Helen's appearance at the end of the sidewalk, though he didn't know what had brought her there or why she'd been AWOL from the soup kitchen that day. It had taken every last bit of hardcore, military discipline he could muster not to reveal his presence; but he knew that Helen would have to be the one to come to him, to cross the divide between them, to take a chance on the gift and mystery of the unknown.

And for the first time in thirty-five years, Hawk prayed.

Chapter 7
Great Expectations

"Good morning, Helen," said Dorothy, and for the first time since Helen began working at the soup kitchen a little over four months ago, she detected in Dorothy's voice the gentleness of the soul within the iron-clad woman who stood at the helm of St. Paul's. Helen admired the way the guests looked up to Dorothy like some kind of hardcore den mother, never sassing her or trying to pull one over on her. They seemed to know that even if they succeeded in doing so, the very act would only serve to diminish their own dignity – not Dorothy's, whose grace under pressure seemed supernatural. She was the sternest and yet the most peaceable person Helen had ever known, for even when she raised her voice it was still infused with a fierce love that covered the multitude of sins afflicting the community of St. Paul's Soup Kitchen. It was this crazy, eclectic, soul-stirring community that Helen prepared to leave in a series of passionate speeches rehearsed deep into the night, none of which she remembered that morning as she walked into the soup kitchen while the volunteer cooks still hovered over steamy pots and pans in the galley. It was barely eleven o'clock, but she didn't want to miss the coming or going of a single guest, knowing it was her only chance to express her gratitude and love for each and every one of them. Now, she wondered if she would get past the lump in her throat that made it hard to respond to Dorothy's surprisingly personal greeting, which was uncharacteristically soft and sympathetic. Normally, Dorothy would simply raise an eyebrow in recognition or glance at her watch to make sure Helen was on time. Surely she already knew, Helen thought, that today was to be her last day. Maybe she even felt a little bit sorry for her.

Helen waved and barely smiled, which in turn made Dorothy frown.

"What is it, child?" Dorothy said, crossing the short distance between them.

"Don't you know?"

Dorothy peered over the thick, black frame of her glasses. "Know what?"

"I've been...laid off."

"Since when?"

"Since Wednesday. This is my last day on the job."

"Why?"

"Funding issues, I guess. You really didn't know?"

"Well, I do know Tristan's nose was out of joint on account of what happened on Monday. But I didn't hear any rumble about you getting fired."

The word made Helen flinch. Dorothy apologized with her eyes.

"So you didn't – complain about me to Stuart? You know, about my being late now and then, or maybe not being so quick to come up to speed here at the soup kitchen?"

"Complain? Helen, I think you're terrific. I have nothing but praise for the way you've loved these poor souls like they were your own brothers and sisters."

"Really?"

"Really," Dorothy said as she put her arm around Helen's shoulder and pulled her to her side like a long-lost daughter.

"I didn't know you felt that way," Helen said, comforted that a saint like Dorothy could hold her in such high regard.

"And on top of it all, I was touched by what you did for Frankie. I had a mind to tell you so when you got to work on Wednesday. I grew worried when you didn't show and no one seemed to know why. Come to think of it, Tristan looked mighty smug that day, even more so than usual. I'm sorry to hear you'll be leaving us."

"Me too," Helen replied, determined not to cry.

"So – what are your plans?"

"I'm just trying to get past goodbye, that's all."

"Goodbye?" Dorothy rebuked. "Now, you know

you can stop by and visit us anytime – or even volunteer to work in the galley. There's always cooking and washing and drying that needs to be done."

"Thank you, Dorothy, but I've been told that it would be better for the guests if they had – closure."

"That's just a bunch of psychobabble, Helen. You don't close yourself off to your family, now do you?"

"You mean the guests?" Helen asked, feeling confused.

"There are no guests, Helen. We're all family here. Some of us just have better teeth and shoes than others." Dorothy winked and smiled, then squeezed Helen's shoulders before loosening her grip. "I got some potatoes that need peeling if you got the time." It wasn't in Dorothy's nature to allow anyone to surrender and feel sorry for themselves – especially those who were blessed with an indomitable spirit, even if they didn't yet know it.

Helen was grateful for the mindless work that allowed her to reconstruct the words she wished to say to the men and women who would stumble, rush, limp or meander through the door in the next thirty minutes. She vowed to keep her explanation simple and avoid getting sentimental. After all, if what Dorothy said was true, maybe there was a chance she could keep in touch with those who had grown closest to her heart without violating Betsy's wishes that she steer clear of the soup kitchen. Perhaps she could invite them to Sunday meetings at Little Flock, or treat them to coffee now and then at the Blue Moon Café on the corner of the city square.

Helen's sadness began to lift as the first of many guests began to walk through the door, creating the customary din that always reminded Helen of the sounds of recess. There were hoots and hollers, teasing and laughter, and always at least a squabble or two in the air. The atmosphere had an almost musical cadence about it, one that had developed its own special rhythm, occasionally spiked with frantic crescendos or long, languid passages that made Helen want to weep at the sheer monotony of it all.

She pulled her denim apron over her head and tossed it on a stack of milk crates that had been delivered by the local food bank early that morning. She hurried out of the kitchen and into the dining area, anxious to greet each person by name. She had finally learned their names, she thought ruefully, and now she was expected to forget them! She found the sight of Tristan sitting on the stage disconcerting. If it was true – if it was simply a matter of funding – why hadn't they thought to let Tristan go? While she understood the concept of seniority in the workplace, she didn't understand why Betsy and Stuart failed to recognize the progress she'd made the past few months; not just with the Vietnam vets but with many of the younger women who gravitated toward her as well. There were but a handful of guests who had ingratiated themselves to Tristan, who favored them with laundry tickets and bus tokens along with the occasional hotel voucher.

If anyone had asked, Helen would have told them that Tristan was clearly burned-out and biding the time until his five-year anniversary of sobriety arrived – at which time his ostracism would be over and he was free to re-enter his family's sphere of wealth and privilege. No so for Helen. She was in for the long haul and barely able to keep from expressing her disappointment to Tristan's face.

"Hey, Tristan," she offered.

"Hello, Helen," he replied, clearly disinterested in further conversation. It galled her to think he could dismiss her so easily! Why, she'd spent nearly as many hours listening to him vent about his own dysfunctional family life and his father's angst over his sexual orientation as she had listening to the guests whose life-or-death issues made Tristan's rants seem like so much bellyaching.

"I suppose you heard this is my last day on the job."

"Yes, Stuart called to tell me the news. I'm sorry, Helen."

"Are you?"

"Of course I am," Tristan said defensively. "Why wouldn't I be?"

"Maybe because you never really thought I was right for this job in the first place."

"Well, that's true, Helen. But that has more to do with your lack of experience than it does with your nature."

"What?"

"Your nature, Helen. You're too soft for this

job. You get too attached."

Helen felt oddly calm in the face of Tristan's criticism. After all, what did it really matter what he thought? He'd made up his mind about her a long time ago and there was nothing she could say now to change it. Still, she could not resist the obvious question.

"Is that what you told Stuart?"

"No, that's what Stuart told me. He got that straight from the top, from Betsy Whitmore."

"Why would Betsy say such a thing?"

"I don't know, Helen. Word gets around. You know that as well as I do."

"So this isn't really about funding. It's about Frankie," Helen declared.

"Maybe he's a prime example as far as Stuart and Betsy are concerned. But if you ask me, I'd say it's about the others, too."

"What others?"

"Look Helen, whatever's going on between you and Hawk is between the two of you. Just be careful. You're playing with fire."

"Me and Hawk?" Helen whispered back. "What are you talking about?"

"Rumor has it that you've been to China Beach."

Helen's heart skipped at the mention of that secret place she'd thought about with wide eyes in the long dark of night far more often than was respectable. How foolish of her to think her indiscretion would stand!

"Is it true, Helen?"

Helen lowered her eyes to the ground and thought long and hard. She didn't notice that Hawk had come up behind her and stood quietly, waiting for her to speak.

"That's ridiculous, I've never been to China Beach. I've heard the guys talk about it, but I have no idea where it is – or if it even exists outside of their imaginations! So the next time that silly rumor comes a-callin', I'd appreciate it if you'd set the record straight."

"Oh, it's real all right, Helen," Hawk said, leaning into her back as Tristan watched suspiciously. "You'd be surprised at how downright homey it is, too. In fact, we have all kinds of creature comforts – hammocks, pillows, radios, cutlery. Why, we even have hot chocolate on special occasions."

Helen turned around slowly. She saw the fleeting hurt in Hawk's eyes before they turned cool and inscrutable once more.

"Tell him, Hawk, will you? Tell Tristan I've never been to China Beach." Helen prayed that Hawk would not betray her. He struggled but couldn't resist the plea that darkened her eyes with desperation.

Hawk laughed derisively. "Trust me, this girl has never been to China Beach. Don't you think I got a little more class than that, Tristan? I mean, what am I going to do with a preacher's wife? Show me a little respect, will you?" Hawk shook his head emphatically.

Tristan's dark brown eyes bounced between Helen and Hawk, searching for some telltale sign that what Hawk said was true or false. Finding none, he shrugged and twisted his lips with scorn, having already written off the significance of their lives within the context of his own.

"By the way, Helen, Stuart asked me to make the announcement."

"What announcement?" Hawk asked, searching Helen's face for a clue.

"Tristan, please. It would be better coming from me."

"I'm sorry, Helen. I've been told to take care of this."

Helen felt the air rush from her chest and her shoulders involuntarily hunch in defeat. She leaned into the stage and folded her arms tightly, curling her fingers into tight fists. "Then just do it," she said, "please, just get it over with."

Tristan nodded and hoisted himself onto the stage where he towered over the crowd that assembled at tables, and in lines, and in pockets of social cliques formed from common miseries. The air smelled of boiled hot dogs and sauerkraut and French fries, a menu inspired by a scarcity of food in the pantry and a lack of money in the bank by the middle of every month. Helen was sure she would remember that moment – and that smell – forever.

"Hey! Listen up! Everybody, I need your attention for one minute," Tristan clapped his hands and shouted as the din began to fade. Within a few moments, the soup kitchen fell silent. The guests had been trained to heed Tristan's calls to attention lest they miss an important clue concerning their health and welfare at the hands of the state. Their response struck Helen as one based on anxiety and dread rather than common respect or any great expectations.

"As all of you know, Helen has become a part of daily life here at St. Paul's Soup Kitchen. She's been a great listener and a big help to many of you who have sought her assistance as an employee of our mental health department. I know she's become quite fond of all of you as well. Unfortunately, Helen will no longer be working with us after today, so please, take a moment on your way in or out to thank her and to say goodbye…that's all."

For a split second, the soup kitchen was speechless and still. Then, like a mighty explosion, the everyday sounds of hustle and grind began anew, with no palpable indication that Tristan's words had made any impact at all. Helen was stunned. Her eyes traversed the room in a frenzied, kaleidoscopic swirl as she scanned the faces of those who were oblivious to any pain but their own. She hesitated to look at Hawk, fearing the worst: that look of disgust he reserved for traitors, war critics, and church ladies who slopped too much gravy on the mashed potatoes and bragged about doing the Lord's work to boot. She prepared herself to glance sideways, to the spot where Hawk had planted himself in anticipation of Tristan's news. All the while, she had felt his potent energy and intense gaze on the profile of her face, reducing Tristan's speech to a hollow sound in her ears. She expected him to be angry, bitter, or aloof.

But she had not expected him to be gone.

Chapter 8
Perfect Timing

Helen drove straight home after saying good-bye to the few soup kitchen guests who understood or cared that she wouldn't be returning on Monday morning. Somewhere along the three-mile drive home from the soup kitchen, she found herself unexpectedly relieved of the indignity and sorrow she'd felt on the way there, discovering a sense of peace in their stead. Perhaps it was the sight of the lone robin staunchly perched on the pitiful remnant of a snow bank that gave her hope that good would follow this day, that a new spring would come with or without her bidding, that her life would start afresh, according to God's will for her. *Christ's bird*, that's what they called this kind back home, the ones that were stained red with the blood of Jesus as they tried to comfort Him on the cross. Helen took it as a sign of God's mercy in her midst. It consoled her to believe it.

"Hey, Chester!" Helen called out as she walked in the door, forcing herself to sound upbeat. Chester had a natural sense for what she was feeling and routinely took it upon himself to try to set things right with a hundred random kisses or by becoming her canine shock absorber. There were days on end back in Dock Watch Hollow when Helen had a mighty bad case of the mulligrubs, those deep-in-your-soul blues that just won't give matter how one tries to vanquish them. They were especially bad on the mornings after. Chester would hop on her thin, spongy mattress and cuddle next to her in the place where she had laid, stoical and still, until groping hands and fierce thrusts had their fill. Only then would Helen let the tears come, tears that spilled onto his silky fur and cries that were muffled in the strong, barreled chest that pressed against her as though to shield her from further harm. Chester would refuse to eat on those days. His dark brown eyes glanced past his food bowl, too preoccupied with the slightest change in Helen's expression to pay it any mind.

She was glad that she was alone in the house, free from the burden of sharing her thoughts about everything that had just happened. Todd had recently moved his office to the new church house on Maple Street. For Helen, it was a welcome change that made their house feel more like a home. She especially liked having the freedom to listen to some of her favorite bluegrass music at volumes that made Todd frown. It was even worse when Helen danced a jig around the living room, inviting Chester to join her after Todd refused. There was something of her spirit in those old mountain tunes with energetic fiddles and plaintive slide guitars that made her grow wistful and sentimental. Life in Dock Watch Hollow had not been all bad. There were times of sheer beauty and bliss, like when she camped out on Rattlesnake Mountain with Joan and Chester on Saturday nights, loaferin' about and drinking honey wine that the locals forewarned "kissed like a woman and kicked like a mule," – then heading out to the ridge at mornglom to see the sun rise over the eastern foothills and stand in shimmering pools of pink and gold in cool, breathless wonder.

She hoped Joan would come to visit her someday. She'd sent her cards, one after another at Christmastime, but had never received a response. She didn't take it personally, knowing that the cost of a stamp and the trip to the post office was often more than a body could bear in any given month. Still, she longed for female companionship, something that had eluded her since moving north. The women in the city were different, Helen noticed, with their tall, pencil thin heels and confident stride, looking more sparkly than any she'd ever seen before, especially in broad daylight. Back home, such girls were likely to be harlots, or flatlanders in mansuits sent by the coal companies to talk nice to the hillfolk and handout free samples of gourmet coffee and fancy perfume. What they failed to understand was that creek and holler people rejected anything they'd never be able to have twice in a lifetime.

That was more torture than treat to them, and Helen was always the first to tell them so. Maybe that's why she hadn't made any girlfriends since her arrival. She was unwilling to trust anyone who hid their eyes behind sunglasses as big as fists and lenses as dark as coal. Likewise, she imagined she looked like some kind of freak to them, with her long, unstraightened hair and unsophisticated gait and naked eyes that screamed she was the antichrist of urban chic.

If for no other reason than companionship, she was looking forward to the arrival of Todd's sister, Jane, whom she had met several times before and after the wedding, but who never seemed to stay in Richmond long enough to become family to her. She was scheduled to arrive in a little more than two weeks, an event that Todd had prepared for by booking himself solid through the end of March. Clearly, it was Helen's responsibility to feed and entertain her – no small feat given Jane's love of traditional southern fare in all its deep fried glory – something Helen abhorred. In fact, Helen didn't much care for the notion of eating meat, much less boiling it in oil and setting it in a basket lined with cheap paper doilies. That was something she'd seen her momma do far too often: running down the chicken in the backyard coop, breaking its neck and plucking it just a couple of hours beforehand so as to honor her guests with the freshest meal they ever had. Helen was glad there was a good fried chicken joint just a couple of miles down the street, knowing her healthy, grilled and whole-grain style of cooking would leave Jane feeling colder than a banker's heart. Jane was what the mountain people called a chuffy girl, one whose healthy, Southern appetite showed on her hips and who might well have been a poster child for the original "plain Jane." As a missionary on behalf of the General Association of Regular Order Baptist Churches, Jane's extended mission trips left her with little or no time for girl talk or other feminine pursuits. Maybe this time would be different, Helen thought. Perhaps they could bond over frothy caramel lattes or department store cosmetic and perfume counters where women in these parts gathered much like traditional Southern belles converged for afternoon tea. It would be a lark for both of them; one she hoped might soften Jane's heart toward her and advance the cause of sisterhood between them.

She looked forward to the task of getting the guest room in order now that Todd had moved his large, oak writing desk, pillars of books, and computer equipment into his new office. In fact, it wouldn't be long before she and Todd relocated to the parsonage that had been designed for them by Jonathan on a lot adjacent to the new church house. More than three-quarters complete, Todd had promised her it would be the home where they would start a family. The very thought made Helen's heart beat faster with joyful anticipation and longing. Perhaps her dismissal from St. Paul's had come at just the right time, Helen mused. After all, isn't that what Todd had assured her – that God's timing is always perfect?

Helen surveyed the empty hallway and noted the stillness of the house. "Looks like it's just you and me, kid." Chester raised his chin from the floor and thumped his tail in reply. Helen glanced at her watch, calculating there at least two more hours of daylight to burn, and three or four more before Todd would come home. "What do you say we go to the dog park?"

Chester scrambled to his feet and stood at the door, prancing and spinning in tight, happy circles. Helen slipped her keys back into her coat pocket, clipped a long leash on Chester's matching red collar, and headed back into the March wind that invigorated Helen with thoughts of the balmy spring breeze that would inevitably follow on its coattails.

The county dog park was located on the outskirts of town where the river branched into a network of narrow brooks that were still running high from the recent thaw. As she followed the river, she couldn't help but glance into the distant woods, wondering what Hawk must think of her. She had vowed upon leaving the soup kitchen not to dwell on the matter, knowing there were things that couldn't – and shouldn't – be undone. And yet, there was a down-to-the-bone feeling that things were unfinished between them.

She hated the way she'd hurt him, the way her denial of ever having visited China Beach made his jaw flicker with tension and his bright blue eyes turn chilly. If she had known he was standing behind her, she might have chosen to remain silent and let Tristan believe whatever he wanted. At least then she would have spared Hawk's feelings and avoided the terrible burden of guilt she felt at having betrayed his trust. For the last few months she had repeatedly assured him she was not like the other outreach workers whom Hawk characterized as little more than the pimps of the charity world, handing out trinkets and tokens to ingratiate the poor masses in exchange for their praise and adoration. Helen had sworn an oath to Hawk that she was there for all the right reasons and not for her own edification. Worse, she had promised to always be there for him and for his band of brothers whose lives meant more to him than his own. Yet despite such lofty aims, she had shot the truth right between the eyes before it revealed a woman who wasn't nearly as noble as her ideals.

It was a rotten thing to do, Helen lamented, but admitting her indiscretion would surely have put her reputation – perhaps even her marriage and her husband's career – at risk. She'd learned over the course of the last three years as a minister's wife that people – church people in particular – were eager to promulgate the seeds of scandal and strife. They would be the first to say that any minister who couldn't keep his own wife in check lacked the right stuff to lead the congregation in the path of righteousness. If only Hawk knew how many feelings raced through her before she'd spoken those faulty words – feelings that were an anathema in the cold, empirical world of social work! But for Helen it wasn't work; it was a ministry of Christian love, one that connected her to the people in the soup kitchen – and to Hawk in particular – in the most intimate way. Perhaps if she could prove to him that her heart was sincere he might yet find a way to forgive her. Maybe then, he might still gaze at her affectionately the next time they met on the street, his blue eyes shrewd and penetrating, urging her as they always did to stand up for herself in the face of every confrontation and circumstance, urging her to be Miss Hell-on-Wheels. She wondered if Hawk had any idea how deeply he had affected her simply by challenging her to be her true self in his presence. She loved who she was and how she felt when she was with Hawk: emboldened by his effortless acceptance of her simple nature – and oddly unashamed of her sordid past. She trusted him to keep the secret she'd revealed to him at China Beach. Over the course of the last few months, he'd come to treat her ever more tenderly, their connection deepened by accidental truths that sprang from random conversations and chance encounters amid the din of the soup kitchen. Those tender moments: an encouraging nod, an appreciative glance, a flash of mirth across his face, were all but imperceptible to others, but Helen gathered them like pearls which she strung together in her bed at night while Todd laid sleeping beside her.

By the time Helen and Chester left the dog park

that day, Helen had made up her mind to pay one final visit to China Beach. She was eager to set things right, to reassure Hawk that she cherished the bond between them. Otherwise, she'd go on and on tearing herself up trying to reconcile what she'd done to a man who confided on more than one occasion that she was the first woman he'd opened his heart to since he was abandoned on a street corner in Brooklyn one Saturday afternoon when he was twelve. His mother had put a crumpled ten dollar bill in his fist and sent him into the five and dime for a pack of chewing gum; by the time he emerged, there was a hooker mulling about in the place where she had been. Even then, Hawk knew his mother wouldn't be coming back. It was a desperate act that had been a long time coming if her frequent, prolonged absences and the proliferation of needle tracks in her arm were any indication. Moved with twisted pity, the hooker took the spare change Hawk clenched in his hand, led him down an alleyway, and turned the hot tears of an abandoned boy into the hot sighs of an angry young man before escorting him to his grandmother's house on Baker Street. He'd lived with his granny for a short while, then with an aunt who didn't care for the young hooligans Hawk caroused with and forced him to choose. From the days of this youth, Hawk had a natural inclination toward the path of greatest resistance, eluding attempts to place him in foster care, living under bridges, and throwing in his lot with fellow creatures of misfortune that morphed from street urchins to hardened criminals to comrades-in-arms throughout the years. Still, he didn't seem to begrudge what had made him the hardcore soldier that he was, a war-horse whose tough luck was encased in bulging biceps and the agile, rock-hard body of a man half his age, courtesy of the boot camp-inspired exercise routine he'd never been able to shake, even if it meant using tree branches for pull-up bars or the snow packed ground for a hundred backbreaking crunches each morning. As a result, he still stood straight and tall in his combat boots and jungle fatigues, giving the impression of an American icon – though many would argue he cut a tragic figure given his preference for a hootch in the woods when he had access to a comfortable apartment of his own. Having spent more than three years in the boonies of Vietnam, there was a certain restlessness incited by the confines of four walls, especially at night when the glare of the streetlamp outside his window resurrected sickening memories of white lights that burned his eyes as the Viet Cong interrogated him in eight hour shifts for days on end before tossing him into a pitch black bunker to reconsider his resistance. People who learned he'd been a prisoner of war often said he should be happy to be alive. But for Hawk, it wasn't about being happy. It was simply about surviving. Any day that he woke up with the sun on his face and breath in his lungs was a day worth having. It was that simple. At least it had been, until Helen walked into his life and made him want for something more.

The jangle of Chester's dog tags heralded Helen's arrival home. Todd grinned at the sound from where he stood watch over a simmering pot of tomato sauce. He heard Chester's toenails tapping out his usual five o'clock bulletin that it was dinnertime in the dog world, then Helen cajole him into being patient while she stripped off her hat and gloves. There was a moment of silence, followed by a tentative voice.

"Todd?"

"In the kitchen, sugar. Come on down."

"Why are you home?" Helen asked as she stood at the threshold, perplexed by the sight of Todd hovering over the stove with a wooden spoon in his hand. Chester stood beside her, watching his mistress' every move.

"Well, I knew it might be a tough day for you, so I rearranged my schedule to be home a little early to – "

"To what? Look after me?" Helen said. She didn't mean to sound surprised but it wasn't like Todd to make such a fuss over her. "I smelled something heavenly from the front door; I thought it was just my imagination. Then Chester caught a whiff of it and I could barely hold him back!"

"It's definitely not your imagination. I'm making tomato sauce," Todd boasted, then he gasped and leaped backward as a hot liquid bubble exploded, splattering the stovetop. He turned and grinned at her sheepishly. "That was close," he said, glancing down at his shirtfront.

"That's what an apron's for," Helen teased, stepping forward to turn down the flame and surveying the pin dots of tomato sauce that landed in every direction. "Actually, maybe you need a sheet."

It felt good to laugh with Todd, to not have to belabor the details of her last hours at St. Paul's Soup Kitchen when all she really wanted was to stand in her own kitchen with the man who at that moment was feting her like she was the prodigal daughter come home.

"What are you looking at?" Helen asked when their laughter subsided and Todd's gaze grew long and unfathomable.

"I'm looking at my wife. I'm looking at her pink cheeks and her pretty smile and the sparkle in her eyes that makes me feel like she's happy to be here with me."

"Of course I'm happy to be here with you. That's never changed."

"I'm glad to hear you say that, Helen."

"Why would you doubt it?"

"I don't know, maybe it's been the distance in your eyes these past few months that made me wonder if you'd rather be...*somewhere else*...."

Helen paused, debating if Todd was alluding to China Beach. If Betsy Whitmore had known about it, surely she would have confronted Helen at their last meeting. No, Helen decided, neither Todd nor Betsy knew any such thing. After all, what would Tristan stand to gain by repeating what he'd heard? He'd already gotten what he wanted: she had been thor-

oughly discredited and dismissed. Making an issue
of her alleged misconduct would only make Tristan
look like a rumormonger or a disgruntled coworker
who was greedy for even greater vindication. He was
too smart for that.

Helen chose not to reply. Instead, she wrapped
her arms around Todd's neck and hugged him
tightly. She liked the crisp feel of his oxford shirt
against her cheek and the broad span of his muscular back under her small hands. Perhaps the neglect
had been hers all along, she speculated, vexed by
the thought. She startled when Todd pulled away.

"So what's this I hear about you visiting Frankie
in the hospital?"

He leaned against the kitchen counter, his lips
still smiling but twitching ever so slightly at the effort it took. He didn't seem angry but she was nervous just the same.

"Who told you?" Helen asked, resisting the tension that made her throat feel like it did when she
got stuck by a swarm of honey bees when she was
ten. No one had even known she was having an al-
lergic reaction until her face resembled a ten pound
pumpkin and she fell to the ground, gasping for
breath. Joan made a run for the nearest house outside the holler that had a telephone to call for help.
She likely would have gone on to meet her Maker if
good old Mrs. Murtha hadn't found her lying in the
middle of the dirt road and quickly concocted one
of her homebrewed medicinal teas. Thirty minutes
later, after Mrs. Murtha removed the last of the

stingers, Helen was near good as new, calling out to Joan from Walker's Ridge to come back home. When Joan saw her, she cried like a baby and begged Helen's forgiveness for daring her to poke her finger in the hive. *Truth or Dare* was a silly game she and Joan often played to amuse themselves as they walked the two-mile path to and from the schoolhouse each day. Unlike Joan, Helen almost always chose the dare.

"Of course I forgive you," Helen said through fat, red lips that made Joan giggle in spite of her tears. "I'da done it to you if I thought of it first," Helen assured her, and together they had trotted home with backs bent by girlish laughter at the folly of it all.

"I heard about it from Carl, Frankie's nurse. You met Carl, didn't you?"

Helen gnawed at her bottom lip and nodded weakly.

"He said you made a real difference in Frankie's recovery – that your visit seemed to be a turning point for him. Did you know that?"

"No. I haven't been back to the hospital since Wednesday."

"Well, I knew Frankie's condition might be weighing on you, so I called the hospital today to check on him. I was told they were about to discharge him but he had no place to go. I made a phone call to Damien House and asked them to take Frankie back into the program. It took some convincing, but they agreed to give him another chance.

They're putting him in isolation, Helen, his immune system is shot. That means *no visitors*," he scolded, "at least for another month or two."

"I understand." Helen nodded emphatically.

"Sit down, Helen, will you? There's something I need to say to you."

Helen was glad to oblige given the leadenness she felt in her body – in her very soul – at the somber tone of Todd's voice and what she expected would be a long overdue announcement: it was over between them, surely that was it. She wasn't fit to be a pastor's wife; she'd known it all along! If only she'd followed her instincts, she never would have found herself in this position of humiliation and regret.

"Helen," Todd began, then tenderly took her hands into his own, caressing them for a moment before continuing. "Helen, I need you."

"What?"

"I need you to be my helpmate. I need you to stand tall with me in this ministry. Now, I've always known you have a heart for the poor. That's part of what I loved about you from the start. But now I need you to use that gift for the benefit of saving souls, not just bodies."

"What does that mean?"

"It means want you to take over the foreign missions program at Little Flock."

"But I thought Jonathan was doing a good job with that."

"He's done the groundwork," Todd conceded,

"but he doesn't have the time to make it grow and prosper – or to travel. After all, he already has a day job – and the elders back in Richmond have set some pretty high expectations for me and my church."

Helen didn't need him to say more. No longer in the employ of the mental health department, she knew the one thing she had plenty of was time!

"But what do I know about running a foreign missions program? And won't that mean I'll have to travel myself?"

Todd shrugged. "Not right away. Not until you're ready."

"What are we talking, Africa?" Helen asked dismally.

Todd laughed. "I was thinking more like Mexico or Haiti for starters. And only for a few weeks at a time, nothing that would keep you away from home for too long. Of course, you'd never travel alone. There would always be a core team with you."

"What about Chester?"

"I promise I'll take good care of Chester. I'll even bring him to work with me whenever you're gone."

Helen hedged at the thought of spending time away from the one being who had been her anchor and unconditional ally for the last thirteen years. He rolled his eyes upward at the sound of his name and sighed when no mention of dinner was made.

"What about starting a family, Todd? I thought

we were going to start a family soon."

"We will, Helen, I promise you that. I don't see how this is going to stand in the way of raising a family together. We'll just have to be creative. Besides, you know what I always say about God's timing...."

"Todd, I don't know – " Helen faltered, unprepared to take the same leap of faith.

"Look, I don't want you to answer me right now. I know you've got some things to get settled in your mind and I don't want to rush your decision. But I know what you've done for Frankie and others like him at St. Paul's. From what I understand, they really took a shine to you, Helen. Let's use that gift to bring the light of Christ to other nations."

Helen caved into the back of her chair, her resistance shrinking as Todd impressed upon her the full force and effect of her Christian duty.

"Take some time to pray on it," Todd suggested softly. "I'll ask you again in two weeks."

"Jane will be here then."

"All the better," Todd said, "I'm sure she can share with you the rewards of her missionary life. No better person to ask than Jane."

"Speaking of Jane...."

"Come on, Helen, I don't have time to entertain her. Jonathan and I are up to our ears in paperwork preparing for our first audit, and besides, we've got a lot of finishing work going on at the parsonage. I know you're going to love it."

"Considering I've yet to see the inside of it, I hope you're right."

"I want it to be a surprise for you, sugar. You don't want to spoil my fun, now do you?"

"I'd like buttercup yellow walls in the kitchen," Helen said, "is that too much to ask?"

"Anything for you," Todd replied, pressing the back of her hand to his lips. It was a sweet gesture but one that fell far short of the intimacy Helen craved.

"That means you'll entertain Jane from ten until three on Monday, Wednesday and Friday?" Helen tested, raising her eyebrows expectantly.

"Ten until two. Tuesday and Thursday," Todd bargained.

"Done!" Helen declared. "You better do it, too, Todd. You better make sure your sister feels welcome and useful when she's with you."

"I'll put her to work painting the walls. *Buttercup yellow*."

"Thank you."

"For yellow walls?"

"For what you did for Frankie."

Todd shrugged. "You're welcome, Helen. I wish there was something more I could do for you."

"That was the very best thing of all," Helen assured him, squeezing his hand tightly as he beamed at the praise, a commodity that had been in short supply throughout his lifetime.

His father, the Reverend Thomas C. Baldwin, was something of an icon among the faithful in Richmond and the surrounding area. Known for his fidelity to a socially conservative agenda and

an old-fashioned hellfire-and-damnation style of
preaching, anyone churched by the fiery Pastor
Baldwin on the radio or in person had perpetual
blisters in his ears and a heart that burned in more
ways than one. But it was that same zeal and inexo-
rable spirit that drew people to his preaching in
numbers that in his heyday were comparable to
those achieved by the more well known televangelists of his time. Todd had always supposed that was
because despite the liberalism that had slipped into
the modern Southern Baptist church like a well-
heeled barbarian at the gate, there were still a fair
number of people who were loathe to hedge their
eternal bets, preferring to be told precisely how to
live their lives in no uncertain terms. His father was
just the man to do that, with an exhaustive list of
sins that started with Adultery and ended with a
lack of apostolic Zeal.

Somewhere near the middle was the sin above
all other sins in his father's eyes: the abomination
of Homosexuality. Short of total apostasy, there
was nothing else that made his father burn with
such disgust and condemnation. He was relent-
less in admonishing Todd to speak, act, and
choose like a "man's man," against his softer nature. Throughout his life that had meant learning
to emulate his father's bold choices and domi-
neering behavior – ultimately, all the way to the
pulpit where Todd mimicked the powerful per-
formances he'd seen his father deliver from seat
eleven in the fourth row, Sunday after Sunday,

for twenty two years. Nevertheless, there was one critical difference: like his father, Todd loved God – but he also ardently loved His creatures. He lacked his father's fervent desire to see them sweat their eternal destiny, preferring that they come to know God's divine mercy as well as His perfect justice. The end result was that Todd also preached a God of forgiveness. Perhaps it was simply because He was the God that Todd was sure he needed most, for reasons that had been branded on his soul from the time that he was ten years old and first knew what it meant to have those unusual "stirrings" that set him apart in an unspeakable way.

"Burnt orange," Helen blurted, breaking the silence between them.

"What?" Todd said, charmed by her playful expression.

"That's what we're going to have to paint the walls of our new kitchen if you're going to be cooking in it. I'm afraid that sauce is burning, Todd. Mind if I take over?" she asked, not waiting for his reply. She stirred the contents of the saucepot, then raised a spoonful to her lips and wrinkled her nose at its charred and bitter flavor.

"It was a really nice thought," she sympathized.

Todd shrugged and pet Chester's head as he sidled up to him in Helen's absence.

"I'll feed the dog," he said.

"I'll call Chen's," she replied.

And for the briefest moment, they were happy.

***

The entire weekend passed before Helen permitted herself to think about the soup kitchen and the daily life she'd left behind. But when the sun rose on Monday morning, it was impossible to ignore the fact it was the first Monday in months that she had not awakened to the joy of getting up and dressed for work. Now, she got out of bed and leaned all too leisurely against the windowsill, regretting the loss and scolding herself for the position she was in. And to make matters worse, for the last two days she'd become increasingly hurt and bedeviled by the urgency of Todd's appeal for her take on Little Flock's foreign missions program.

There was something about it that just didn't sit right with her. Why, she brooded, would he want to send her away for weeks at a time when he knew that what she wanted most was to settle into their new home and start a family? She didn't share his optimism that such diverse goals could coexist and still bear the necessary fruit. The more she thought about it, the more angry and resentful she became until she could barely muster enough goodwill to accept his customary kiss and blessing on her forehead as he headed off to work that morning. Looking back, she hated that Todd hadn't seemed to notice the hurt and disappointment in her eyes as he brushed her concerns aside with yet another nod to God's impeccable timing. If God's timing was so perfect, where was He all those times when her father skulked into her bedroom, bolting the door behind him? Or when Granny Hicks got killed when the car she was riding in got broadsided by a coal truck that lost its brakes coming down a mountain pass? Or when Joan's daddy raised his fists to beat her senseless for speaking out of turn or refusing to tell him where her mother hid the milk money? Or when innocent hillfolk got tossed about and washed downriver like rag dolls left out in the rain?

Helen twirled a strand of her hair in furious circles as she stared out the window, her eyes focused on the green tips of the crocuses pushing through the soft brown earth. Oh, she would do her husband's bidding, of that much she was sure, she thought bitterly; she couldn't deny the plea in his eyes nor bear the guilt of failing the one who had plucked her from a life of poverty and woe at a time when he needed her most. *The elders back in Richmond have set some pretty high expectations for me and my church,* he had said, *my church*, as though it was his one true bride and Helen a mere earthly metaphor.

Yes, she would become the dutiful preacher's wife that he so desired. But she would do so with a broken heart, knowing that Todd's love for souls exceeded his love for her. It was a hard truth that she could only accept by yielding to her own calling, the one that hissed and churned like an approaching locomotive on some days and cooed with the quiet urgency of a mourning dove at the dawn of others. Today, just for today, she would not resist her own vocation: to love and to be loved, not because she was good and obedient and holy, or young and vulnerable and physically over-come, but simply because she was Helen, Miss Hell-on-Wheels.

Chapter 9

A Pearl of Great Price

Helen waited until well after the soup kitchen closed before heading out to China Beach. She knew there was a chance it would be deserted when she arrived. Hawk and the others sometimes wasted away the afternoon at Jake's Place, the local pool hall, before some or all of them proceeded to the drop-in center at the Methodist Church across the square where they could check for mail, make two phone calls apiece, and take a four-minute shower.

She'd thought long and hard about what to wear, how to fix her hair, and whether or not to put on her everyday perfume or something more exotic – or none at all. She avoided the thought that anything might happen between them, knowing only that she wished to make a distinct impression when she met Hawk on his own terms in his own territory; one that confirmed she found him worthy of a concerted effort to look beautiful for him. For him alone.

She settled on a simple white cashmere sweater and a pair of faded jeans tucked into sage green suede boots that were lined with lamb's wool and assured her firm footing. She swept her wavy hair into a soft twist at the nape of her neck, fastening the twist with a gold filigree butterfly clip with pale green crystals on its wings. A few loose tendrils framed her face, which she dusted with a translucent powder that made her cheeks softly shimmer in the mid-afternoon sunlight. She glossed her lips with a wholesome shade of pink and took a deep breath before spraying her everyday fragrance on her wrists and into the air, walking through the jasmine-scented mist on her way to the door.

She bid Chester to be still as she reached for her coat and keys, then drove to the edge of town and darted into a parking space behind the Pour Man's Pub, where no one would think of looking for her and no God-fearing Baptist would be seen in the light of day. From there, she set out on foot, tracing the path that led to the end of the sidewalk and the broad field separating ordinary civilians from the anarchy of China Beach.

This time, Helen didn't hesitate. She stepped off the sidewalk with a sense of purpose, her stride long and sure, her eyes eagerly searching the woods ahead for telltale signs of life. It didn't take her long to reach the unmarked trail that led her deeper, through stands of oak trees and aspens until the unrest of the river could be heard and the outskirts of the campsite came into view. There was no acrid smell of smoke in the air, no orange flame to point the way, just instinct that propelled Helen forward until she reached the edge of the clearing and the weather-beaten welcome sign that no longer struck her as quite so odd. She stared at the cold ashes and charred wood in the fire pit, her heart plummeting at the sight. She glanced in every direction, hoping her senses were wrong, that there was more to this emptiness that stretched out before her; that Hawk would mysteriously appear as he had a knack for doing from the very first day they met. Now *there* was a man with perfect timing, Helen mused, releasing a bitter little laugh that seemed to ricochet off the trees and make a resounding mockery of her standing there.

Now what? Helen muttered as she glanced at her watch and mulled her options. She could make haste for home and forget this ever happened, that was the obvious choice. But it wasn't Helen's choice. She took a seat on the same chunky log where she'd sat before with a tin cup of hot chocolate and trembling hands. Her hands weren't trembling now. This time it was her heart that trembled in anticipation of Hawk's arrival. She prayed he would come soon; she prayed he would come at all! She knew with Hawk there were no guarantees that he would be the same man in the same place on any given day. His military training had broken him of any inclination or desire to become a creature of habit. That was a deadly disposition in the killing fields of Vietnam where the element of surprise was key to a man's survival.

Helen picked up a nearby stick that had been sharpened and set aside as a makeshift fire poker. She began to idly stir the ashes, pushing them this way and that until she uncovered a small pocket of embers that pulsed faintly against the odds. She leaned over and breathed on them, sending warm streams of air to revive them, even if just for a few moments longer. There was something poignant and commiserate in their struggle to survive, Helen thought, something of her own soul mirrored in the black pit before her.

"Didn't your mother teach you not to play with fire?"

Helen slowly lifted her gaze to the spot where Hawk stood less than five feet in front of her.

"If she had, I wouldn't be here," she replied, surprised by her own boldness.

Hawk stepped forward but remained at arms length. She hoped he would sit down beside her but he didn't. Instead he stood over her, his eyes absorbing every detail of her appearance: from the emerald green butterfly she wore in her hair that glittered in the afternoon sunlight, to her dark lashes swept with glossy black lacquer, to her lips that were dewy and soft and trembling ever so slightly.

"Why are you here, Helen?" Hawk asked brusquely.

Helen stood and shortened the distance between them. Hawk allowed his gaze to travel further, over her pretty curves and long slender legs and back to her face where she met his wandering eyes with the hope and longing that he knew she had come as gift and atonement. God Almighty, she had not meant to hurt him; she could tell by his demeanor that she'd done a fine job of it, too. Worse, he seemed angry, standing with crossed arms and a stiff back that made her feel like she was facing an impenetrable brick wall.

"I'm here to explain what happened at the soup kitchen…about what I said, or rather what I didn't mean to say," Helen stumbled.

Hawk tightened his arms across his chest, resisting the urge to touch Helen's face which he could tell she had painted for his benefit. He preferred her natural beauty: the sheen of her pink, freshly scrubbed cheeks, her soft, feathery eyelashes, and her chestnut-colored hair unpinned and undulating behind her like a satin sheet in the wind. She had clearly come to him with feminine persuasions and a tentative plan. He was willing to hear her out, willing to see how far she would go to cross the abyss between them.

"What do you want from me, Helen?"

"I want your forgiveness. Please, forgive me, Hawk."

She found his silence unnerving, yet she was grateful for the small flicker of interest in his eyes. It was a start, she reasoned, and enough encouragement to go on.

"I never should have denied coming here when

Tristan asked me about it. I guess I was just afraid of what would happen if Todd found out about it, or people at our church heard about it, you know how people talk, right?"

"You *are* a married woman," Hawk replied, "and yes, people will talk. Fuck them, Helen."

Helen stiffened, determined not to cower at the hardness of his tone, knowing it would be contrary to everything Hawk had tried to teach her these past few months.

Hawk waited for her to offer something more, something more substantial than her misery and the superficial gift she made of her physical beauty, even if she did look like an angel and smelled like a breath of heaven, too.

"Is that it?"

Helen nodded, looking down at the embers which had since given up the ghost. She was comforted when Hawk reached out and lifted her chin, leveling her gaze to meet his. Her heart beat faster in anticipation of the softening of his eyes to that shade of dusty blue that was more beautiful than eveglom in the mountains, that magical moment when starlight and daylight melded to form a velvety blend of indigo and sky blue. At that very moment it was what she needed and wanted more than anything else in the world: the magic of eveglom in this far away place that was anywhere but home.

"Go home, Helen," Hawk said tersely, releasing his hold on her.

Helen flinched at the finality in Hawk's tone,

sure she must have had heard him wrong. She hesitated, then watched in stunned silence as he turned his back to her and began to gather kindling for a new fire.

"Hawk?"

"You heard me, Helen. Go home to your husband."

This time, there was no mistaking the ridicule in his voice. She would not endure the humiliation of being asked to leave a third time. She was glad for having chosen a flat-heeled boot that made it easy for her to sprint from the woods before she could embarrass herself any further. It wasn't until she had locked herself inside her car that she allowed the tears to come and relieve the ache in her chest that was more painful than any she had ever known. But in the wake of her tears there was clarity. She'd had this coming, she realized, this comeuppance from Hawk that served to restore the balance of power between them, the power to hurt and the power to heal. Knowing Hawk as she did, it would have been easy for him to feign forgiveness and take advantage of her vulnerability; instead he had taken the harder path: he had refused her and sent her home – home to her husband. There was something of a challenge in the taunting way he'd said it, like it was some kind of test of wills. Clearly, it wasn't enough for her to simply show up at China Beach. He expected her to risk all or nothing. Lord have mercy, she didn't know if this attraction she felt in the depths of her soul for a quasi-homeless man with a fierce chip on his shoulder and the devil on his back was worth losing everything she ever thought she wanted. All she knew was that when she was near him she didn't feel broken anymore, or dirty anymore, or poor anymore. Perhaps that was at the root of it all – despite all the comforts her life with Todd afforded, she still felt pitifully poor inside and no matter how many compliments he paid her, or gifts he bought her, there was no recompense for the empty space in her bed as he worked long into each and every night, for her unfulfilled longings to be touched and loved, for the sorrow of knowing she could never attain the perfection he required of her in her daily life and in service to his God.

If she was a different kind of woman she might have left him by now. But if nothing else, she was a thankful woman. He had saved her from ever having to return to the hardships and sorrows born in Dock Watch Hollow and given her a fresh start in life. She owed him for that and would pay her dues by being his obedient wife and partner in ministry. Beyond that, she could offer no guarantees.

Helen spent the next five days planning her strategy and biding her time, knowing that with every hour that passed she was moving closer to the day when Jane's presence would make it nearly impossible to steal away to China Beach. Helen had done her spring cleaning three times over, prepared the guest room for Jane's arrival, and aimlessly wandered the local mall until she could beat a path from one end to the other with her eyes closed. She resisted the urge on weekdays at noon to hover in the department store across the street from St. Paul's to catch a glimpse of Hawk coming or going. Sunday couldn't come soon enough; it was the one day she knew Hawk would be alone at China Beach. That was the day the Korean church on Trumbull Street hosted their elaborate Sunday afternoon dinners for the poor. His comrades didn't share his aversion to the feast offered at the hands of the Asian community. It didn't matter to Hawk that their hosts were Korean, not Vietnamese; he thought it was an affront to the marines who had died fighting against the North Korean Peoples Army to accept their belated charity. There was no convincing him otherwise.

Likewise, Helen knew Todd would be busy with his usual round of activities that followed Sunday services, too busy to know or to care what she might have planned for herself. He had already informed her that he and Jonathan were in the thick of preparations for the upcoming audit and would be occupied most of the afternoon. Helen simply nodded and smiled sweetly. Todd had come to expect her full cooperation and indulgence. Anything less would have given him instant cause for concern. He still monitored her carefully, wanting to be sure her dismissal from the soup kitchen hadn't done any permanent damage to her psyche or spirit. He had never meant to hurt her by orchestrating the demise of her position at St. Paul's, only to redirect her energy to something more fruit-ful for the glory of God. He thought she was hold-ing up all right; she seemed a little sad and humbled, but that was to be expected. He marveled at how good it felt to have her back in the fold where she belonged.

Helen dressed slowly and prudently for Sunday services, careful not to look conspicuous. She used to wear blue jeans until Todd pointed out to her that the other women at Little Flock found it disrespect-ful. Now she was acutely aware that everything about her was fair game, from her choice of nail polish color to the length of the hem of her skirt. As a result, she was mindful to wear only the most con-servative colors and styles of clothing on Sundays, taking special care to gather her hair into a low, neat ponytail and cover her head with the requisite silly, broad-brimmed hat. On that particularly balmy Sunday, Helen chose to wear a flowing, pale blue skirt that brushed her ankles and a fitted, plain white blouse buttoned tightly at the collar, topped by a simple straw hat with a blue-and-white floral band.

Come the early afternoon, just as soon as the congregation dispersed and Todd disappeared be-hind closed doors, Helen pattered down the side-walk in gold-colored flats, rushing headlong toward China Beach. This time would be different, she vowed; she wouldn't falter under Hawk's steady gaze or second-guess her own intentions. She would look him in the eye and tell him what she wanted, what she needed, and what she was willing to give to have it all….

Hawk cocked his head at the sound of the woods stirring in an unnatural way. Throughout the years he had retained his built-in radar for incoming threats and this was no exception; this time it came in the form of a beautiful woman wending her way through the budding trees in a floppy hat, with a hurried gait. He forced himself to be still, resisting the urge to rush forward to meet her as she came into view.

"Miss Hell-on-Wheels," he said, trying to sound indifferent. "You're back."

Helen stood at the edge of the clearing with her hands on her hips, slightly breathless from her eager pace. "Yes, I am."

"Come on over," Hawk said, beckoning her with a nonchalant wave of his hand. "Have a seat."

Helen walked toward the pit which blazed with a young fire.

"Perfect timing, I just got here," Hawk said, giving her a thorough once-over and smirking at the sight. "That's some get-up, Helen."

"I just left church," Helen said, not sure if he was mocking her or not. "Don't be mean, Hawk," she pleaded as she took a seat by the fire. "It wasn't easy for me to come back here."

Hawk paused, tossing a handful of twigs into the fire. "So why did you?" His voice lacked emotion but his eyes were the piquant blue of a man who had a stake in her answer.

"I didn't get what I came for the last time."

172

"Oh? And what was that?"

"Your forgiveness. That's what I wanted and you refused me."

Hawk tilted back his head and laughed, amused by her directness. "And why do you think that was, Helen?"

"I don't know, maybe you're punishing me."

"You do a fine job of punishing yourself. You don't need me to make you feel any worse, now do you?"

Helen glanced at the fire and shrugged, then made a heroic effort to keep her gaze level with Hawk's. She wouldn't have him thinking she was defeated before she even got onto the battlefield.

"Look, I did you wrong, Hawk. I lied about coming to China Beach and maybe it *wasn't* because I was afraid of what people might think. Maybe I was afraid of how it makes me feel to be here."

Hawk stared at her intently, resting his chin on his knuckles as he leaned into the orange licks of flame that flashed between them. He had been waiting for this day, for this revelation that could only come from the mouth of a woman who had spent some time searching her heart and soul. He knew it was a tenuous moment, a tender thread that spanned the chasm between them, but it was a start.

"Tell me how it makes you feel," Hawk said, forcing her to go further, deeper, than she had expected.

"Protected...accepted...."

"Beautiful?"

Helen laughed softly. "Yeah, except when you make fun of my clothes."

Hawk arose from his customary place at the fire and took a seat next to Helen. It was a tight fit and as his muscular thigh pressed against hers, she felt the heat of his nearness pierce the thin cloth of her skirt and permeate her skin.

"Let's do something about that, then," he said, tossing Helen's hat into the fire and freeing her hair from the elastic band that loosely held it in place.

"Hawk!" Helen exclaimed as she watched the straw fibers spark and burst into flame. She tossed back her head and squealed with laughter at the sight.

Hawk couldn't resist her glee. He found himself laughing with her, releasing the tension that had them in a stranglehold and only now unloosed its grip. When their laughter subsided, Hawk straddled the log so as to face Helen head-on, then boldly reached out and put his hands around her neck.

She startled and for a split second thought the worst. His hands were sinewy and strong, capable of crushing force that on more than one occasion had easily dispatched stray Viet Cong foolish enough to engage him in hand-to-hand combat. She willed herself to be still, to trust her own instincts.

Hawk slowly unfastened the top button of her blouse, then the second one, then the third. She wondered if and where he would stop, unsure that she wanted him to stop at all. Then he peeled back the collar of her blouse, exposing the hollow of her throat.

"That's better," he said, his eyes traveling the tantalizing arc of Helen's neck and returning to her dream-worthy face. "Now you don't look like such a prissy church lady." This time when they locked eyes there was no trace of the usual awkwardness or uncertainty – just an awestruck silence that acknowledged the passion that was rising between them.

"Helen," Hawk said, turning aside and exhaling the urges that threatened to overcome him. "What about your husband?"

Helen forced a tight-lipped smile.

"He doesn't want me," she stated flatly and shrugged.

Hawk nodded, knowing it was true. He knew what people on the street said about Pastor Todd and felt sorry that Helen had yet to hear it for herself. Not that it mattered; she had reached the inevitable conclusion on her own. The whys and the wherefores wouldn't make any difference in the end.

"Do you love him?"

"Not that way, not anymore," Helen confessed. "I mean, how can a woman love a man who can't see past his own needs and blind ambition? I've been lonesome far too long…but I won't leave him," she declared.

Hawk nodded calmly. "So then we're back where we started," he sighed, shifting so as to face the fire once more. "What do you want from me, Helen?"

Helen wrapped her arms around herself and glanced skyward. It looked like rain, she thought, perhaps even some thunderclouds were gathering overhead. She wondered what the homeless men did in the rain, sheltering under tall trees that were the last place a body ought to be….

"Helen?" Hawk prodded.

"I want you to say you forgive me. Please, Hawk, I need to hear you say it," Helen persisted, knowing there could never be anything worthy between them until they were fully reconciled.

"I forgive you," Hawk replied, disappointed that she had not asked for more. He was about to get up and walk away when Helen spoke again, softly.

"And I want you to be here for me."

"I'm not going anywhere, doll," Hawk avowed, stirred to pity by her earnest expression. Hell, if he didn't feel like a sap, but there was something about Helen that made him lose his edge every time.

"Can we just leave it at that for now?" Helen smiled bravely, fighting back the tears. It was an act of valor that elicited in Hawk an overwhelming desire to gather her into his arms and hold her. And that's what he did for the rest of the afternoon, amid occasional bouts of meaningless conversation until the rains came and the thunder rolled and Helen reluctantly peeled away from him like a tender vine divided from an iron trellis.

"Are you coming back?" Hawk called out after her, just before she stepped over the invisible boundary of China Beach. Her intentions had been implied but he needed to hear her to say it aloud.

Helen glanced behind her at the sight of Hawk standing in a driving rain beside the smoldering fire, his gaze as firm and demanding as ever.

"God willin' and the creek don't rise," Helen shouted through the rain. She treasured the broad white smile she brought to his face, knowing she would add it to the imaginary string of pearls that made up her most cherished memories. This day was the pearl of great price, the kind of day her momma would have called a keeper before urging her to quit while she still running a few short steps ahead of trouble.

Helen hadn't known how tired she was of running until that very afternoon when time stood still, and at last so had she in Hawk's strong, protective arms. It was a relief and a revelation to know that nothing bad would happen to her if she let herself be still…if she let herself just *be*. Unwilling to surrender her bliss to her ordinary household routine, she drew herself a hot bath the moment she got home, languishing in steamy water and savoring every new and fervent sensation that had coursed through her body that day. It was as though the bud of her sexual being had awakened for the very first time and burst into bloom in a new and long-awaited spring of her own choosing. That something could feel so sinful and so beautiful at the same time was a mystery to Helen, one that she refused to contemplate or question.

She was already thinking about when she would

return to China Beach and what might happen when she did. She closed her eyes and let her mind drift over the possibilities, gathering pearls along the way, knowing all too soon there would come a time when they would be all she had to comfort and sustain her.

***

For each of the next five days, Helen fought and then surrendered to the urge to return to China Beach, knowing that with every visit she was one thread less connected to the simple but satisfying life she had planned, the one with two children and a dog and buttercup yellow walls. Each afternoon, just before two, she parked her car at the Pour Man's Pub, discovering ever more discreet alleyways and shortcuts through abandoned lots to reach China Beach. When she did, she didn't stay too long, just long enough to sit with Hawk by the fire until they ran out of things to say and the awe of simply being together overcame them. Sometimes they sat across from one another, their gaze penetrating through steady, controlled flames as they tentatively explored the details of one another's lives; the things that made them Helen and Hawk; the things that bound them and the things that kept them apart. Other times, the fickle late March winds came and fanned the flames between them, inciting their restlessness and frustration until Helen would rise to leave in a state of panic and confusion. Hawk would jump to his feet with the fleetness and precision of a seasoned soldier and intercept her before she could get too far, reaching out and pulling her into his arms where he covered her in his benevolent will until she yielded to the comfort and surety of his embrace. When that moment came, it was as though her bones thawed and her flesh melted and she poured like spring rain into every groove and hollow of Hawk's body, which was as strong and resolute as any mountain she had ever known.

"Stay with me, Helen," he would whisper into her ear. "Be with me."

It was an invitation and a command she could not refuse, and yet even as the days grew longer, she knew their time was slipping away faster than a country fiddle playing to a hot summer night. It was already Friday; Jane would be arriving in just a couple of days and once she came, Helen would be sorely tested to find a way back to China Beach.

"Jane's a-comin', Hawk," Helen said, often reverting to her lost mountain twang and manner of speech without even realizing it. It was a phenomenon that only happened in Hawk's presence. He never called attention to it, either. He thought it revealed glimpses of the woman she was at heart, the essence of a strong, mountain girl who had sacrificed and endured much to survive the hardships particular to her upbringing, the ones she rarely talked about but alluded to every now and then with a stoic expression that failed to mask her wounded spirit.

179

Hawk had been reluctant to take things further, to touch Helen in a more intimate way for fear that she would bolt like a frightened pony at the unfamiliar touch of a hand that did not intend to break her body or her soul. Thus far, that was all Helen had ever known of a man's love: the domination of her body followed by the tyranny of her soul under the strongarm of faith and family. It tore him up inside to resist the soft pink shine of her lips and the tangle of her hair and the curve of her back that arched toward him whenever they embraced like a taut bow yearning for release. But there was still a part of Helen that was untouchable; that was the part he wanted first and foremost, the part that made him lie awake in his bed at night imagining what it would be like to possess her heart. Until he did, he couldn't lay a hand on her without feeling as though he was exploiting her loneliness and her most primitive, unfulfilled sexual desires.

It was in his blood to aspire to the ultimate *coup*, defined by his Cherokee people as a feat of bravery during battle that enabled a man to overcome the enemy without harming him. Helen's distrust of her own feelings was the unseen foe that stood between them, a shadow he boxed at with all his might and had not been able to defeat. For all his combat experience, he was helpless to obliterate the doubt that shone in Helen's eyes every time he reached for her – the doubt that she was free to choose him, to love him, and to open her heart to all the crazy possibilities that came with those choices.

If her fear had a face, he'd do what he did best: blow it to bits with his military issue M-16 and be done with it. As it was, he couldn't attack the enemy without hurting Helen at the same time; all he could do was hold her until she stood still long enough to feel what he did, the heat of his body, the strength of his will, the rock-solid conviction that there was something truer and deeper between them than either one of them had ever hoped to experience in their broken lives.

"I know Jane is coming, Helen. But there's nothing we can do about it."

"I don't want to be away from you, away from here," Helen said with a sweep of her hand over the expanse of China Beach. The other Vietnam vets had become accustomed to Helen's presence, treating her like a soul sister in the family of exiles they considered themselves to be. They didn't know what she was hiding from but if Hawk allowed it, they didn't second-guess him. He was the voice of reason among them, the only one who hadn't succumbed to the escape of alcohol or drugs to manage his psychic trauma, the only one who took his flashbacks on the chin and was able to keep himself clean and clothed and housed with his military pension from Uncle Sam, who as far as his comrades were concerned owed them a living in exchange for the loss of their right minds and souls.

"It's only for a week," Hawk said, patting Helen's knee in consolation as they sat by the fire.

"Easy for you to say."

"Have a little faith, doll. We'll figure something out."

"I just know she's a-comin' at Todd's bidding to turn me into some kind of Bible-thumping missionary lady," Helen complained. Hawk tried not to laugh at her blunt assessment.

"Maybe. So what?"

"So what?"

"Yeah, so what? Just tell her you got a new religion."

"Really? And what is that?"

"Tell her you joined the Church of Hard Knocks. There's only one problem, though. I hear they let anybody in – as long as they're not wearing a big, floppy hat." Hawk winked, trying to ease Helen's misery.

"Refresh my feeble memory, Hawk, just what is their theology?"

"Well, it used to be *don't mistake my kindness as a sign of weakness*, but they've had a revelation."

Helen raised her eyebrows expectantly.

"Now it's all about the love, baby."

Helen laughed in spite of herself. She was intrigued by the way Hawk could change his demeanor from dark and foreboding, to cool and mysterious, to light and heat as easily as the weather vacillated in the early throes of spring. He was akin to what was known in the mountains as a dogwood winter, that peculiar time of year when the dogwood trees bloomed amidst a surprisingly late spring snowfall. She had a notion to tell him so, then

182

changed her mind as her thoughts drifted to the past winter and the last snowfall that had dumped so much misery.

"So how is Frankie? Any news on his condition?" Helen asked.

"I guess he's doing all right," Hawk replied. "I haven't seen him at the soup kitchen since he got out of the hospital."

Helen nodded. "I surely wish I could see him."

"Why can't you?"

"Todd told me he's in isolation at Damien House. He's not allowed to have visitors, at least for a month or two."

"Todd tells you a lot of things," Hawk said matter-of-factly, tossing more kindling onto the fire.

"Are you telling me that's not true?"

Hawk shrugged. "Ask your husband, Helen."

"I'm asking you, Hawk."

There was a quiet tension in Helen's voice that turned it soft and low. Hawk knew what she was really asking was for him to tell her the truth; if he failed, it would be another battle lost to the devil of doubt that stood between them.

"Let's just say that Frankie has been well enough to pay his Costa Rican friends on Mechanic Street a number of visits since he's been home."

"You mean he's still..." Helen's voice trailed off, crushed by the thought.

"He's an addict, doll. It's just not that easy...don't cry, Helen," Hawk said. It was more of a plea than a reprimand.

But Helen couldn't help it. She wept at the thought that there was no relief for the poor, that no matter how hard the spirit rallied there was always the greater likelihood that the flesh would win the day, just like the Bible said. And was it any different for her, sitting in the middle of a campground populated by homeless and traumatized veterans of war, flirting with temptation that appeared in the form of a ruggedly handsome, enigmatic man with a criminal past and a bold, penetrating gaze that took turns making Helen's blood run hot and cold? Was she really any better off?

"What the devil, Hawk? Why are we all so messed-up? I mean, what's the point of going on if we're all no better than a heap of broken down cars that can't hardly get from here to there without blowing out a wheel or smashing into a concrete wall or running out of gas in the middle of the highway to heaven? Tell me, what's the point?"

Helen wiped her tears away with the back of her hand and sniffled loudly. "I got to go," she said, rising to her feet and brushing off the seat of her pants.

"Did you want me to lie to you, Helen?" Hawk demanded. He was angry that Helen was leaving for no other reason than that she wasn't able to handle the truth.

Helen stopped in her tracks and let out a long sigh. "If I wanted lies, I reckon I might as well stay home." She closed the distance between them until she stood face to face with the man who, for better or worse, was more forthright than any she had ever known. "I can't come back tomorrow. Todd booked me for lunch with the volunteers who serve on the foreign missions committee. And I have to pick up Jane from the airport on Sunday afternoon."

Hawk didn't reply, nor did he avert his gaze. Helen waited to see if he would reach out and take her in his arms, then kiss her lightly on the forehead as he was accustomed to doing. He made no move to do so, but Helen didn't mind. She lifted herself on her tiptoes and braced her hands on his sturdy shoulders. Then she leaned into him and pressed her lips to his, lingering just a moment longer than was necessary.

"Thank you for being honest with me," she said.

Hawk nodded, but didn't otherwise flinch. Jesus, if she didn't smell like the wild jasmine that bloomed on the hillsides of 'Nam, whose heady fragrance had haunted him and now would be impossible to forget.

"I'll be back, Mickey Lightfoot. Can't say when, but sure as rain, I'll be back."

Hawk understood there was a shift in Helen's heart that day, one that had both embittered and emboldened her. In her own tacit way, with a single kiss, she had let him know she was ready to take the next step with him; that he was no longer just the persona of Hawk, the brash Vietnam vet who had made her blush that first day on the job and slowly stripped her of her own peculiar form of camouflage until Miss Hell-on-Wheels was fully exposed. Rather, he was becoming her most intimate, trusted friend and guilty pleasure, Mickey Lightfoot. It felt odd and perhaps a bit sentimental, but all he could think of to say was *thank you, Jesus.*

Chapter 10
Waking the Dead

"Jane!" Helen waved her hand overhead to attract the attention of the chuffy, short-haired woman who funneled out of the gateway with a bulging, purple paisley backpack strapped across her shoulders. She ambled forward at twenty-degree pitch, careening her thick neck like a swamp turtle coming up for air.

"Over here, Jane!"

Helen smiled as Jane squinted through prim, wire-framed glasses that were two sizes too small for her broad, manly face.

"Helen!" Jane said as she cut across the swell of passengers outpacing her. "Well, aren't you a sight for sore eyes."

The two women hugged awkwardly, neither accustomed to each other's size and frame. Jane had Todd's height, which seemed ungainly in a woman. Helen blanched at the feeling of her face in Jane's bosom.

"You look as pretty as ever," Jane remarked,

taking a step backward to Helen's great relief.

"Thank you, Jane, you look wonderful, too! How was your flight?"

"Can't complain. Anytime I have a hot meal and fresh, filtered water it's a treat."

"So how long were you in India this time?"

"Four months, flew by like a racehorse. Feels darn good to be back in the States, though. I've been dreaming about deep-fried chicken and collard greens like a mad woman on death row."

"I think we can put that right," Helen said, suspecting that the collard greens would be a tougher order to fill. She didn't quite remember how to prepare them properly so as to purge their bitterness …boiling water, a little salt…five minute, too bitter, ten minutes, no flavor…or was it the other way around?

"Is something wrong, Helen?"

"Heaven's no! C'mon, let's get your bags – you *do* have bags?"

"What I got is on my back," Jane replied.

"That's it?"

"I got my Bible, a few changes of clothes, my toothbrush, a comb, a bar of soap. Something else I need?"

Helen shrugged. So much for spending the afternoon at the cosmetics counter or the designer shoe department at the mall. She'd have to come up with a better plan!

"Well, then, let's get on home. I know Todd is eager to see you."

Jane furrowed her scruffy eyebrows as they walked toward the busy concourse ahead. "Where is my baby brother, anyhow? Why didn't he come out to get me himself?"

"Aw, don't take offense. He's a mighty busy man these days."

"Busy how?"

"He's done y'all right proud. His congregation is already over two hundred strong and growing by the day. He's got a powerful good way of winning souls, Jane."

Jane's eyebrows transformed from flat lines to rugged arches at the lapse in Helen's proper manner of speech. It made her sound uncouth, Jane thought, and was an unpleasant reminder of her brother's misguided choice to marry a poor girl from the coalfields. Jane had urged him to be more prudent, to reconsider his choice before the differences between them reared their heads and undermined his calling. Todd had pointed out to her on more than one occasion how hard Helen worked at improving her grammar and elocution so as to present a more polished image for his benefit. "There's nothing wrong with a girl wanting to better herself," Todd admonished Jane, sure that Helen would do everything in her power to become the ever more gracious, dignified wife he knew she was capable of being. Besides, Todd reasoned, better a simple girl from the coalfields than a high-bred one from Richmond whose constant demands and expectations would only distract him from his ministry.

Jane had reluctantly agreed and given Todd her blessing. Now, she wondered if she'd made a mistake, seeing how refined Helen looked in her fancy clothing and made-up face, like a hillbilly playing dress-up.

"I guess I can't argue if winning souls is what kept him away," Jane sighed, anxious to see if he looked any worse for the wear of having to raise up a wife who was clearly not on par with Baldwin standards.

"Well, that – and Jonathan."

"Jonathan?"

"He's Todd's right-hand man. He started out as Little Flock's architect but I guess he's a man of many talents 'cause Todd is always wanting his help or his opinion."

"It's good for a minister of God to have a person like that in his life," Jane said, fighting the urge to declare that person ought to be his wife.

"I reckon so. But it makes for some real lonesome days and nights just the same," Helen confided. "I'm so glad you're here, Jane."

"Me too," Jane said, patting Helen lightly on the back as they meandered through the airport terminal. She wouldn't tell Helen she had come at Todd's bidding, despite having planned a relaxing, two-week hiatus for herself in Richmond before leaving for a six-week stint ministering to the unchurched poor in Port-au-Prince. *"Please, Jane,"* Todd had begged, *"it would be a big help if you could spend a week preparing Helen for the mission field. If anybody can help her understand what's expected of her, it's you."* Helen had yet to learn that when Jane left for Haiti, she would be sitting beside Jane's chuffy bottom in seat 12E. Todd had been saving that announcement for another day, knowing his timing would have to be perfect.

Jane took a week in Richmond to recover from the rigors of ministering in the slums of Mumbai before flying north to continue her mission work, only this time it was within the heart of her own family. She didn't begrudge the time, knowing it was for Helen's eternal good. Todd had told her all about Helen's lapses in judgment at the local soup kitchen. A poor, misguided soul like hers could get lost if left to its own devices; she'd seen it all too often and had sensed the urgency in her brother's voice.

"Jane!" Todd bellowed as Helen and Jane walked in the door. Chester scampered excitedly around their knees. Helen stepped aside and watched Todd and Jane embrace, the affection between them clear.

"What are you doing home at his hour?" Helen said, glancing at her watch. It had been months since Todd was home at two in the afternoon.

"You think I'd miss welcoming my big sister?"

"Todd, you're looking hale and hearty," Jane said, casting an approving glance in Helen's direction. "Helen must be taking good care of you."

"Of course she is," Todd gushed, quickly drawing Helen near.

"Trust me, he's a moving target," Helen said.

Jane laughed. "So what else is new? Our mama used to call him the original rolling stone. He's had high ambitions since he was just a boy."

"I guess it runs in the family," Todd replied.

"All for God's glory, baby brother."

"Amen!" Todd declared, sporting the broadest smile Helen had seen in a very long time. She fought hard to keep her eyeballs from rolling as Todd and Jane exchanged spirited high-fives. It was going to be a wearisome week.

"Well all right then! Jane, why don't I show you where you'll be staying and give you a chance to settle in?"

"I have to admit I'm feeling a bit peaked. I'm afraid I haven't quite made the adjustment back to the States. My body still feels like it's two in the morning."

"All the more reason to rest for a spell. I'll wake you in time for dinner."

"Thank you, Helen."

Helen nodded, grateful for the few hours until suppertime. She hadn't counted on having time alone with Todd, a commodity that had grown so scarce that she hardly knew how to spend it.

"This is a pleasant surprise," she said, joining Todd in the kitchen after showing Jane to the guestroom and helping her to make herself at home. Todd sat at the head of the table, pushing some leftover macaroni and cheese around on his plate.

"Why so downhearted?"

"It's nothing."

"Surely it's something or you'd be tearing into that plate with a lot more gusto."

Todd sighed and leaned back in his chair.

"Is it me? Did I do something to upset you?"

"It's not you, Helen. It's just that seeing Jane always reminds me –"

"Reminds you of what?"

"How far I've missed the mark."

"What are you talking about?"

"I see Jane and I know there's a holier path, the one she walks with the poorest of the poor."

"Just cause you're not in Mumbai doesn't mean you're not serving the poor, now does it?"

"Yes, I think it does," Todd argued.

"Well, I'm no expert in religion, but didn't Jesus say there's more than one way to be poor? Remember that story about the widow who put everything she had into the poor box, and the rich man put in a few gold coins, or something like that? She gave her all and he gave his spare change. I mean, you can be right rich and still be poor – can't you?"

Todd nodded pensively.

"Well then, quit your bellyachin' and enjoy your macaroni, Todd. I'm on my way to the grocery store to hunt down some collard greens."

"Overcook them and they'll lose their flavor."

"I know that," Helen declared, putting a hand on her hip for good show.

"Thanks for the kitchen homily," Todd said. "Whether you know it or not, you're going to make a fine missionary, Helen."

"I haven't agreed to it just yet."

"I know," Todd said, as he put down his fork and took note of Helen's peeved expression. "But I'm confident you'll make the right choice. You know how much this means to me – and to Little Flock's ability to meet the articles of our Constitution. A lot is riding on your answer, Helen."

"We'll see."

Helen turned her face aside, fighting the unexpected tears that sprang into her eyes. No matter how bad things were, there was still a part of her that found it incomprehensible that Todd could banish her to some far-flung destination without a second thought. When, she wondered, had he stopped loving her, stopped wanting her, stopped looking at her as though she was the other half of his soul like he did that hot summer day when they married in his daddy's big white church and danced till duskydark on the sweeping veranda of his family's fine home on the outskirts of the city?

Now, he looked at her like she was just another soldier in the army of God as it marched toward Judgment Day under his command, his blind ambition obliterating the promise of milk and honey she once beheld in his eyes, the promise that had made her consent to this life of urban exile. She had already made up her mind to do her husband's bidding. She supposed that now was as good a time as any to say so, restrained only by the knowledge that the moment she consented, the fate of their relationship would be irrevocably sealed. There was still time for Todd to set things right, to recant his will for her – but it would have to happen now, this very instant in time. Once spoken, her *fiat* would be the final word between them and as it hung on her lips, she began to cry.

"Helen? Helen, why are you crying, sugar?"

"I'm going to miss you, that's all," Helen said.

"But you're only going to the grocery store." Todd's forehead rippled with confusion.

"No, I mean, I'll do it, Todd. I'll go to Haiti or Mexico – or even Mumbai, if that's what you want. I owe you that much."

"What do you mean, you owe me?"

"You took me in, Todd. You gave me a new home and a new life, and I know I didn't deserve it at all. I know I'm just a girl straight out of coal country with inferior raisin'...."

"Stop right there, Helen," Todd said, hastening from his chair. He grasped her by the shoulders and held her tightly, a little too tightly for Helen's liking.

"First off, I didn't just take you in, I took you for my wife. I didn't do it out of pity, I did it because I loved you. And I still do, Helen. Asking you to work shoulder-to-shoulder with me to build up Little Flock is a testimony to every good thing I think about you. Not the other way around."

"You really mean that, Todd?"

Helen thought Todd just might unloose a tear or two of his own, the way he suddenly released her

195

and turned aside. Helen's childlike trust made Todd feel guilty and ashamed, so much so that he nearly aborted his plan to send Helen away as a sure means to avoid experiencing those same feelings every time she curled up next to him when he arrived home well past midnight and slinked into their bed; inevitably, she would stir and look at him with a sleepy gaze that was soft with unspoken forgiveness and love. He wanted to reassure her that what he said, what he felt, was the pure and simple truth. But the truth was neither pure nor simple.

"Of course I mean it, Helen."

"Then why don't you want to lay with me? Why haven't you touched me for so long?" Helen whispered, her gaze intensifying as she asked the questions that had burned on her lips far too many nights.

"I don't know, Helen, it's – complicated. There's a ton of pressure on me to succeed. Don't you think that weighs heavy on a man's mind?"

"I guess that depends. What's your definition of success?"

"Standing room only, every Sunday morning." Todd shrugged unapologetically, recalling the capacity crowds that filled the interior of his father's church and spilled out onto the sidewalk where two weatherproof loudspeakers amplified the sermons that made grown men weep.

"Well if that's all you're a-wantin' that's likely all you'll ever get." Helen couldn't keep from sounding bitter. She longed for him to choose the rewards of a happy home, a blissful marriage, the blessing of children – things that mere mortals could neither endow nor steal from them. She would have settled for any one of them, but Todd's priority was clear. At least now she could choose for herself without the twin stakes of fear and self-loathing piercing her heart.

"You're angry."

"I'm not."

"Did you want me to lie?"

"I don't know, Todd. Have you ever lied to me before?"

"No."

"Are you sure?"

"Yes, I'm sure."

"What about Frankie?"

"What about him?"

"Remember when you told me he was in isolation? And that he wasn't allowed to have any visitors? I know for a fact that isn't true."

Todd's jaw tensed as he considered the weight of Helen's words. She gazed back at him defiantly, not the least bit compelled to twirl her hair into a nervous knot.

"I said it for your own good."

"My own good? You know how much Frankie means to me."

"Which is why I rescued his sorry soul in the first place. If it wasn't for me, he'd be strung-out and sleeping in a hollow refrigerator somewhere down by the river."

197

"But you still lied!"

"Look, I don't want you exposed to him, Helen. The man is dying of AIDS. You've already compromised us once. Wasn't that enough?"

"Us?"

"Think about it, Helen. Besides the enormous pressure I have bearing down on me at work, why do you think I won't make love to you?" Todd shot back, this time without reserve. "You brought this chastisement on yourself. Come and see me in six months when you're given the all-clear."

Helen gasped as Todd's condemnation slammed into her ears. She wanted to flee but her feet were leaden and immobilized her where she stood. Besides, Todd clearly wasn't finished....

"So you've been loitering around the soup kitchen, Helen? Is that how you spend your time while I'm at work?" Todd's eyes were cold and accusing.

"No," Helen whispered as her fingers instinctively curled into tight little fists, just like they did when she was a young girl crushed under the weight of a family man who professed his love for her in thick, clumsy whispers that tunneled into her ears like a cyclone, imploding her from the inside out.

"Are you sure?"

"Yes, I'm sure!" Helen shouted, unable to restrain herself any longer. "But so what if I *did* see Frankie or anyone else from the soup kitchen? Those people are still my friends whether you like it or not."

"I don't like it – and I won't have it. Don't you see how damaging it is to have my wife socializing with lunatics and felons? Damn it, Helen, I have too much to lose!" Todd slammed his fist on the kitchen counter. Helen flinched at the sound and wondered: *Did he not care he was losing her?*

"I'm sorry to interrupt – "

Helen and Todd startled at the sound of Jane's voice. They turned in unison to see her standing in the doorway with a glass of water in her hand. "I was looking for some aspirin. The bottle in the medicine chest was empty."

"It's fine, Jane," Todd said with a limp wave of his hand.

"I was just on my way to the grocery store," Helen sniffed. "I'll get some aspirin while I'm out." She hurried past Todd, knocking her knee against the chair he'd been sitting in so meekly just moments before. She softly swore, eliciting a quiet gasp from Jane as she stampeded from the kitchen and down the hall.

Jane and Todd stood silently in the aftermath. A full minute ticked by before either one of them spoke.

"I want you to keep a close eye on her, Jane. I don't care what you have to do, I want to know everywhere she goes and everything she does, you hear?"

Jane nodded as the front door slammed and Chester woofed at the commotion. "She's just upset, Todd, she'll settle down if she knows what's good for her. Give me a week; I'll give you a miracle."

"Don't blaspheme, Jane," Todd said dully.

Jane sighed and tousled her brother's curly hair. "I won't let her out of my sight, baby brother, you have my word on it."

Helen seethed at the words Todd had spoken, words simultaneously too cruel to forget and too painful to contemplate. She drove in a series of left hand turns around and around the city square, thankful for the lengthy red lights she usually found nothing short of maddening. She was in no hurry to get home, having already gone to the grocery store but too distraught and embarrassed to face Jane in light of what she'd obviously seen and overheard. Dinner would have to wait!

The blue lights in the window of the Pour Man's Pub flashed and beckoned at each go-round until she felt she could no longer resist. Given Todd's accusations, she was sure all bets were off, that he'd sic Jane on her like a junkyard dog and insist they spend every waking moment of the next six days together. Admittedly, she only had herself to blame. If she hadn't confronted him with his lies and neglect, none of this turmoil would have come to pass. Instead, they'd all be fixing to sit around the kitchen table to feast on bitter greens and store-bought country fried chicken like one big happy family right about now.

Helen pulled into a parking space and reconnoitered her surroundings. The moment all was clear, she bolted from the car toward China Beach. Her feet couldn't carry her fast enough and as she reached the edge of the woods, she briefly paused to catch her breath for fear she would appear as reckless and wild as she felt inside. Todd had made it clear that she was as unclean – as untouchable – as any leper in the gilded pages of his Bible. His fear of getting sick felt like a sorry excuse from a man who had simply lost interest in bedding his wife – or had loftier things on his mind or in his heart. But Helen couldn't belabor the point. She knew where to find relief from her particular malaise, the one that had reduced her to a bootlicking woman who had all but forsaken her own needs and desires. Even if it only came in stolen moments like this one, it was powerful relief just the same.

"Henry?"

"Miss Helen! What are you doing here this time of day?"

"Where's Hawk?"

Helen clutched her side where a stitch had formed and leaned over to catch her breath. She imagined she was a sorry sight, but Henry looked sorrier, she thought, with his bulging, bloodshot eyes and wiry, unkempt hair, standing forlornly in a torn, white tee shirt and baggy, mud-crusted cargo pants that emphasized the toll the past winter had taken on his body. It was clear that he had been on some kind of bender, the smell of alcohol on his breath a sure sign that he had no idea he was pitifully underdressed for the cool March afternoon that was quickly fading into dusk.

"He's not here." Henry shuffled his feet and looked down at his sneakers. Helen was pleased to see that he had not yet lost them or traded them for some iniquitous pleasure. It had taken her a long time to find someone in the congregation with a size-thirteen foot who was willing to part with an extra pair of shoes! Still, there was something odd about his demeanor.

"Henry?"

Henry glanced at Helen and shrugged.

"Is Hawk all right?" Helen felt her breath catch in her throat as she asked the question. She was only slightly reassured by Henry's nonchalance, hoping it wasn't simply because he was too inebriated to care!

"He's downriver, Miss Helen. But you can't go there."

"Why not?"

"You can't get near him when he's in-country, if you know what I mean."

"What are you talking about, Henry?"

"I told him to take his meds, but he's a stubborn man. Last time it was a helicopter," Henry said, pointing toward the darkening sky. "I don't know what set him off this time."

"Flashbacks?"

"Yes, ma'am. Sometimes they last a minute or two, sometimes hours or days. The fourth of July set him off something awful. Didn't eat, didn't drink for two days straight; just laid on his belly, naked in the mud holding a long, skinny stick like it was an M-16, scoping out the gooks in the grass and blowing them to pieces. It was fearsome, all right, but you know, when he came out of it he didn't remember a thing. I suppose that's something to be grateful for."

"Can you take me to him, Henry?"

"Oh no, Miss Helen. I can't, I won't."

"Then I'll find him myself. Maybe I can help him snap out of it."

Henry massaged the sides of his head with the palms of his gangly hands in a gesture fraught with weariness and frustration. "Jesus, that's not how it works, Miss Helen. Please, just let him be."

Helen ignored Henry's pleas as she marched westward, following the flow of the river. It didn't take her long to spot Hawk kneeling on a flat rock that jutted into the swift current, made all the swifter by the spring rains that flooded the city streets when they came, but without the same fury as the gullywashers in Dock Watch Hollow that obliterated the local roads and isolated hillfolk for days at a time.

There was something grotesque in his posture, in the way he held his muscular arms overhead, palms pressed together, his eyes closed, and his head tilted toward the sky. His broad chest was bare and his rippled abdomen was tense with resistance, rising and falling with rapid, labored breaths that were nearly in sync with her own. She waited for him to sense her nearness as he was apt to do, but he seemed oblivious to everything but the drama

playing out behind the curtain of his fluttering eyelids as he shouted the same two phases into the air
in five second intervals: *La dai! Caca dau!*

Helen didn't know what language Hawk was
speaking, or to whom he barked the odd-sounding
words with such defiance that his voice had turned
hoarse. She darted behind a tree trunk, her desire to
come to his aid overpowered by the terror of stepping into a hellish scene that was as real to his
senses as the fading sunlight on her upturned face.
Instinctively, her mouth silently formed the invoca-
tions she had learned in her youth, the fervent *Hail
Marys,* the solicitous *Our Fathers,* and most especially the militant *Prayer to St. Michael,* which Sister Perpetua, who had helped her make her First
Holy Communion, taught her to invoke in defense
against the devil and every form of evil:

*Saint Michael, the Archangel, defend us in bat-
tle! Be our protection against the wickedness and
snares of the devil. May God rebuke him, we humbly pray, and do thou, O Prince of the Heavenly
Host, by the power of God, thrust into Hell, Satan
and all the evil spirits who prowl throughout the
world seeking the ruin of souls. Amen.*

Helen squeezed her eyes shut as she prayed
harder and louder within the confines of her soul in
an effort to drown the sight and sound of Hawk's
fury. She was relieved and thanked God when his
shouts diminished to a whisper. Only then did she
open her eyes to see him curled on the rock in a fe-
tal position, facing the river. *La dai! Caca dau!*

His voice trailed off as a fleeting surge of sunlight flooded his flinty bed and the rise and fall of his chest became rhythmic and peaceful once more.

In slow, disciplined movements, Helen retreated from the riverbank, tracing her steps to the campsite where Henry walked in uneven circles, wringing his hands and muttering nervously. He startled when he saw her, his eyes widening as though he had not expected her return. He shook his head long and hard at the sight of her. She felt the weight of his reproach.

"It's okay, Henry. He's going to be all right."

"Ain't Hawk I was worried about," Henry scolded.

"He didn't even know I was there."

"Lucky for you, Miss Helen, ain't no telling what would have come to pass if — "

"If he'd seen me?"

"Seen you? More likely he would have seen a gook in the grass and cut you to pieces with that shiv of his. Nobody knows what a Marine will do when he's in-country till it's already done."

"How often does he get like this, Henry?"

"Often enough. It comes and goes."

"Can't it be stopped?"

Henry shrugged.

"There's pills for it, but Hawk won't take them unless it gets real bad."

"It looked pretty bad to me," Helen said as the shock of what she'd seen began to set in and registered on her face. Henry laughed and hooted loudly. She hated when he did that.

"Shhhh! You'll wake him!"

"Can't wake the dead, Miss Helen," Henry quipped. "We're all as good as dead."

Helen softened at Henry's bravado, which in a moment of introspection reminded her of her own. After all, she knew firsthand what it felt like to be dead inside while the world turned without her. Horace Hicks – and now, her own husband – had seen to that.

"What is it that vexes him so?" she prodded. She had always known Hawk to be a highly-disciplined soldier who rarely let down his guard enough to let his softer side shine through. His bro-kenness was haunting. She wished she hadn't come.

"Could be a hundred different things, but I'll wager a guess. Was he like this?" Henry said as he stretched his arms overhead.

"Yes, just like that."

"And this?" Henry extended his long, skinny neck and tilted his head backward.

"Yes!"

He swore and released a heavy sigh. "Sounds like a dip in the Song Hong River. Factor in a four-by-eight bamboo cage…iron shackles... let's just call it the Viet Cong version of dunking donuts. You get the picture?"

Helen felt sick to her stomach as she imagined Hawk undergoing the torture Henry described with a matter-of-factness that defied comprehension. She found his smile unnatural, bordering on cruel.

"*La dai! Caca dau!*"

This time it was Henry who looked shocked as Helen mimicked Hawk's mantra flawlessly. "What does it mean, Henry?"

Henry sank to his knees and ceased to smile. Hatred and anguish invaded his eyes at the sound of the words she had spoken, words Helen wished she had never heard and instantly regretted having repeated.

"Rough translation? *Come here you dirty VC bastard. I'm gonna fucking kill you.*"

Helen nodded as a bilious lump formed in her throat. She didn't look back at Henry cursing and kneeling in the dirt, not even once. All she could think about was the fresh air in the field that lay just beyond those forbidden woods where she could draw life and breath as she knew it, as she understood it, in plain and simple terms that no matter how miserable was largely sane and reliable just the same.

I praised God that Helen had discovered the supernatural truth that China Beach was nothing short of the devil's playground, and that for Hawk and for Henry and for thousands more like them, the war had never ended, only relocated to the muddy trenches of their minds. What she failed to see was that the battle for her own precious soul escalated with each thought she had of Hawk's sinewy body awash in sunlight and her overwhelming desire to lay beside him in comfort and relief. She knew what it was to be held against one's will, to be tormented and humiliated by forces beyond one's control. But Helen's compassion was tainted with lust and anger that tempted her to confuse vindication with love.

I dared to hope that she would keep on running, as she did now in earnest toward the parking lot of the Pour Man's Pub. I prayed that she would choose spirit over flesh and never again return to China Beach. But I knew in my heart that as much as it terrified her to think of entering Hawk's shadowy world, where the perversities of war and death and destruction floated like a ghoulish mist that crossed time and space to settle where it pleased, it terrified her more to think she might never see him again. And so I was consigned to a vigil of prayer and fasting as the day of Helen's reckoning drew near.

***

"Helen, we were getting worried about you!" Jane said as Helen bustled into the kitchen with two sacks of groceries and a barrel of deep-fried chicken.

"No need," Helen replied. "I had to make a few extra stops on account of the collard greens. I finally found them at the organic food market across town. The traffic was horrendous, besides. Where's Todd?" she asked, as she set about finding the right pot in which to boil the greens, unaware that Jane was scrutinizing her every move.

"He's on the phone with Jonathan. Is it raining

out, Helen?"

"Raining?"

"Yes, your nice, fancy shoes are all muddy."

"Oh!" Helen glanced down at the soles of her brown leather loafers. "Spring thaw. It's muddy everywhere. You'll see." Helen paused and prayed for a soaking rain before the morning came.

"Speaking of shoes," Helen said, forcing herself to smile as she donned an apron and began to fill a two-quart pot with water. "I was wondering if you'd like to take a ride with me to the mall tomorrow. I've had my eye on the cutest pair of oxford pumps…."

"Exactly how many pairs of shoes does a girl need, Helen?"

"As many as her moods, I suppose. And I have *many*, just ask Todd," Helen quipped, trying to keep things light. She was banking on the notion that Jane would find the entire idea distasteful and opt for a quiet day of rest and relaxation at home, leaving Helen free to do as she pleased.

"Well, I suppose that might be an interesting diversion, to see how the other half lives, that is."

"Come on, Jane. You don't exactly come from the wrong side of the tracks."

"I admit I had a comfortable upbringing, but that doesn't mean I ever felt compelled to indulge my every…whim. I'm a simple girl with simple needs, Helen."

"So I see," Helen replied, setting the pot on the front burner and turning up the heat.

209

"Don't forget the salt," Jane said sweetly.

"Helen." Todd's intonation teemed with indictment. Helen could hear the unasked questions: *Where were you, Helen? What took you so long, Helen? Do you really expect me to believe that, Helen?*

"I couldn't find any collard greens."

"I saw some at the supermarket just the other day."

"Oh? When do you ever go to the market?"

"I occasionally have to pick up a few things for Little Flock's kitchen."

"I could help you with that," Jane said. Helen bristled at the offer. It was just like Jane to try to make her feel like she was shirking her wifely duties.

"Well, if Todd would make his needs known, I could help him, too."

"I believe I make my needs abundantly clear," Todd interjected. Helen didn't miss the innuendo and responded by clamping the lid atop the stainless steel pot with a noisy flourish.

Todd and Jane exchanged rueful glances. Helen picked up a wooden spoon and tapped it impatiently on the stovetop, trying not to come undone. It was all she could do to stay focused on the mundane task of boiling a mess o' greens, as her momma used to say. She had never taken a liking to them herself, always refusing them whenever they were served. That made some folks uncomfortable, like she was less than a true southerner for it, but Helen had no mind to eat anything that stank like swamp water and tasted like bitter tears.

"A watched pot never boils," Jane said gently, trying to defuse Helen's ire. "Didn't your momma ever tell you that?" She made a mental note to buy Helen a simple cookbook with tried-and-true southern recipes for Christmas.

"I suppose I was too busy working two jobs and minding the family farm to spend much time with momma in the kitchen," Helen said politely. She lifted the lid with the hem of her apron and dumped the bundle of collard greens into the pot, grimacing as droplets of hot water splashed her hands. She glanced at her watch, marking the time so as not to overcook them. Such an offense would surely give Jane more cause for reproof.

"Todd, would you mind giving me and Helen a moment?"

Todd arched a wary brow but conceded to Jane's authoritative nod. "I'll be back in a few minutes. Greens should be about done by then."

Helen was grateful for the clue.

"Helen, come and sit with me a spell."

"I've got to watch the stove. Go on. Speak your mind." She refused to turn around and give Jane the satisfaction of seeing the tears in her eyes.

"Look, it appears we've gotten off to a bumpy start. I'm not here to judge you, honey, I'm here to visit with you and to get to know you a little better, that's all. I'm terribly sorry if my being here has upset you."

Helen swallowed hard and nodded. "It's not your fault, Jane. It's just been a stressful time for me."

"Why?"

Helen found herself daunted by Jane's pointed question. What was she supposed to say? *Because I'm fixated on a man who sets my heart on fire, and oh, by the way, he's not your brother? Because your visit comes at the worst possible time and I know you never cared one whit for me from the start? Because I'm fit to be tied over being forced into a missionary life like yours?*

"I think it's just a bad case of the mulligrubs, Jane. It's been a long, hard winter."

"Believe me, I understand. It's like the rainy season in Mumbai, when I feel like I can't stand so much as one more drop of rain on my face or another gray cloud rolling in from the sea, or one more breath of hot, humid air that nearly chokes the life out of me. Not to mention what 110-percent humidity does to a girl's hair for months on end. Why, I felt like a circus clown most of the time I was there. In fact, I still do." Jane poked her fingers through her choppy hair and shrugged.

Helen smiled at the realization Jane was as self-conscious about her appearance as any other woman. While her hair was cropped short to minimize its care, Helen guessed from its hopelessly frizzy and uneven shape that it had been repeatedly cut by Jane herself. She wondered how long it had been since Jane had treated herself to a professional's touch.

"Well then, what do you say I book us appointments at the hair salon in town? I'll see if they can't squeeze us in some time this week. I know I could use a little sprucing up myself."

"Kind of like a spring makeover?" Jane ventured.

"Exactly." Helen glanced over her shoulder and smiled, grateful for Jane's effort to make peace between them.

"Sounds like fun."

"Well, I'll make that call first thing in the morning. Mind having a look at these greens? Maybe you can tell me if they're done."

"I'd be glad to," Jane replied, neither one of them noticing that Todd stood in the doorway with a satisfied grin. He knew he could count on Jane to bring the peace of Christ to his household, just as she had done to countless tribes and villages in her twenty years in the mission field. It bothered him that he'd been unsuccessful in mitigating peace under his own roof. The tension had not gone unnoticed, especially by the female members of his congregation. The older ones arched their penciled brows and clucked at Helen's waning enthusiasm towards him and his Gospel message, while the younger, prettier ones closed in, in anticipation of an inevitable split. It was an embarrassment that would be instantly set right when they saw Helen step up in support of his work and in obedience to his will as the head of the household. Yes, a three-week stint in Haiti under Jane's mentorship would do them both a world of good. He toyed with the idea of telling her so and then changed his mind. The announcement could wait a couple more days, until after Helen and Jane had sufficient time to bond as sisters and friends.

Helen glanced at Todd. She forced a weak smile and set about draining the pot of collard greens under Jane's direction. She was grateful for the bustle of getting food on the table and Jane's constant chatter in her ear. In fact, she dreaded the silence she knew the night would bring, when the house was still and her husband's breath was slow and deep beside her, when all she had were her own thoughts ricocheting in her brain like a hailstorm as fierce as the ones that glazed the poplars and oaks in Dock Watch Hollow and bent the sweeping arms of stately mountain pines to the ground until they fractured and died a slow death come the spring.

"Supper's up," Helen beckoned. Todd rubbed his hands together in anticipation of freshly cooked collard greens. He hoped that Helen would see how easy he was to please and the gratitude he felt for authentic, home-cooked southern fare like his momma used to make. It was only collard greens, but it was a start.

"So, Jane, tell us about your latest mission trip," Todd said.

"Dear brother, I fear you have a one-track mind. Can we please talk about *civilian* life for a change? I mean, what's happening here in the States? Read any good books? Seen any good movies?"

Helen laughed, surprised by Jane's easy defiance. Perhaps there was more she could learn from Jane than she thought.

"I'm afraid I don't have the time or stomach for the mass media," Todd sniffed.

"Oh, come on, Todd. Lighten up. Is he always like this?" Jane asked, turning towards Helen who had frozen with a fork to her mouth.

"It's no wonder this poor child is as stressed out as she is. When was the last time you took her out on a date, Todd?"

"Well," Todd thought for a moment. "We went out for a nice dinner on our anniversary."

"Your anniversary is in July! It's nearly the end of March, Todd, according to the Gregorian calendar. Or maybe you only count Sundays? For the love of God, take your wife out on a date. Tonight."

Helen put her fork down.

"Honey, you have a nice dress to go with those fancy shoes?"

Helen nodded.

"I'm sure there's a movie you've been wanting to see, right?"

Helen shrugged. On more than one occasion she had circled movie times in red ink on the local pages of the newspaper for Todd to see. He'd never once taken the bait and she had long stopped trying.

"There's a good love story playing at the theater downtown," Helen said softly, hesitant to look up from the napkin on her lap. She was sure Todd was fuming by now and she braced herself for a

full-scale brawl between brother and sister. A few
seconds passed before Helen dared to peek at
Todd's face. When she did, she saw Todd was smiling and staring at her like a lovesick cow.

"Helen, might I have the pleasure of your company tonight?"

"Of course," Helen replied, expecting a litany of
conditions and perplexed when he merely gave her
a satisfied nod.

"It's settled then," Jane said. "So tell me, are
y'all Yankee fans now?"

Helen marveled at Jane's natural charm, thoroughly enjoying the ease with which she shifted
between topics and not one of them religious or
missionary-minded. It was refreshing to talk about
matters that were earthy and real and of no eternal
import. It occurred to her that perhaps she'd figured
Jane all wrong; that the coming week just might be
a welcome respite from the loneliness of daily life
with Todd as she knew it.

"I'll take care of the kitchen," Jane said, shooing
Helen from the sink as soon as the table was
cleared. "You go put on your prettiest dress and
have yourself a good time tonight, you hear me?
Shame on my brother for neglecting you so. I'm
sure the good Lord would agree that charity begins
at home."

"He's a very busy man," Helen replied, repeating the mantra that had gotten her through a lengthy
chain of long and miserable nights

"Don't make excuses for him, Helen. I could tell

by the amount of time he spent on the phone with Jonathan this afternoon that he's got his mind too fixed in one place."

"That's just his nature, I guess. He's very dedicated to Little Flock. He just wants it to be successful."

"Well, I always say that God doesn't call us to be *successful*, he calls us to be *faithful*. Actually, I didn't say that, Mother Teresa did. She was a spirit-filled woman all right, a fine missionary considering she was a Catholic."

Helen nodded politely.

"I don't think there's much chance of changing him."

"Let's just start with tonight and see what happens." Jane winked and set about washing the dishes, glad that Todd had taken to heart the swift kick she'd delivered under the table. "And don't you worry; I'll mind the dog."

"Thank you, Jane."

"It's no bother, I like dogs."

"I meant thank you for coming – and for overlooking my contrariness today."

"Don't be so hard on yourself, Helen. I know Todd isn't an easy man to please but his heart is in the right place."

Helen wondered if what Jane said was true, if Todd merely had her eternal good at heart. She hoped they could put aside the hard words and feelings that had come between them, at least for one night. In many ways, she considered their impromptu date an eleventh-hour reprieve from an altogether different kind of mission she was about to undertake on the shifting sands of China Beach. Just maybe, if she really set her mind to it, she could learn to love Todd all over again, this time with her eyes wide open. After all, her momma had always said: *the devil you know is better than the devil you don't!*

"Ready?" Todd said, peering in the doorway.

"Almost," Helen replied as she donned a pair of blue crystal earrings and finished her lips with rose-tinted gloss.

"You look beautiful in that dress, Helen. It's always been one of my favorites."

"Thank you," she said, fussing with the prim white collar that pinched the back of her neck.

"Shall we?"

Helen smiled shyly at Todd's outstretched hand. She grasped it lightly and he responded by curling his fingers around hers and squeezing them tightly.

"Take your time," Jane called out as they passed by the kitchen. "Why don't you stop and get yourselves a cup of fancy coffee on the way home?"

"Thanks, Jane," Todd replied. "We just might do that."

"Has she always been so...." Helen stumbled, searching for the right word.

"Bossy?" Todd whispered.

"*Nice*, I was going to say. I'm sorry I didn't get to know her a little better before I passed judgment on her."

"A peculiar kind of nice," Todd conceded,

"once you get past her prickly shell. She can seem a bit fanatical at times but I think you'll find she's also very compassionate and fair."

Todd held the car door open for Helen. She was grateful for shelter from the stark light of a three-quarter moon, for the seconds that separated them just long enough for her to think about Hawk and what he would say if he were to see Miss Hell-on-Wheels dressed up like a delicate, porcelain doll with a demure smile etched on her face and a limp look frozen in her dark green eyes.

Todd glanced at her keenly as she turned her head aside to stare out the window. He admired the strong profile that reflected her Appalachian roots, with sculpted apple cheeks and lush pink lips that offset the sharpness of her nose and the strength of her jaw. Her eyes were framed by long, full lashes that fluttered like black butterfly wings and exposed her nervousness. She had turned into a gorgeous woman, Todd thought, appreciating her exquisite beauty with the same impersonal regard an artist has for the object of his creative energy and relief. He inhaled the sultry fragrance of her jasmine perfume and wished he were a better man.

Helen sensed Todd's gaze upon her but chose to continue looking aimlessly out the window. She couldn't help but contemplate the last time they had shared what was supposed to be a romantic evening out on the town. Instead, Todd had chosen the night of their third wedding anniversary to ambush her with the announcement that they were moving up north to plant a church in a small city that was known for its Revolutionary War provenance. While she still bristled at the memory, she was determined not to fire the first salvo this night, to keep the conversation courteous and polite until the house lights dimmed and the movie began and gave her 108 merciful minutes to think about how she felt and what she was going to do next.

Todd brought her a barrel of buttered popcorn and three different kinds of chocolate candy, which only served to remind Helen that he still knew or cared precious little about her preferences in life. If he had asked, she would have opted for a small cup of salted, unbuttered popcorn and the soft, jellied candies that stuck to her teeth; the kind that she and Joan used to eat by the box until their tongues turned psychedelic colors and stayed that way for hours and made them giggle every time they opened their mouths to speak.

One hundred and six minutes later, as the music swelled and true love triumphed and Todd reached for her greasy fingers, Helen knew there was nothing more to talk about, that it was all but over between them. While she would never shame Todd or his ministry with the stigma of divorce, she craved the soaring passion she'd seen two lovers display on the screen that night, knowing it had its essence in truth. Somewhere, a writer had the heart to conceive it; a producer had championed it; a believer had bankrolled it; a man and a woman had enacted it with confidence and grace. Surely then, this phenomenon was native to the natural world, in hearts that extended from Hollywood to China Beach. It was a truth she was committed to knowing and to experiencing in her lifetime, in her flesh and in her very soul.

God help her, she would no longer settle for less.

Chapter 11
Stolen Hours

"Jane?" Helen rapped on the guest room door. "You up?"

She heard a muffled groan, then Jane's faint reply.

"I'm awake. Come on in."

Helen peeked inside the doorway. She tried not to laugh at the way Jane's hair stuck out like the tail feathers of a chicken on the lam. "Get up sleepyhead. We have ten o'clock appointments at the beauty salon downtown."

"This bed…" Jane groaned.

"Oh no, what's wrong with it?"

"It's the closest thing to heaven I've ever known." Jane sighed contentedly. "That's it, I quit the mission field. I'm selling my soul for a Swedish mattress."

Helen laughed. "Coffee's on. You do drink coffee?"

"Only if it's black and strong."

"You're in luck. That's the one way I know how

222

to make it."

"I'll be right there. I just need a few minutes to tidy up." Jane rubbed the top of her head and grimaced. "My hair must look a fright."

"I've seen worse – down on the farm," Helen teased. She was pleased to see Jane smile, which Helen took as confirmation of their budding rapport.

"Hey, how was your date last night? You came home early."

"I reckon that was all the excitement we could stand for one night. We're going to have to ease back into this dating thing."

"But you had fun?" Jane persisted.

Helen didn't have the heart to tell her that she and Todd barely uttered a word on the ride home, that he had sullenly retreated to his side of the bed after a perfunctory kiss goodnight that had made her weep into her pillow for want of something more.

"Sure, we had fun."

Jane clapped her hands and grinned. "Praise God, it's a good day!" Helen was touched by Jane's childlike display of innocence and faith. It pained her to think of her plans to deceive her in the hours and days ahead, but it didn't seem to Helen that she had much choice.

"I'll be in the kitchen."

Jane nodded and threw off the covers, making Helen blush as she caught a glimpse of Jane's nakedness on her way out the door.

"Don't mind me!" Jane called out. "It's hot as blazes in Mumbai. I got used to sleeping *au naturale*."

Helen chuckled as she walked down the hall and past her own bedroom, relieved that Todd had risen early and left for work before they had a chance to lock eyes – or horns. He was angry she had rebuffed his offer to stop for coffee on the way home from the movie. She got the sense that there was something he wanted to tell her, something he'd been holding back all night for lack of time and opportunity. It no longer mattered to Helen what that something might be and so she had feigned fatigue, entreating Todd to take her home. He obliged in stony silence, which had yet to be broken.

"Helen, do you think I'll be warm enough?" Jane ambled into the kitchen dressed in a pink and purple cotton blouse and baggy blue jeans topped by a brown, knee-length sweater that had hopelessly lost its shape.

"It was near sixty degrees when I took Chester for a walk early this morning. I think you'll be just fine."

"Good, because I don't have anything else to wear."

"I've got plenty you can borrow."

"It's been a long time since I fit into single digits."

"Well, how about your shoes, then. What size are you?" Helen said, glancing down at Jane's feet which were shod in cheap rubber sandals.

"Seven and a half, I think."

"Perfect. Try these," Helen said, lifting the stylish, gold-tone ballerina slippers off her feet.

"I couldn't impose," Jane said, unable to hide her admiration for them.

"Never mind just put them on."

Jane kicked off her sandals and stepped into Helen's shoes. She wiggled her toes and giggled. "I feel like Cinderella."

"I hope that doesn't make me the ugly stepsister."

"On the contrary, Helen. I'm quite surprised by you."

"What do you mean?"

"I expected someone with a lot less – grace."

"Well, I'm no Princess Diana, if that's what you mean."

"No, I mean you have a deep goodness inside of you, Helen. I can see that now."

Helen shuffled her bare feet and shrugged. It had been a long time since anyone had said something so stunningly kind to her. She didn't quite know how to respond.

"But I'm afraid I'll wind up far too attached to pretty things if I stay here much longer," Jane said, looking sternly at her feet.

"It's okay to like pretty things," Helen said quietly, "so long as you don't covet them at the expense of people's needs and feelings, isn't that right, Jane?"

Jane nodded. "Well said, Helen. Thank you."

"So we can go get our hair done now?"

"Absolutely."

Helen glanced down at her bare feet, then raised

one finger in the air. "Just a minute," she said, racing down the hall. She returned with a pair of brown leather mules on her feet and Chester trotting behind her.

"You watch the house now, Chester," Helen said, offering him a biscuit from the bone-shaped cookie jar on the kitchen counter. "We'll be back soon."

"Todd says you spoil him."

"Todd says a lot of stuff and nonsense."

"Amen, sister," Jane replied wearily. She had already made a note to speak with Todd about his unfair treatment of Helen. She didn't like his sore neglect of her and had a mind to tell him so before he got too steeped in the sin of self-righteousness. He had always been a proud boy, too concerned with appearances and the weight of his reputation to pay much mind to the rest of the world around him. She knew he came by it honestly, the way their father raised them to a standard of perfection that led them to work longer and harder than anybody else to be worthy of their calling. Jane had worked out her salvation with the fear and trembling that came from tending to Jesus in the broken bodies of the poorest of the poor. Todd, on the other hand, had yet to surrender the notion that his salvation was somehow connected to his ability to make *others* fear and tremble. That was such old-school religion, Jane lamented, wishing that Todd himself would spend a week or two changing the diapers of grown men or feeding amputees who had lost their limbs but not one iota of their hope in Jesus.

Jane listened eagerly to Helen's vivid descriptions of the historic fields and buildings they passed on their way into town. Helen slowed as they drove by the iron gates of St. Paul.

"Now that's a lovely church," Jane said.

"That's where the local soup kitchen is. And behind it is Damien House, for people living with AIDS."

"That's the soup kitchen where you used to work?"

"Yes."

"Do you miss it?"

"More than words can say."

Jane reached over and patted Helen on the shoulder. "I understand, Helen. It gets in your blood, doesn't it?"

Helen nodded, fighting back a sudden assault of tears.

"I've only been stateside for a couple of weeks and already I'm itching to get back to work. If it weren't for these shoes, I'd be gone tomorrow."

Helen laughed through her tears. "You can take the shoes with you, Jane."

"I have a better idea."

"Oh? What's that?"

"Why don't I take *you* with me?"

"What?"

"Helen, you have a real heart for the poor. I'll show you the ropes and you can ease into it at your own pace. You don't have to stay in Haiti the full six weeks. Just come for a week or two and see."

"I couldn't."

"Why not?"

"I'm not ready."

"Who ever is? Simon Peter and Andrew might have dropped their nets at the first call, but most of us aren't willing to give it up so easily. Think about it, will you?"

"Yes, I'll think about it," Helen replied, hoping that would put an end to the matter.

"Better yet, pray on it."

"I will, Jane."

"I'll take you up on the shoes just the same," Jane said, stretching out her legs and admiring them once more. "They sure are comfortable, too."

"That's good because we have to walk a few blocks from here."

Helen pulled into a parking space and turned off the car.

"I'll walk you to the salon."

"Aren't you getting your hair done, too?"

"Yes, but they couldn't take both of us at the same time. Your appointment is for ten. Mine's at eleven, but don't worry. I've told my stylist, Camille, exactly what to do for you. I've got a short list of errands to run around town. I won't be long, I promise."

Jane nodded, feeling guilty that she had already breached the promise she'd made to keep Helen squarely in her sight – and it was only day one! And yet somehow she didn't see Helen as being untrustworthy the same way that Todd did. Confused, perhaps. Lonesome, for sure. But neither devious nor deserving of such hard scrutiny and discipline. She made up her mind not to tell Todd that she and Helen had been separated for the better part of an hour. Not unless he asked her outright. Then she'd have no choice.

Helen waited until Jane had donned the prerequisite black vinyl cape and was sitting contentedly in the shampoo girl's chair with a glossy fashion magazine in hand before leaving. She smiled encouragingly and waved, then calmly departed from the salon, walking several feet past the plate glass window before breaking into a spirited run.

She didn't stop until she reached the perimeter of China Beach, pausing just long enough to catch her breath, inhaling the sweet scent of balsam mingled with the ashy fragrance of burning wood that told her before her eyes could confirm it that Hawk was near. He was the only one who kept the fire ablaze in the middle of the day, unafraid that the smoke rising above the treetops would draw the police or well-meaning social workers into their makeshift camp. He figured it was no secret that he and his troops were at home there. Over the years, he had negotiated a truce with law enforcement that assured their undisturbed peace – as long as they kept their end of the bargain and didn't emerge from the woods in drunken stupors that upset the general public. It was Hawk's own sense of discipline and commitment to keeping his word that had kept his

troops in line and China Beach on the map; under
his leadership, it had become a refuge where men
who had lost virtually everything in the combat
zones of Vietnam could retain the only thing left
that mattered to them: the brotherhood they shared
with their comrades-in-arms, with other men like
them who could never again feel at home in a place
with four walls and only one exit; who would never
again sleep in a bed beside their pre-war wives and
lovers for fear of mistaking them in their twisted
dreams for a comely, female Viet Cong soldier who
was no less a threat – and sometimes more so – than
the Victor Charlies who prowled in the tall grass.
No, they were loathe to be among the ranks of soldiers in the news who had attacked or maimed their
sleeping loved ones in midnight firefights that
seemed as real to them as the flesh and blood that
spattered their pit helmets when the man beside
them was fragged by a grenade wielded by a skinny
Vietnamese boy with a baseball-worthy arm.

"Helen."

Helen didn't remember crossing the distance between them, only the warm, familiar dent of Hawk's
shoulder into which she buried her face and wept
with profound relief that he had risen from the
muddy waters of the Song Hong River and now
stood soundly in mind and body before her. She
didn't notice the way Hawk stood with his arms
held out stiffly in front of him, stunned by the force
of Helen's embrace and the heat that radiated from
her body. After several seconds, he gingerly curled

his arms around her back and held her lightly, fearful that the wild beating of her heart pressed any closer to his own would render him helpless to ever let her go. The comforting fragrance of jasmine arose from her feverish skin like incense and he fought to keep from burying his face in the soft waves of her hair.

"Why are you crying, Helen?" This time there was no chastisement in his voice, just a desire to know who or what had given her cause for such unbridled sorrow. He knew there were several scenarios that could bring her down low – but he was reluctant to venture a guess as to which had come to pass. He knew when Helen was ready, she'd talk. Until then, she'd cry.

As her tears subsided and gave way to delicate sighs, Hawk stepped backward and held Helen at arm's length, examining her from head to toe for a sign of hurt or trauma. She refused to look at him, embarrassed by the unexpected siege of emotion that overcame her at the mere sight of him. She'd already made up her mind never to tell him that she'd seen him half-crazed down by the river. She hoped Henry had enough sense to do the same.

She glanced at her watch, disappointed that several precious minutes had already ticked by. Jane was probably halfway through her haircut by now and fixated on the front door like a fox on a henhouse.

"I'm crying because I'm happy," Helen said, blotting her eyes with the hem of her sleeve. He looked at her sternly and she realized he thought she was being sarcastic.

"No, I really mean it. I couldn't wait to tell you."

"Tell me what?"

"I know what I want, Hawk. I can finally tell you what I want. Right here, right now, if you're still interested in knowing."

Hawk released his grip on Helen's shoulders and crossed his arms over his chest. His square jaw rippled with tension as he fought the hope that swelled within him, hard pressed to believe that a woman like Helen would choose a soldier of misfortune like himself over a man of God who offered her a life of privilege and stability. He knew Helen had come looking for him the day before and that Henry had informed her he'd gone to visit friends at the VA Hospital. He was grateful to Henry for the lie, humiliated at the thought of Helen witnessing the flashbacks that left every muscle in his body sore from being taut with rage and every thought wrapped in a foggy haze that lasted for days thereafter. He wanted to match Helen's enthusiasm but found himself thwarted by the dullness of his mind.

"You don't look so excited, Hawk." Helen's smile began to fade.

Hawk took Helen's hand and held it to the pulse point on the side of his neck, just above the swirling tattoos that reminded Helen she was about to stir up hell with a long spoon.

"Feel that?"

"Laws a mercy, your heart's beatin' faster than a hillbilly jig!" Helen whispered, and for a moment Hawk felt the pall of his exhaustion lift. He smiled and drew her closer, revitalized by her nearness. She glanced into his eyes before shyly lowering her gaze to the soft, muddy ground that had finally given way to the moist breath of spring.

"Then don't keep me in suspense, Helen. Tell me what you want," he urged, unable to keep himself from tangling his hands in her hair and tilting her face upward so that she couldn't avoid his gaze a second longer.

"I want *you*, Hawk."

Hawk didn't flinch, though the slightest cock of his head made it clear that he was second guessing what he'd heard Helen say, the blunt force of her words wrapped in the camouflage of a sweet mountain twang.

"What does that mean?"

"It means I want to be with you. You know, *be* with you…." Helen blushed and tried to look away. Hawk did not allow it. He exhaled slowly, his body beginning to ache in an altogether different way as he contemplated Helen's declaration.

"You mean like this?" he said, his lips brushing against her forehead, then trailing down her tear-stained face until they skimmed Helen's lips, which she parted to murmur her assent.

"Yes," she barely uttered before Hawk's mouth covered hers in a long, deep, penetrating kiss that had been far too long in coming. Hawk's powerful arms encircled her waist and pressed her tightly to his body until she knew without a doubt that his desire mirrored her own.

"But not just like that..." Helen sighed in the breathy spaces between their fervent kisses. "This is yours, too," she said, placing the palm of Hawk's left hand over her blouse in the center of her chest. It was not in her nature to give a man her body without surrendering her heart and soul as well. She hoped he understood the full extent of her offering that was manifested by a fierce throbbing against the gentle pressure of his hand.

Hawk forced himself to pause and reconnoiter their surroundings. His years of military training prevented him from letting down his guard without first assessing the risk of doing do. In this case, however, he was far less troubled by his coordinates than he was by the prospect of allowing his emotions to overrule his instincts. There was something Helen hadn't said...something he had to know.

"So you're leaving your husband?"

Helen hesitated and then shook her head. "I can't leave him, Hawk, I know that's hard for you to understand. But it's over between us. Ours is strictly a marriage of convenience. You know I wouldn't lie to you about something like that."

Hawk stood tall, his hand dropping from Helen's chest like a lead weight.

"Convenient for who?"

"For Todd, I suppose."

"And what about you, Helen? Is it convenient

for you?"

Helen couldn't lie. "Maybe, in some ways."

"That's what I thought. You got no business walking down this path unless you're prepared to go the distance."

Helen put her hands on her hips and stared at Hawk defiantly. The deep, cherry red of her lips reflected their ardent kisses and made him sorry he'd pulled away from the heat of her mouth and the warm flesh radiating from beneath her tidy white blouse.

"How can you say that? I'm risking everything to be here – and you're risking nothing," she argued.

"Nothing? You call the risk of falling in love with you nothing?"

"What?"

"Never mind."

"Say it again."

"I won't.'

"Fine. Then kiss me again."

Hawk grasped Helen at her waist and in one powerful motion pulled her tightly to his chest. She pressed her hands firmly to the sides of his face, kissing him as deeply as he kissed her, matching his every attempt to close the tiniest spaces that stood between them.

"I have to go," Helen finally murmured into Hawk's ear, cherishing the smoothness of his cheek next to hers. The face of her watch glared at her from where it peeked out under the collar of

Hawk's black leather jacket.

"Stay with me," Hawk whispered back. He had entreated her that way before, but never with the same urgency he felt that day.

"I can't. Jane's a-waiting on me at the beauty parlor. She'll get suspicious if I don't show up right soon."

Hawk stared at her intently. "When are you coming back?"

"As soon as I can. Maybe tomorrow, maybe the day after."

"No more *maybe this* or *maybe that*, Helen, I need to know."

"Jane's leaving on Saturday. It'll be easier after that. Heck, I'll come see you every day if you want me to." Her eyes sparkled with a captivating blend of devotion and desire.

Hawk nodded, turning his back to Helen in an awkward and confused spin. Damn, if she hadn't succeeded where a thousand Viet Cong had failed, ambushing him in the light of day, no less. He had anticipated the physical attraction between them would eventually have its way, but he hadn't seen this coming – this stirring of his soul which had been numb for almost thirty-five years, a casualty of war and death and dismemberment and every evil thing under the sun. It was an awakening that left him alternately exhilarated and pained. He turned to face Helen once more, her expression soft with supplication.

"The question is, will you be waiting for me,

Mickey Lightfoot?" Helen asked, hoping that when she returned she would find the same vibrant man she was leaving, not the tormented soldier she knew coexisted within the confines of his well-conditioned body and shrewd, disciplined mind.

"God willing…" Hawk's voice drifted.

"And the creek don't rise," Helen finished, basking in the gleam in his eyes. This time she didn't feel the faintest urge to cry as she took her leave. There would be no more futile tears, she vowed, remembering that she had chosen this stolen hour for her heart's return from exile and this un-holy place for the opening of her body and soul like the waters of the Red Sea, blindly trusting the one in whose seductive blue eyes she found her prom-ised land; in whose powerful desire for her was true redemption; in whose battle-scarred body she found her refuge and her strength.

Oh yes, God willing or not, she would be back!

***

"I'll be with you in a minute, Helen," Camille called out from beside the black hydraulic chair where Jane sat and managed a wave from beneath the black cape still draped around her blocky shoul-ders.

"Well look at you!" Helen cried out, approach-ing to admire Camille's handiwork. She reached out and caressed the waves of light that Camille had painted into Jane's dun-colored hair, giving it a quiet radiance that Helen thought befitted Jane's saintly nature.

"Do you like it, Helen?" Jane scrunched her nose as she looked at herself in the mirror.

"Like it? I think it's magnificent, Jane. It really suits you!"

"I feel vain."

"Nonsense, Jane, say it with me: *I feel pretty.*"

Jane turned her head from side-to-side, secretly enchanted by the shimmering highlights that bounced off the mirror and the hot lights overhead. She barely stifled a giggle and made Helen and Camille laugh at her giddy expression.

"Okay. I feel pretty. Are you happy now?"

Helen nodded slowly and deeply. "Happier than you'll ever know."

"Good Heavens, first the shoes, now this," Jane said mournfully. She ran her fingers through her expertly coifed hair as Camille removed the vinyl cape and dusted the back of Jane's neck with a brush full of baby powder. "You're going to make a reluctant missionary out of me if you keep this up, dear sister."

Helen eyes grew misty at the endearment.

"Then we'll be quite a pair someday, won't we?"

"Someday?" Jane's spirit lost its buoyancy as she searched Helen's face for a remnant of hope. She thought Helen seemed open to the idea of taking some time to pray on the idea. Now, it was abundantly clear in the way she crossed her arms over her chest and shifted uneasily from foot-to-foot that Helen had her mind dead-set against the idea of accompanying her to Haiti at the week's end. Like it or not, Helen would be aboard Flight 232 – yet she had dared to hope it would be at Helen's own choosing. More troublesome than the battle that lay ahead, though, was the sight of the fresh clumps of mud that clung to the sides of Helen's brown leather mules – the same ruddy mud Helen had tracked home the day before. *Spring thaw*, she had said. Jane glanced down at her own feet, noting there was not a speck of dirt along the soles of her own shoes, nor had she noticed any particularly soggy turf among the burgeoning green grass lining the city sidewalks.

"I'm sorry, Jane. I'm just not prepared to go with you this time around. I'd take it kindly if you don't hold it against me."

"Of course, I understand," Jane replied curtly as she awkwardly slid out of the stylist's chair. Jane fussed with the buttons on her floral blouse that looked to Helen like a close cousin to the riotous pink tablecloth Granny Hicks used to set on the table when good company was coming.

"Are you upset with me?" Helen asked, begging a moment from the tattooed shampoo girl who impatiently tapped her foot and rolled her eyes at Helen's deferral.

Jane shook her head. "I'm not upset, but it's only natural that I'm disappointed. I think we could do some mighty fine work together, Helen."

Helen shrugged, momentarily distracted by the exquisite soreness of her lips as she pressed them together resolutely. Lord have mercy, if she didn't like kissing Mickey Lightfoot even more than she had ever dreamed she would.

"So where did you go, Helen?"

"Excuse me?"

"I mean, where do you suggest I whittle away the time while you're having your turn?"

Helen pointed abstractly to her left. "There's a wonderful café just a block up the street that serves the most heavenly coffee this side of…well, heaven. They have all sorts of interesting books and magazines to read. More than enough to hold your interest, I'm sure."

"Oh, is that where you were?"

"Well, I just picked up a coffee to go and then I went every which way. You know, the post office, then to the ATM…."

"Then I guess I'll do the same. I think I'd enjoy taking a little walk myself."

"I'll meet you back here at noon?" Helen pointed to the face of her watch as she hurried toward the glossy black sink and the shampoo girl whose expression was turning hostile. Helen knew what was likely to happen when the shampoo girl got annoyed – how the cold water line oddly managed to cross with the hot water one and send an icy stream down a client's bare back.

"Yes, at noon," Jane confirmed, waving merrily as she headed towards the door.

Helen breathed a heavy sigh, relieved that all was well between them. Once settled in Camille's chair, she gazed into the gilded oval mirror and smiled softly as she recalled the sensations of Hawk's broad, strong hands stroking her cheeks and his mouth firmly pressed over hers in bold yet tender exploration.

"So what are we doing today?" Camille asked, rifling through the crown of Helen's hair and frowning at the length. "You have the perfect face for something short and sassy, you know."

Helen laughed. "You say that every time."

"Well? What's it going to be?"

"Just a trim. I think a girl should have a head of hair a man can run his fingers through."

"Jeez, Helen, I can't argue with that," Camille said. She sighed and picked up a long black comb, the look on her client's face far too distant and dreamy for small talk. She'd seen that look before, on PTA moms who were Planning Their Affair and starry-eyed teens who gazed longingly at Hollywood's bad boys in tabloid magazines. She hoped whoever he was, that Helen would be careful. She was just a sweet country girl who had likely never even heard of Sex in the City, let alone practiced it. Camille gave Helen a knowing wink, then began humming softly to the radio as she set her hands to work.

It was that same dreamy look that sent Jane in the direction of St. Paul's Soup Kitchen. She had a hunch that there was something more to Helen's attraction to the impoverished guests who stood out-side the imposing red door in a ragged line that snaked down the granite steps and along the wrought iron fence bordering the street. She had heard of lay missionaries who had been dismissed for becoming too emotionally involved with their charges, their own neediness or lack of self-control overpowering their Great Commission to preach the good news to all nations and all people with dignity and grace. More than once, she had heard Todd complain of Helen's fascination with the poor, es-pecially with the residents of Damien House and the Vietnam vets who posed a particularly menacing threat to the core Gospel message of peace and temperance.

I watched Jane approach us with a purposeful, lumbering gait that was accented by metallic gold shoes that glinted in the sunlight. As she drew near the steps, Marcy took notice and stopped Jane in her tracks.

"The end of the line is that way," she said. Her red hair stuck out from beneath a brittle straw hat that wobbled on her head as she shook it furiously from side to side. "We got rules around here, Missy. The first one is *no jumping the line!*"

"I beg your pardon," Jane said, offering her hand. "I'm not here to eat, I'm a Baptist missionary and I've come to see the fine work that goes on here at St. Paul's. My name is Jane Baldwin. Perhaps you know my brother, the Reverend Todd Baldwin?"

"Nope," Marcy said, vigorously pumping Jane's

hand just the same. "But any friend of God is a friend of mine." Marcy smiled, her gapped teeth gritty and dark. "I'm Marcy Floyd. You want to have lunch with me?"

"Well, I can't stay too long, but I'd sure like to sit with you for little while."

"Come on," Marcy said, just as the red door opened with a ceremonious thump. "This way…you sure you don't want nothin' to eat? Smells like ziti. Ziti for the needy, we call it. You should try it."

"No, thank you."

"Then wait for me at that table over there," Marcy said, pointing to a round table near a tall metal cart lined with slices of fresh apple pie. "Stay away from *that* table," Marcy cautioned, speaking in a clumsy whisper. "That's where the Vietnam vets sit…crazy bastards."

Jane nodded, taking note of the few bedraggled men who had already congregated there – Henry, Butch, and Hawk among them.

"And definitely don't go anywhere near that one," Marcy continued, pointing in my direction. "Not unless you want to catch AIDS."

Jane's eyes traveled in the direction of Marcy's finger until her gaze came to rest on me. I smiled at her and waved. She seemed unnerved by my friend-liness and wavered in her golden shoes. But to my surprise, as soon as Marcy departed, she approached me and extended her hand to greet me.

"Hello, I'm Jane Baldwin."

"I know, I heard you introduce yourself to

Marcy outside."

"And you are?"

"Frankie. Frankie B."

"Nice to meet you, Frankie."

"So, are you any relation to Helen Baldwin?"

"You know Helen?"

"Yes, she's a good friend of mine."

"Helen is my sister-in-law. My brother is the pastor of the Little Flock Baptist Church. Do you know him also?"

"We met. Once."

"Only once? I hope his fire and brimstone delivery didn't turn you off."

"Not really. I'm a Catholic."

"Oh." Jane nodded, counting me among the lost.

"So, how do you know Helen?"

"Well, she used to work here. Didn't she tell you that?"

"Of course she did. That's why I'm here, to see what keeps her coming back," she tested.

"Helen hasn't been here in weeks. Not since the day they let her go."

"Really? Not even once?"

"Not even once."

Jane's eyes skirted the room, lingering on the spectacle of Norman as he hobbled toward the lunch line, his aluminum cane clanging against metal chair legs as he zigzagged drunkenly across the room. She looked at me questioningly. I pointed to the sign on the wall. *Judge not lest you be judged.* I smiled politely. Jane stifled a huff, but not the frown that tugged at the corners of her pale, thin lips.

"So how is Helen?" I ventured, anxious to redeem Jane from the sin of pride. Jane looked at me intently, clearly trying to decide if there was any guile in me.

"She's doing fine," she finally replied with a cordial smile, having decided I was a harmless and credible witness.

"Will you tell her I was asking about her? And that I miss her?"

"I surely will."

"And if it's not too much trouble, would you give her this?" I removed the wooden Tau from around my neck and handed it to Jane.

"What is it?"

"It's a Tau…the cross venerated by St. Francis of Assisi. I know it doesn't look like much, but it's a cross just the same."

Jane inspected the blocky looking "T" that dangled from a leather cord. I could tell that she thought it odd, but accepted it as just another ancient Catholic eccentricity.

"Please, tell her I'm hanging in there…but that I wanted her to have this as a remembrance of me."

My reference to my terminal condition was not lost on Jane. She gazed at me sympathetically – almost lovingly – as she took the cross and then covered my trembling hands with her own.

"It was a blessing to meet you, Frankie."

"You too, Jane."

I thought I saw tears welling in her eyes just before she turned and took her leave. She was a good and tender soul, one whose principles sometimes thwarted her deeply compassionate nature. I wished her well. But even more, I wished her the strength and wisdom to be an instrument of God's peace in a household that was soon to explode with the devil's fury.

Jane hastened to rejoin Marcy, who stood on her tiptoes searching for her new friend. Halfway across the room, Norman careened recklessly with a tray of ziti tipping on the fulcrum of his feeble hand. I thought Jane would soon be baptized with ziti for the needy, but she saw it coming and banked left just before Norman lost his balance and fell to his knees, his cane clattering over the tile floor, skipping in her direction. Jane expected the mishap to bring the noisy kitchen to a grinding halt; she glanced around and raised her eyebrows in disbelief that no one seemed to notice or care about what had just happened. She reached down and picked up Norman's cane, hooking it over the back of a chair as she helped him to his muddy feet.

"Goddamn gooks!" He cursed and shook her off. "Where's my stick?"

"Here," Jane said, thrusting his cane toward him. Much as she wanted to look him in the eye and ease his pain, she was mesmerized by the sight of his shabby sneakers – sneakers that were caked in the same moist red clay that glazed the soles of Helen's trendy brown shoes.

"What are you looking at?" Norman growled as he snatched his cane and shook it threateningly.

Jane wobbled her head and put up her hands defensively, then bolted toward Marcy and sat down beside her.

"I told you they were crazy bastards," she clucked.

"Tell me more about them," Jane said as she watched Norman resume his unsteady trek toward the table of camouflaged men who paid him no mind or sympathy – except for, she observed, the fierce-looking one in the black tee shirt, who noticed Norman's distress and pulled a chair out for him when no one else was looking.

"Nothing to tell," Marcy snapped, eager for another woman's opinion on her philandering boyfriend, Manuel, and annoyed by the distraction. "They're just a gang of ex-marines who think they own the place. They got a campsite down by the river, about a quarter mile from here. Half of 'em think they're still living in the jungle. *Freaks...*" she said dismissively.

"Who's the one in the black tee shirt?"

"That's Hawk. You don't want to mess with the likes of him."

"He's quite a – *presence.*" Jane said, intrigued by the contrast of his scary tattoos against his subtle show of kindness.

"That's what all the women say. But not me, I got Manuel."

"Marcy, do you know Helen Baldwin?"

"Helen..." Marcy tilted her face towards the ceiling and paused with a finger pressed to the bottom of her chin. "You mean the Outreach Lady?"

"Yes."

"Sure, I know Helen. She was real nice."

"Have you seen here around here lately?"

"Nah. Not since she got kicked to the curb by the mental health department."

"So she was nice?"

"Yeah, and real friendly, too. Even the jungle rats loved her."

"You mean the Vietnam vets?"

"Especially Hawk. He kind of took her under his wing, you know. There was even a rumor awhile back...."

"What kind of rumor?"

"I heard she went to China Beach once or twice to see Hawk. I don't know if it's true, but I do know those two were real tight. Hawk doesn't seem quite the same since she's been gone."

"China Beach?"

"Their campsite."

"Oh."

"But Helen, she always said she was happily married, and I believed her. I want to get married someday. Manuel says he ain't ready to settle down just yet."

Jane nodded sympathetically. She glanced at her watch and gasped.

"Mercy me, I've got to go!"

"Go where?"

"I'm supposed to meet someone at noon. But it was so very nice to meet you, Marcy."

"Same to you. By the way, your hair is real pretty. I like the way it sparkles."

Jane had all but forgotten about her new hairdo and raised her hand to her head self-consciously. "Really? I just had it done."

"Yeah? Can you hook me up?"

Jane cocked her head and pondered the expression. She wasn't sure what it meant, but it didn't seem to imply any real harm. "Sure. Why not."

"Thanks, Jane!"

"You're welcome, Marcy. God bless you!"

Jane hurried toward the door, not wanting to be a minute late. As she turned the last corner, she was surprised to see Helen sitting on a bench outside the beauty salon. It was only ten till noon. She hoped she hadn't been waiting long.

"You're already done?"

"Camille just finished spraying me down like I was a king-size gallynipper."

"Gallynipper?"

"*Mosquito*," Helen explained. "And *a katynipper* is a dragonfly. Silly mountain talk, isn't it?" Helen shrugged, suddenly feeling awkward.

"You look lovely."

"Thanks, so do you."

"What's the damage?" Jane said, reaching into her backpack for her wallet.

"Don't be silly, it's my treat."

"You shouldn't."

249

"But I did. Well, Todd did. But it's his pleasure, I'm sure."

"So now what?"

"Well, I was hoping to have a look-see at those oxford pumps at Macy's...."

Jane bristled at the mention of shoes. She didn't want to contemplate shoes or the idea that Helen's carried the telltale sign of a woman who had been where she had no business being. She hated the thought that Helen had been misguided at best – or as wanton as any Jezebel at worst. But how would she ever know the truth of the matter without confronting her directly? Sadly, Todd had been right; Helen required a firm, disciplined hand and a vigilant eye. She would not let her out of her sight again!

"By all means, dear sister, I believe you've made a shoe junkie out of me as well!"

Jane smiled and clasped Helen's hand tightly.

***

That night, Jane treated Todd, Jonathan, and Helen to a home cooked meal of chicken and dumplings, topped off by a fried apple pie; she knew that people tended toward an open mind when they had a full belly, and so she waited until after supper to pull her brother aside.

"Todd, I know you're a liberated man so I'm sure you won't mind if I ask you to help me clean up the kitchen. I'm sure Helen can keep Jonathan entertained for a spell, isn't that right, Helen?"

"Of course," Helen replied, smiling warmly as Jonathan blinked self-consciously behind the lenses of sleek, square eyeglasses that Helen thought made him look like a cross between a professor and a gigolo. "I'd love to hear more about how our new home is coming along. Todd tells me we're on track for moving in by early summer."

Todd didn't wait to hear Jonathan's reply. He was far more interested in what Jane had to say, given the solemn look in her eyes. He'd seen that look too many times before; the last time was when she'd broken the news to their parents that she was in a relationship with a Catholic man whom she'd met on a retreat for lay missionaries in Mumbai. Whatever Jane had to say, it was bound to be a grim announcement.

Jane turned on the faucet full stream and spoke in a careful whisper.

"I'm afraid we might have a problem."

Todd folded his arms across his chest and waited.

"I'm not sure, but I think that Helen went to China Beach today."

Todd's jaw rippled with tension as he pondered the meaning of Jane's revelation.

"It's a place where the homeless Vietnam vets congregate. I understand it's in the woods, somewhere near the soup kitchen. And not far from where we had our hair done today."

"But how could she? I mean, you were with her, right?"

Jane reached for a dish and began to wash it zealously.

"Jane?"

"I'm sorry, Todd. I didn't know she planned to leave the salon while I was being held hostage with my head wrapped in tin foil."

"How do you know where she went?"

"At this point I can't say for sure, but the mud on her shoes was just as wet and red as the mud on the shoes of this guy at the soup kitchen who lives at China Beach. It's river mud, Todd. There's no mistaking it."

"So you went to the soup kitchen?"

"Yes, while Helen was having her turn. I don't know, it was just a hunch. Or maybe the leading of the Holy Spirit. But if it's any consolation, I'm pretty sure Helen hasn't been back to the soup kitchen since she was fired."

"No, now she goes into the woods," Todd retorted.

"Well, if she does, you're partly to blame."

"What?"

"Your sore neglect of your wife is a disgrace and I've been meaning to tell you so. You can't expect a woman to follow your lead if you don't love her into submission. Now, how can you love someone you hardly see? She needs time and affection, Todd. And if she doesn't get it from you, she'll get it somewhere else. Open your Bible. That's a story old as time."

Todd unfolded his arms and leaned on the

kitchen counter with his head in his hands. He knew
that Jane had spoken the truth and yet he had precious little regret for his treatment of Helen. He'd
made it clear to her from the start that his priorities
were his ministry and to building as fine a church as
any his father had ever seen or planted in his time.
He hadn't foreseen the temptations that had since
crept into his life like a thief in the night to steal the
hours and the better part of his intentions. Nor had
he ever contemplated the notion that Helen might
become equally as restless and vulnerable. He found
it preposterous to think that Helen – his simple,
faithful girl from the coalfields – could be having an
affair. Surely this was all one big misunderstanding!

"Maybe you're jumping to conclusions, Jane.
You know – making a mountain out of a little bit of
mud?"

"Helen explicitly said she went to the ATM this
morning, sometime between ten and eleven o'clock.
Is there any way for you to check on that?"

"Sure, I can see online if there's been any activity on our account today."

"Well, why don't you do that while I finish up
here?"

Todd nodded, then returned several minutes
later with an expression that hovered between anger
and disbelief.

"I'm so sorry, Todd. But look, in a matter of
days, she'll be far enough away from whatever it is
that's gotten under her skin and have a chance to
come to her senses. My guess is that she'll tame

right down."

"What's this place called, Jane? China Beach?"

Jane nodded. "You're not thinking of going there, are you?"

"No. Not myself, anyway."

"What does that mean?"

"I don't know. I need some time to think. But in the meantime, don't you let her shake you off again, you hear me?"

"She says she has a doctor's appointment on Thursday morning."

"What's wrong with her?"

"What are you asking me for? You ought to know."

Todd let out a long, slow breath and rubbed the back of his neck to release the tension that had settled there.

"Wait, Todd. There's more."

Todd rolled his eyes and threw up his hands. "What is it?"

"Again, it's just a hunch, but if there *is* a man, I think he goes by the name of Hawk."

Jane was surprised by the flicker of recognition in her brother's eyes.

"I've heard of him."

"Be careful, Todd. From what I understand, he's not to be trifled with."

"We'll see about that. But until I know something for sure, I've got to give her the benefit of the doubt."

"Of course you do. I feel the same way."

"Then it's settled. Not a word of this to Helen, understood?"

Jane nodded as she dried and stacked the last dish in the china cupboard. Her sister-in-law had developed extremely fine taste, she noted, marveling at the lovely pattern of roses that graced the edges of dinner plates rimmed in gold. And yet, the rose has thorns, she mused with a tinge of sadness. She didn't wish to see her brother's heart pierced by them, nor Helen's wounded by his lack of care. She vowed to take the matter to prayer and to trust the Lord to set things right according to his divine authority.

Chapter 12

The Wind of the Spirit

By the time Thursday morning arrived, Jane and Helen had visited every mall, museum, and coffee shop within a forty mile radius. Helen's only consolation was the certainty that she had invested enough time to warrant a solo trip to the doctor's office without resistance from Jane or Todd. She declined Jane's last-minute offer to accompany her, which had seemed half-hearted anyway. As she left the house, Jane was curled up on the sofa with her Bible in her hands and Chester's head resting on her lap. It had been a pure and lovely sight, one that set off sudden pangs of guilt that dissipated the instant Hawk came into view.

"Jesus, Helen, where have you been?" he said, his words not a reproach but an admission of longing as he rushed forth to meet her. He didn't wait for her to answer. His movements were fleet and precise as he took her into his arms and kissed her softly and deeply. It was the first such kiss between them, unhurried and tender with joyful release.

"I came as soon as I could," Helen said. Hawk smoothed her brow and scanned her face for signs of tension or worry. Finding none, he drew her close again and held her tightly for several moments more.

"C'mon, sit with me by the fire and tell me what's going on."

"There's not much to tell," Helen said as she sighed contentedly and settled in beside him. She liked the way he smelled fresh and earthy like mountain laurel and the way his skin had turned lightly tan under a radiant springtime sun. "I've been spending night and day with Jane. She's been fine company and all. It's just that a body can only take so much fuss and commotion. I swear, she's asked me a thousand and one questions since she's been here."

"And where is she now?"

"Home, studying her Bible."

"And where does she think you are?"

"I told her I had an appointment with my, you know, female doctor. I figured that might get me the right to a little privacy."

Hawk was amused by the blush that crept into Helen's cheeks and her awkward, halting explanation.

"I see. Looks like it worked."

"Why, are you laughing at me, Mickey Lightfoot?"

"I'm not laughing," Hawk said, forcing a

somber expression. "You just surprise me sometimes, that's all."

"Why is that?"

"Because you blush like a virgin and kiss like a
goddess."

"And which do you prefer?" Helen teased.

"I'll take you any way I can," Hawk said, inch-
ing closer and stopping just short of her lips. Helen
turned aside, noticing the licks of yellow flame that
struggled to rise from a pool of glowing embers.
She glanced at her watch worriedly. Try as she
might, she was unable to abandon herself to the
moment, knowing it would end much too soon and
leave her with little more than a want in her body
and an ache in her chest.

"Fire's burning out," Helen said, averting her
eyes from Hawk's.

"The fire's just getting started."

Helen's heart quickened. "So…what are we
supposed to do now?" she asked as she began to
twist a strand of hair around her finger.

"You tell me, Miss Hell-on-Wheels." Hawk's
gaze was fierce and unrelenting, a piercing blue
stare that reminded her of Appalachian skies in the
fall when there was such a depth and purity of color
that every other shade of blue seemed pale by comparison, maybe not even blue at all.

"Can we just sit and talk for a spell?"

"Sure. We can talk," Hawk replied noncha-
lantly, releasing his tenuous hold on Helen and
settling for the nearness of her hip pressed against

his. He would not rush her into loving him, despite the deep, antagonizing longing that penetrated his flesh and felt like a new and particularly effective form of torture. Jesus, he would give anything to lie naked with her in the tall, sweet-smelling grass of the meadowlands down river.

"Tell me what's going on in the soup kitchen. How's Frankie?"

"He's doing all right. I saw him on Monday talking to a new outreach worker. I think that's who she was anyway."

"Stuart promised he'd call if they were hiring."

Hawk nodded thoughtfully, sensing her disappointment. "She's a plain looking woman if I ever did see one. Not even in your universe when it comes to pretty. She'll have a hard time getting anyone's attention."

"Is that supposed to make me feel better?"

"That and the fact she almost got plastered with ziti for the needy. I thought Norman was going to nail her head-on, but she managed to swerve just before he fell. I think maybe her golden slippers got splashed with a little marinara sauce, but she seemed to get off pretty easy."

"Golden slippers?"

"Yeah, and one badass, ugly backpack."

Helen stiffened. "Was it purple?"

"Yeah, I think it was. Purple and black, with some swirly design," Hawk replied, tracing his fingers in tight curlicues through the air.

"That was Jane," Helen declared, her voice rising

with shock and disbelief.

"What?"

"That was Jane! I put those golden slippers on her feet myself. What was she doing there?"

"I don't know, Helen. She spent a few minutes talking to Frankie and to Marcy, and then she was gone."

"Oh my God," Helen repeated over and over again until the words became a string of syllables that had no real beginning or end.

"What are you so upset about?"

"What if she knows?"

"Knows what?"

"About this!" Helen said with a sweep of her hand over China Beach. "About us! God only knows what Marcy might have said to her. You know she was always giving us the big eye, like she knew there was something going on between us! And what if Jane said something to Todd? What if he knows I've been sneaking off to see you?" Helen tried to recall every snippet of conversation she'd had with Jane over the last couple of days, turning them this way and that to uncover the slightest trace of innuendo or suspicion. She didn't notice the subtle tightening of Hawk's strong, square jaw, or the coolness that invaded his eyes at the mention of Todd's name.

"Would that be such a terrible thing?" Hawk challenged, his eyes once again trained on Helen with sniper-like intensity and precision. He willed her to look at him and reach deep for the feisty girl from the coalfields he had gradually come to know and adore.

"Yes!" Helen stumbled. "I mean, no...I don't know!" She leaned over her lap and buried her face in the cradle of her arms. Much as she wanted to abandon herself to the wind of the spirit and a life of reckless passion and adventure with Mickey Lightfoot, she suffered no illusions as to what such a life would cost: her marriage, her security, her confidence that she'd never be poor and wanting again in the hill country of Appalachia or anywhere else there was such misery and woe. Besides, she'd given Todd her word that she would stand tall beside him. If nothing else, she had always been a woman of her word.

Hawk slapped his thighs and rose to his feet. He marched purposefully toward his rucksack and returned a minute later with a piece of scrap paper in his hand. He knelt beside Helen and firmly pressed the folded square into the palm of her right hand, closing her fingers around it.

"What's this?" Helen said, lifting her head.

"It's my address."

"Your address?"

"Yes, my apartment. It's an old duplex with red shutters. I live on the second floor. Do you know where Mechanic Street is?"

"It runs by the railroad tracks?"

Hawk nodded and began to pace. The muscles in his forearms rippled as he broke a thick, craggy tree branch into pieces and jettisoned them into the fire pit, creating sapphire-colored sparks. "It's not that complicated, Helen. If you can't get here, then come to my apartment after dark. Not only will I be there, but the minute I see your face at my door I promise you I will take you in and hold you in my arms and kiss you again and again until there's not an inch of you I haven't covered with my mouth and my breath and my whole being, body and soul. I'm a patient man, Helen. But I won't play the fool and I sure as hell won't force myself on you – now or ever. In fact, I think you should leave."

"What if I don't want to?"

"Suit yourself." Hawk shrugged and began to walk towards the river.

"You're a cruel man, Mickey Lightfoot," Helen called out after him. "Is that all you have to say?"

Hawk continued to walk along the riverbank, his head held high and his back stiff with pride.

"*Semper Fi*, my country ass!" Helen called out after him. She didn't see the smile her insult brought to his lips. He was grateful for the years of military discipline that enabled him to keep on walking despite the urge he felt to relent and turn back. He considered it a risky maneuver, one that would force Helen to stand down, to confront her own worst demons and win. As it was, she had yet to discover that neither Jane nor Todd nor her father – or any other human being was her true nemesis; it was the enemy within, that dark, shadowy spirit of fear that pinned her heart to the ground and held it captive. If there was one thing Mickey Lightfoot and I agreed on, it was that Helen's heart was made for better things – for deeper love and greater heights – than she had ever known.

Helen departed slowly, in no great hurry to reach the end of the woods and the grassy field that stood between the two separate lives she was leading, with no real footing in either one. She walked with her head down, contemplating the new blades of grass and the resiliency they showed in having sprung from dull thatch into dark, vibrant little...*soldiers of spring*, she thought, muttering at the comparison which only made her resent Hawk all the more.

When at last she glanced up, she froze where she stood, pondering what she was going to say to the tall, daunting figures waiting for her at the end of the sidewalk. There was no mistaking Todd's thin, athletic build or Jane's chuffy bottom. Oddly, she didn't feel panicked anymore. Just weary and dull and reconciled to the thought that the gig was up. In fact, she thought it might even be a relief to simply submit once more to God's will and humiliations, the same way that she had mutely rolled onto her back at her father's perverse bidding, played the meek, subservient wife, and now suffered Hawk's cruel and unusual punishment. At least now she could stop thinking, stop wanting, stop praying for something more. It was all so much wasted energy better spent making herself as happy as a slaughterhouse pig in sunshine, as her momma used to say. Momma knew it didn't serve a woman to bemoan her lot; a man will only stand it so long before he gets a misery in his heart and bids her a better life with a better man – only there weren't one man better than another. In Dock Watch Hollow they were all carved from the same lump of coal. Maybe even in Richmond and the northern states, too.

"I'm ashamed of you, Helen."

"Don't say that, Todd. I've done nothing to shame you."

"Then tell me, what are you doing here?"

"Taking a walk."

"I've heard that before. What's out there?" Todd demanded to know, pointing toward the tawny woods and shaking his head in reproach before she had a chance to respond.

"Nothing. Just the river."

"And China Beach?"

Helen glanced upward, her eyes latching onto a patch of sky that peeked out from between a cavalcade of low-slung clouds – clouds that would have touched the mountaintops back home and covered them in a pale blue veil, making them look mysterious and forlorn. At that moment, that was exactly how she felt: a deep and terrible sadness at the realization she was a vast wilderness, a great unknown, even to herself.

"Come on, honey, let's get you home," Jane said kindly, grasping her gently by the arm. "We can sort this out later, after we've all had a chance to simmer down."

Todd opened his mouth to protest.

"Not another word, brother. It'll keep!"

Helen dispatched a grateful glance and smiled apologetically. Jane nodded and increased their pace as they walked toward the parking lot of the Pour Man's Pub, holding her own tongue until Todd trailed several steps behind them.

"I'm so sorry," Jane whispered. "I admit this is my doing, but I just know in my heart I was sent here to help bring light into the darkness. It's for your own eternal good, Helen. Surely you'll forgive me." Jane didn't tell Helen that she and Todd had trailed several car lengths behind when Helen left the house that morning; that they'd waited the better part of half an hour for her to emerge from the woods – or that it was all she could do to keep Todd from going in after her. She didn't want to see her brother hurt, nor humiliate Helen with the scandal of being caught in the act of adultery. Just the same, the deep red hue of Helen's lips served to confirm that she'd been freshly kissed and justified her worst suspicions. She desperately hoped Todd hadn't noticed.

"I forgive you, Jane."

"God has a plan, dear sister. We'll talk more when we get home."

Helen nodded, glad for the silence that endured until Todd flung the front door closed behind them and banished Chester to the kitchen with a resounding roar.

"You!" Todd growled. Helen glanced over her shoulder at Chester who had patently disobeyed the command and hovered stubbornly behind her. Instead, she realized Todd was pointing his finger at her and was now shaking it mightily.

"How could you do this to me?"

"Todd! Do not speak to your wife in that manner," Jane admonished.

"This is between me and Helen," Todd replied as he sidestepped Jane's outstretched arm, gripped Helen's shoulder, and ushered her down the hallway. Helen neither flinched nor fussed as Todd steered her into their bedroom and slammed the door shut. He motioned for Helen to sit on the bed and began to pace slowly, his finger to his lips in self-restraint, intent on choosing only the most necessary words.

"You betrayed me, Helen."

"I didn't. I was simply visiting my friends."

"Hawk and his crew?"

"Yes."

"Why?"

"Because I care about them."

"All of them?"

"Yes."

"Not just Hawk?"

Helen paused at the sound of his name, which in itself was typically enough to make her heartbeat quicken and her senses stir; now, all she could muster was the faint realization that his icy rebuke had numbed her soul to the extent that she no longer cared what happened to her in this or any other moment.

"Helen?"

"He's just another lonely and traumatized Vietnam vet. They're a dime a dozen in these parts," Helen replied dully.

"Are you telling me the truth?"

"Yes."

Todd stopped pacing and hovered over Helen's upturned face. She flinched at the savage flare of his lips and the thinness of his eyes that made him look like a biblical wolf in sheep's clothing.

"I'm glad to hear that, Helen, because I won't stand for another man's mark on my wife." With that, Todd toppled her onto her back, his weight pressing down like an iron anvil as he pinned her arms overhead and kissed her with a brute force that made her gasp for air.

"Todd, no!" she protested, wrenching her face aside. Her rejection only seemed to fuel his passion as he grabbed her face and drove his tongue deeper until her muffled cries were silenced. She knew too well that it was hopeless to resist the sweaty palms and probing fingers, the clumsy tongue and dead weight of a man hell bent on forcing himself on a woman. Several minutes later, Helen languished beneath Todd's limp body, his hot sighs branding her cool, pale skin.

"So – we're good?" Helen asked, thankful Todd couldn't see the sarcastic twist of her mouth.

"Yeah, sugar, we're good," he whispered in her ear, confident he'd made it clear that his authority over her would not be compromised. If there had been any doubt as to the extent to which he would go to prove and defend it, surely he had put an end to it.

"I thought you were afraid of catching the virus from me."

"Maybe I'm more afraid of the thought of losing you to another man." Todd propped himself on one elbow and studied Helen's face for her reaction. He was pleasantly surprised to see a fleeting smile cross her face – a smile that took Helen's every last ounce of will to form. "Jane is right. I've neglected you and I'm sorry."

"And I'm sorry I made an error in judgment. I don't know what I was thinking. I was only trying to find my place in the world. You know, my own calling. Surely you can understand that."

"A noble thought – just poorly executed." Todd rolled onto his back and chose his next words carefully. "That said, I've asked Jane to book you a seat on her flight to Haiti on Saturday. I've arranged for Dr. Reid to give you all the necessary shots and clearances you'll need at his office tomorrow morning."

Helen nodded. "That's fine."

"Really?"

"Really. I think it might do me a world of good to get away. Jane's been a good friend to me and I reckon there's a lot she can teach me about being a servant-hearted woman."

"You don't know how happy it makes me to hear you say that, Helen."

"I'm glad you're happy."

Helen pulled the pale blue coverlet around her body and staggered to her feet.

"How long will I be gone?"

"Three weeks."

"Then I'd best get busy packing. You'll look after my baby boy, right?"

"He won't miss a meal."

"And you'll let him sleep with you on the bed?"

"At least at the foot of it."

Helen nodded and strode toward the bathroom, mindful of Todd's eyes on her back. She imagined he expected her to rise up and rebel any minute now. But she had never been more at peace with the thought that she had always been – and would always be – at the mercy of one man or another. This, she realized, was the bitter fruit of life in a tin can holler, where crumbling, stone mountains and dark, running streams drowned out the sounds of girl children crying out in the night; where young men fancied women with strong backs and wide hips capable of bearing enough young'uns to run their farms or their stills and ease their loins and burdens; where old men gathered in little white church houses on Sunday afternoons to handle venomous snakes in the name of God and then blamed the womenfolk for not praying hard enough to keep them from suffering a lethal strike. Until that moment, she had dared to hope there was a female side to God, one that had compassion for the plight of hillbilly Eves locked out of Paradise for generations on end. Instead, there was clearly just another Man at the helm of it all who permitted her and her Appalachian sisters to suffer a timeless legacy of toil and tears and riled serpents who smote the heels of any woman who dared to reach or want for more.

By the time she emerged from the bathroom in her flannel robe and fluffy blue slippers, Todd was gone. Helen reached under the bed and retrieved her pretty pink suitcase. It had been a wedding gift from her mother, a symbol of her tacit approval that Helen should travel far from the confines of Dock Watch Hollow in pursuit what she had simply characterized as *a beautiful life.* Inside the suitcase were remnants of her honeymoon: a thin trail of Bermuda's pristine, pink sand; a brochure from Palm Grove Gardens where she and Todd had strolled arm-in-arm among exotic royal palms and kissed for luck under the fabled, arched Moongate made out of coral and stone; a ticket stub from a horse-and-carriage ride through the historic city of Hamilton under piercing, white starlight that seemed to vibrate with intensity. Now, she was packing for the slums of Port-au-Prince where she'd be lucky to find a drop of clean, running water and a sturdy roof – let alone a Moongate – over her head. Yes, she was fairly sure her momma was turning in her grave right about now.

"Helen? Mind if I come in?" Jane tapped the door and waited. Helen was in no hurry to reply. "Helen? Are you okay?"

"Come on in," Helen finally replied, barely glancing at Jane as she entered. She stood awkwardly for a few seconds before deciding to sit at the foot of the bed and wait for Helen to acknowledge her. She sighed and fussed with the fringe of her new purple shawl as the silence grew longer.

"I'm not mad at you, Jane, if that's what you're frettin'."

"I'm glad to hear that. I was worried you'd hate me."

"I couldn't ever hate you." Helen offered a weak smile.

"I'm just thrilled you've agreed to come with me to Haiti. Believe me when I tell you it will be a life-changing experience. I know you won't regret it."

"I expect you're right. You seem to have good enough instincts." Helen paused, debating between a pair of white patent leather sandals and the blue rubber flip flops she wore when she walked Chester on summer mornings. Jane pointed to the flip flops and nodded.

"About what happened – "

"Nothing happened," Helen interrupted.

"What I mean to say is that Todd knows he's failed to give you the kind of attention a woman needs and deserves. He wants to set things right between you."

"I'm sure we'll be just fine."

"Of course," Jane stammered, realizing she was quickly losing ground. She found Helen's lack of emotion troublesome and sensed her withdrawal from the conversation.

"Well, you just let me know if there's anything at all I can do to help you. I'd tell you to bring hairspray but I can pretty much guarantee it's not worth a dime in those parts. Bug repellant would be a much better choice. The gallynippers are ruthless!"

"Thank you, Jane."

"Sure," Jane replied, sidling off the bed and pausing to see if Helen would stop her from walking out the door. "Our flight leaves at ten o'clock on Saturday morning."

"Yes, I know. I suppose we were lucky there was still a seat available."

"Maybe it's not luck. Maybe this is God's will for you, Helen."

"I reckon so."

Helen nestled a framed photograph of Chester in the folds of her clothing, then began to zip the suitcase shut. It struck Jane as odd that Helen would take a picture of the dog and leave a photograph of Todd behind, but she wasn't about to belabor the point. She figured the good Lord would make sense of it all in His own time.

"Todd asked me to go with you to the doctor's tomorrow."

"That's great. We'll have a nice lunch somewhere in town."

"I'd like that."

Helen nodded and set about the task of stripping the bed, knowing she wouldn't be able to sleep in sheets that smelled like fear and domination. Jane hovered in the doorway, then sighed and closed the door behind her softly.

***

Saturday morning came wrapped in a thick, soggy blanket of fog that grazed the tips of the purple crocuses and refused to budge. The last twenty-four hours had been a whirlwind of activity leaving Helen with precious little time to contemplate Todd's relentlessly cheerful demeanor or Jane's sidelong glances that seemed anxious and unsure. She briefly considered sending word to Hawk that she was leaving town, then reminded herself that he was a man who believed in freedom at any price. She preferred to let him think she had simply gone AWOL, knowing he had no stomach for those who took the path of least resistance or surrendered to the enemy. She could bear to suffer his fury but not the loss of his respect.

Would he understand that she had not surrendered but been commandeered, much the same as he'd been captured and held hostage in a bamboo cage? Would he believe that she was as much a prisoner of circumstances as he had been a prisoner of war? That her heart felt as tortured and broken as his own body had once been?

Hawk had spoken just once of his own confinement at the hands of the Viet Cong, saying only how he would have preferred to have been captured by the NVA and relegated to the Hanoi Hilton or some other organized POW branch camp under the paper-thin protection of the Geneva Convention. Instead he'd been shackled and forced to march from one makeshift Viet Cong camp to another for months on end, engendering the official status of MIA by the Department of Defense. Not that it mattered, he'd said with a crooked grin. There was no one stateside to miss him anyway.

He said it was dumb luck that a thin green line of Marines on a reconnaissance mission stumbled on their encampment one night and rained hellfire on his captors, setting their M-16s on full automatic in a show of fury reserved for those who dared to mess with one of their own.

Helen knew there would be no such luck for her. No infantry to rescue her, no one to log her as MIA despite the fact that she felt soulless and invisible and utterly lost. The minute she got on that plane, she knew it would be the end of Helen Hicks, the girl from the coalfields who had what the locals called a bodacious nature: bold, audacious, and strong in spirit, despite the indignities she suffered after dark and camouflaged in plucky tones each sunup. Now, she could barely feign the bravado to kiss her husband goodbye as they approached the airport's security gate and the imperceptible line that would be their breakpoint. Once through the gauntlet of grim, robot-like screeners, she smiled weakly and waved as Jane placed her hand on her back in silent consolation and ushered her down the long, narrow terminal that stretched out before her like a highway to hell.

"Might as well get comfy," Jane said as she glanced at the blinking yellow letters that signaled the delay of Flight 232. "My guess is this fog is going to set us back at least a couple of hours. Can I get you a magazine or something, honey?"

Helen had a misery on her face that Jane had never seen before. She clasped Helen's hand and squeezed it gently.

"It's going to be all right, Helen. By the time you get back, things will have tamed down and y'all will start fresh."

Helen turned her face aside, choosing to remain silent. If she'd had a rank and serial number, she would have bitterly recited only that and nothing more. Jane let go of her hand and reached into her backpack for her Bible. It was as dog-eared and tired a book as Helen had ever seen and she wondered what it was that kept Jane coming back for more.

She was grateful for the quiet of Jane's prayer time which effortlessly transcended from one hour to the next. Helen simply stared blankly into space, unwilling to give any one thought free rein lest it should turn into a hope or worse yet, a prayer. She was plumb tired of both, having exhausted her store of faith in a God who knew or cared that her heart was broken and her spirit was crushed. What she didn't know was that Jane was praying for her without ceasing, imploring God's wisdom and strength for her, calling on the Holy Spirit to move in Helen's heart and direct her path.

Three and a half hours later, the fog lifted and a slow, steady buzz of activity began to permeate the ranks of weary travelers who stirred and swarmed like a colony of bees in springtime. Jane and Helen startled at the sound of their flight number being called for boarding. Helen grasped the handle of her petal pink suitcase and trudged forward, her ankles feeling weighted with invisible chains. Jane mutely fell in beside her, trusting the Holy Spirit to do His best work.

Jane handed their boarding passes to a young, pretty gatekeeper who examined them and smiled politely as she waved them through to the jet way.

Helen hesitated.

"What's the matter, Helen? Did you forget something?"

"I'm not going."

Helen stepped aside, forcing Jane to follow.

"What do you mean you're not going?"

"I can't do it, Jane. I don't want to."

"Are you afraid of flying?" Jane asked cautiously.

Helen laughed, feeling giddy as a sense of relief overcame her.

"No, I ain't ascared of flying. I just decided, right now, I don't want to go. I don't know what's come over me, but I know it sure as I know my own name."

Jane nodded in understanding. *The wind of the Spirit blows where it will,* she thought, untroubled by Helen's declaration. "What do you think Todd will say?"

"I reckon whatever he wants to. But it won't change my mind."

"Whatever you decide to do, Helen, be gentle with him, will you? He's just a poor sinner like the rest of us. He knows not what he does," she said solemnly.

"You're not mad at me?"

Jane shook her head and dabbed the corner of her eye with her purple shawl. "God wants you to be happy, Helen. And so do I. Even if that pursuit of happiness leads you to China Beach."

Helen began to weep, overcome by the depths of Jane's mercy.

"I love you, Jane," she blurted.

"I love you too, dear sister. Now, you go on and make a good and godly life for yourself."

"I'm not sure I know how, Jane. I'm afraid I've made a complete mess of it all."

"Look here," Jane said, drawing forth her Bible from her backpack and effortlessly flipping to a page near the end. "*As you have heard from the beginning, his command is that you walk in love,*" she recited, pointing to the words written in the first book of Peter. "That's not so hard now, is it? Where there is love – there is God, I can assure you of that." She closed her Bible and glanced toward the dwindling line approaching the jet way. Jane reached out to give Helen a hug and then stopped short, remembering the wooden cross in her pocket, the one she'd pledged to give to Helen but had decided to withhold until they arrived in Haiti lest it add to her sorrow.

"I almost forgot. This is for you." Jane held out the wooden Tau to Helen who instantly recognized it as mine.

"Frankie's cross?" Helen asked, choking back a sob.

Jane nodded. "He asked me to give it to you to remember him by."

Helen reached out and took the cross from Jane's hand. "How is he?"

"Weak in the flesh, but remarkably strong in the Lord. At least that's how he seemed to me...maybe it's a sign, Helen. Maybe you've already found your calling. These soup kitchen friends of yours sure do love you."

Helen nodded, dumbfounded by the joy that flooded her chest and made it impossible to give breath to any of the words she thought to say. Yes, we did love her, she realized; many of us with clear signs of affection, some with shameful secrets and woeful tales shared only with her, and still others with harsh complaints and coarse words, trusting her not to turn away. And then there was the one, the one who loved her like no other.

"I have to go. God bless you, Helen," Jane said as she bestowed a kiss and a hearty embrace.

"Goodbye, Jane," Helen replied, basking in her blessing as Jane disappeared down the jet way. She clutched the wooden Tau tightly, drawing from it the strength and wisdom of the ages as it pulsated in the palm of her hand as if it were alive with the passion of Christ. She knew there and then what she had to do, no matter what the cost would be. And for the first time in a very long time, she walked with her head held high, mingling with the saints in the city who closed ranks behind her and propelled her forward like a wind at her back, gently steering her towards home.

Chapter 13

Lonesome Water

Helen pressed a twenty dollar bill into the hand of the cab driver.

"Please, sir, wait for me down the street, at the corner of Maple and Locust. If I'm not there in ten minutes, go ahead and leave. By the way, do you like dogs?"

"I don't mind 'em," the cabbie said roughly. "Why do you ask?"

"Just wondering," Helen replied as she stepped from the cab, dragging her suitcase behind her. "Ten minutes," she reiterated, glancing at her watch.

The driver nodded and pulled his checkered cab away from the curb, leaving Helen to ponder Todd's car in the driveway. It was unusual for him to be at home on a Saturday afternoon; normally, he spent a solid three hours rehearsing his sermon from the pulpit, playing to the empty pews and tweaking his delivery until he thought he had every gesture and inflection honed to perfection. She approached the front door slowly, hoping to escape Chester's detection. She reached for the spare key duct-taped to the inside of the downspout, slid it into the brass lock, and then glanced down the street to make sure the cab driver had followed her instructions. She had desperately hoped Todd would be gone for the afternoon, giving her time to make all the necessary arrangements. Seeing his car had made her alter her plans on the spot, knowing it was likely he'd fly into a rage at the sight of her or bully her into re-turning to the airport to board the next flight to Haiti. The morning after Todd's punishing assault, she'd looked into the mirror at the pale bruises pooling beneath her skin and swore on her momma's grave that no man would ever take con-trol of her body – or her destiny – by brute force again. There'd be a new face in hell should any man try!

Comforted and emboldened by the sight of the yellow cab hovering at the end of the street, Helen unlocked the front door and stepped inside. She could hear Chester scramble to his feet and his nails click sharply on the hardwood floor in the living room. She gave him a stern *shush!* as he came into view and commanded him to lie down by the coat tree.

"Good boy," she whispered, patting his head and motioning for him to stay. She cocked her head at the sound of murmuring coming from somewhere down the hall. Perhaps Todd had taken advantage of a quiet house to do a dry-run through his sermon, she thought. She hesitated to disturb him, knowing it would only add to his ire – yet she had no choice. There were but eight short minutes that remained between this life and another. She hoped that Todd would not prolong their agony. She had a ride to catch!

Helen tiptoed down the hallway and stopped outside her bedroom door. There was more than one voice, one sigh, one deep, throaty groan coming from within. She turned the brass knob and pushed at the door, letting it swing wide open.

"Helen!"

"Todd?" Helen felt her breath catch in her throat. "Jonathan?" She couldn't help but stare at the tangle of bare arms and legs that formed a most peculiar mound of flesh. She watched with an odd sense of detachment as Todd freed himself from Jonathan's domination and glanced furtively for something with which to cover himself, his eyes round with horror. By contrast, Jonathan looked remarkably satisfied – perhaps even relieved – by Helen's presence. He stood shamelessly and walked into the bathroom, closing the door behind him.

"What are you doing here?" Todd's voice trembled despite the indignation he tried to infuse into his words.

Helen didn't reply but merely stepped closer, strangely fascinated by the deceit and hypocrisy of it all. Her eyes swept over Todd's beautiful, naked body which she saw for the first time as being as ramshackle and hollow as any tin can trailer she'd ever known back home, and a sorry house for the Holy Ghost at that!

"What are you staring at, Helen?"

Helen smiled.

"For the love of God, Helen, say something. Look, I can make this up to you, sugar. I can set this right…Helen?"

Helen opened her mouth to speak, to say every last thing she'd ever planned to say when this day of reckoning came. And yet when she spoke, it was as though another voice had been reborn in her, one that had been silent, repressed, and neglected far too long….

"*I ain't a-hurtin' for you Todd Baldwin,*" she said. And then she was gone, with three minutes to spare.

***

"You said you don't mind dogs, right?" Helen said, pushing Chester's rear end into the waiting cab.

"I did say that, Miss. But I didn't expect to be seeing one in my back seat."

"Please – Joseph, is it? Give a girl a break, will you? I just need you to take us as far as the Pour Man's Pub. You know where that is, don't you?"

"Yes, Miss."

"Helen. My name is Helen."

"I hope you don't mind my asking, but…you

running away, Helen?" Joseph asked, surveying the pink suitcase, rolled up bag of dog food, and long leash tangled around Helen's arms and legs.

"You bet I am," she replied, climbing into the cab and tugging the door shut. "Let's hit the grit, Joe. I'm in a bit of a hurry."

Joseph tipped his hat and rolled away from the curb, grieved that a pretty girl like Helen would want a ride to the Pour Man's Pub. There was nothing there but a few Saturday afternoon ne'er do wells who made a weekly habit of surfacing from the woods for a little jukebox music and a cold draft of half-price beer. Some of them came out to look for a woman, too. Helen didn't seem like that kind of girl, but after twenty-seven years of driving a cab there was precious little that surprised him.

They drove the three miles into town in silence, but for the slow, steady tick of the meter that clocked Helen's time in limbo. She knew once she exited the cab that she had only a short sprint to go before she'd land headlong in another world, one that bore not even the slightest resemblance to the one she was leaving behind. She paid Joseph his due, plus an extra five dollars for his trouble. He wished her luck and watched her race across the open field at the end of the sidewalk, her speckled dog pulling jubilantly ahead and her pink suitcase bobbling behind. He sighed and supposed that he hadn't yet seen it all….

"Miss? You with the dog!"

Helen startled at words that had been shouted

through a megaphone and were clearly directed at her. She stood still, then slowly turned and glanced toward the sidewalk. A uniformed policeman exited from his cruiser and walked purposefully in her direction. It didn't take him long to reach the center of the field where she stood bewildered and slightly peeved.

"Can I see your identification, please?"

Helen reached into her purse and fumbled for her wallet.

"What are you doing out here, Miss...Baldwin?"

"I was just going for a walk, sir."

"A walk?" the policeman replied, perplexed by the sight of her suitcase.

"Yes, I have some time to kill before my ride comes for me and my dog. I thought I'd let my boy here burn off some energy before being cooped up in the car for a long time."

The policeman handed Helen her driver's license, satisfied by her explanation.

"I know what you mean, I got a crazy dog myself. But I can't let you go in those woods."

"Why not?"

"We conducted a raid there just last night. You know there was a whole band of vagrants living down by the river. Mostly homeless Vietnam vets. A crying shame if you ask me. But the town council and the local clergy were pretty adamant that we get these men out of the woods and back into the system. At least the ones we can sober up."

"And the rest?"

"Well, I suppose they'll wind up in jail or the VA hospital, or some other institution, depending on their needs. But the point is, these woods are off-limit."

"I understand," Helen said. "I'm sorry for the trouble."

"No trouble, Miss Baldwin. You have a nice day."

"Thank you, officer," Helen said, barely suppressing her rage. She suspected Todd had been among the most vocal complainants, if for no other reason than to retaliate against the men who had stolen her affection. In fact, it wouldn't have surprised her in the least if Todd had solicited the influence of several councilmen who just happened to be members of his congregation. It wouldn't be the first time he had used his pulpit as a means to advance his own agenda!

Helen wound Chester's leash tightly around the palm of her hand, shortening the distance between them. "Heel, Chester," she whispered gruffly as she trudged to the end of the sidewalk. She paused outside the Pour Man's Pub, then took a deep breath and walked through the front door.

"Hey! No dogs allowed!" the bartender growled.

"Calm down, I ain't a-stayin', I'm just looking for someone. Besides, he's right friendly."

"Yeah? So are they," the bartender said, gesturing to the far end of the bar. "I'll bet they wouldn't mind being pet by a pretty girl like you."

Helen ignored the coarse guffaws that followed. She pulled Chester closer and squinted into the darkness, hoping to find a familiar face, someone who could tell her where to look for Hawk on a Saturday afternoon. Finding none, she took her best shot.

"You seen Hawk?"

"What do you want with Hawk? You his attorney?"

"Attorney? No, I'm his friend."

"I only know he spent last night in the slammer on some bogus charge – trespassing, or something like that. My guess is that they just wanted to shake him up. I hear they sprung him this morning."

"Nobody's seen him since?"

The bartender shook his head. "I ain't seen none of 'em since then." He shook his head at the row of empty barstools and grimaced. "Bad for business, all this politicking that's going on," he grumbled.

"I thank you kindly," Helen said, turning to leave.

"You're welcome," the bartender replied, softening at the way Helen's voice had turned sweet and forlorn. She looked like somebody's left-behind little sister and he was sorry for his disrespect.

"If I should see him, who should I say was asking?"

"Helen. Helen Hicks."

"Take care of yourself, Helen."

Helen nodded and walked out the door, fearing

the light of day and the possibility that Todd would come looking for her. She walked to the corner and thought to hail a cab, then looked at Chester and thought better of it. She walked briskly down the street, clinging to the inside edge of the sidewalk and prepared to duck into the nearest doorway should Todd's car come into view.

"Need a ride?" she heard someone call out. Helen saw Joseph's cab double parked just two car lengths ahead.

"Joseph?"

"I figured it might be hard to find another cabbie willing to take a chance on a runaway and her dog."

Joseph popped open the trunk and reached for Helen's suitcase. She smiled gratefully and climbed into the backseat, bidding Chester to lie down beside her. He obliged by curling into a tight ball, his nose pressed to Helen's knee.

"So where to now, Helen?"

"Mechanic Street. It's down by the train station."

"I know where it is," Joseph replied. "You sure you want to go there?"

"Why wouldn't I?"

"It's a pretty rough neighborhood for a girl traveling solo."

"It's okay. I know someone who'll look after me."

"I hope so," Joseph replied, steering into the flow of traffic. "You got a house number?"

"Fifty six. It's a duplex with red shutters." Helen leaned back and closed her eyes, savoring the unexpected sanctuary she'd found in the backseat of a checkered cab. It wasn't until Joseph announced their arrival that she opened her eyes and inspected her surroundings. She had to admit, Joseph was right; the sidewalks were tagged with graffiti and more than one rusted car languished in a row of stubby driveways alongside broken down basketball hoops and bicycles with bent frames and chipped metallic paint. Chester pricked his ears at the report of a dog barking nearby. It was not a welcoming sound.

"You sure you're going to be okay? I can wait around if you want." It seemed more of a plea than a proposal. Helen was thankful for the offer.

"If you wouldn't mind, can you wait just long enough to see if my friend answers the door? I'll give you a wave if everything is all right."

"You got it," Joseph replied. He retrieved Helen's suitcase from the trunk and set it down on the sidewalk. "You want me to come back for you later?"

"I don't think so," Helen said. "I believe I might just lay low here for awhile." She smiled broadly in an effort to reassure him that all was well. "Now what do I owe you?"

"Nothing, it's on me," Joseph said with a wave of his hand.

"A man's got to make a living," Helen pro-tested.

"I get by," Joseph replied. "Besides, I know what it's like to have to get out of town in a hurry."

"I'm much obliged," Helen said, humbled by her good fortune and Joseph's big heart. God only knew she was going to need every last cent to reach her final destination!

"Good bye, Joseph."

"Take care, Helen."

"C'mon Chester, there's someone I want you to meet," Helen said. She climbed the stout, brick stairs and hovered between two identical doors. She had no idea which one led to the second floor and she searched for a clue. Finding none, she knocked sharply on the narrow black door to the right and waited.

She heard the deadbolt slide and the latch click. Seconds later, she gazed into keen blue eyes that registered neither surprise nor concern. In fact, it was as though Mickey Lightfoot had expected her all along and was merely a bit perturbed that she was late.

"It's about time," he said, observing the suitcase, the dog, and the pitifully wrinkled, half-torn bag of dog food Helen clutched in her arms. She turned around and waved to Joseph who nodded sagely and then slowly drove away as the sky turned dusky-dark.

Hawk reached out and wordlessly took hold of Helen's suitcase, lifting it over the threshold. He grabbed the bag of dog food from Helen's hands and hoisted the suitcase off the floor, then turned his back and ascended the narrow stairwell. Helen followed silently, knowing there was something at work beyond the scope or power of words.

When they reached the top of the stairs, Hawk set down his cargo and stooped to stroke Chester's head. He took the lead from Helen's hands and encouraged Chester to enter through the open doorway. Once inside, he unfastened the leash and allowed him to roam freely. Helen smiled at the tenderness with which Hawk treated her beloved companion. He didn't smile back at her. He only proceeded to do what he had promised: to take her in, to hold her in his arms, and to kiss her until there was not an inch of her that he had not covered with his mouth and his breath and his whole being, body and soul.

"Hawk," Helen whispered, naked and trembling at the sight of him as he descended upon her softly, gently, like the mist over the mountains. "This is crazy. You're near old enough to be my father..." she murmured, the distant past and the present and everything in between converging to create a storm of memories and sensations that confused and frightened her.

Hawk gazed at her tenderly. "But I'm not your father, Helen. I'm not your husband or any other man who has violated or betrayed you. I just want to love you like you deserve to be loved. Will you let me do that, Helen?"

Helen allowed Hawk's words to tunnel deep inside of her, to saturate every cell of memory and

skin and the darkest, most secret places in her heart.
Never before had a man asked her permission for
anything. And here was the consummate warrior,
whose calling was to divide and conquer, giving her
a choice to love – and to be loved. She smiled a
deep, satisfied smile that reached all the way to her
eyes…vibrant, green eyes that locked with Hawk's
in a potent meeting of earth and sky.

"Yes, Hawk. I will," she said, breathless and
exultant with newborn feelings of passion and em-
powerment. And so it was that Helen and Hawk became lovers that night – not just lovers, but soul
mates as their wounded spirits intertwined and
sought to rise above their infirmities.

In the interludes between their bouts of pleasure,
Helen shared with Hawk the chain of events that
had brought her to his door. Later, she feel asleep in
his arms, lulled by the sound of train whistles and
the clatter of the rails that came in steady, thirty
minute increments. Somewhere around midnight
she awoke to find Hawk sitting in a chair beside the
bed, staring into the darkness.

"Hawk?" she said, struggling to sit upright.

"Shhhh…" he commanded softly. "Go back to
sleep, Helen."

"What's wrong?" she persisted.

"Everything's fine, doll."

"You just watching me sleep?" Helen found the
thought a bit peculiar. "C'mon, Hawk, come and lay
with me."

Hawk reached out and stroked Helen's hair re-

assuringly. He didn't wish to frighten her with the
grim reality of what was likely to happen when he
closed his eyes to sleep – the reliving of firefights
and bloodbaths and ambushes in tall, spiky elephant
grass that made him thrash and curse and sometimes
lock his pillow in a stranglehold until he choked the
life out of it. No, he couldn't take the chance it
would be Helen's soft, supple neck he wrapped his
hands around instead, or her tender heart that he
pierced with powerful arcs to her chest with his
shiv.

"What, you can't get enough of me now, is that
it?"

"You're incorrigible." Helen grinned sleepily,
then curled her arm beneath her head and closed her
eyes once more. It wasn't long before her breaths
came in slow, deep succession and her eyelids fluttered with what appeared to be sweet, untroubled
dreams.

When the streetlight outside the window
dimmed at the break of dawn, Hawk climbed into
bed beside Helen and drew her to his chest. She
stirred and pressed into his muscular flesh which
did not give way for her but rather surrounded her
like a stone fortress. Confident in his strength and
protection, she surrendered once more to his bold
and nimble touch. It awed her that hands that had
maimed and killed with cold, premeditated precision could just as easily, tenderly, revive her bedeviled body and redeem it from the past. Helen
blushed at the thought of things she'd said and done

the night before in the throes of a heady passion that was like no other she'd ever known. She didn't care that the burgeoning sunlight would bring with it a host of unexplored questions and decisions. She only knew beyond a doubt that she was free to choose this moment in all its natural splendor. And so, with an arching back and outstretched arms, she welcomed that new day, sight unseen, and basked in its budding glory.

***

"You're going to make a fisty woman out of me if you keep this up," Helen said as she snuggled in Hawk's arms and pulled the scratchy gray blanket up to her chin, unaccustomed as she was to such a chilly morning draft.

"Fisty?" Hawk laughed. "What is fisty?"

"You know," Helen chided. "A girl who's just a little too fast and free."

"You mean feisty?"

Helen glared. "No, I meant what I said. We say *fisty* where I come from."

"I see," Hawk replied, amused and satisfied by her explanation. He loved the fight and the sparkle in her eyes that made her seem more beautiful and alive than she'd ever been before. He imagined they were the green of Appalachian hills and the tangles of laurel that Helen had described with such poetic longing in stolen hours at China Beach. "And being a fisty woman is a bad thing?"

"Depends on who she's fisty with, I guess."

"Well, for the sake of argument, let's say it's someone like me."

"Oh my," Helen said, shaking her head ruefully, her brown curls spilling over the pillow. "That could be a downright misery."

"Oh?" Hawk did his best to feign indifference.

"Only because she'd likely get too attached for her own good."

Hawk propped himself up on one elbow and traced the outline of Helen lips, which had curled into a melancholy smile.

"What about you, Helen? Are you getting attached to me?"

"I've been attached to you since that first cup of hot chocolate at China Beach. Or maybe it was that beautiful, long-stemmed rose that made me all a-twitter."

"What rose?"

"The one you had that sweet girl, Tess, deliver to me at the soup kitchen."

"I didn't send you that rose, Helen."

"You didn't?" Helen replied, mindful that Todd had denied it too, scowling at the mention of it.

"No, I didn't," Hawk confirmed.

"Well then, if it wasn't you and it wasn't Todd, who was it?"

"Hell if I know – but I hope you're not too disillusioned."

"I reckon there's time for you to make it up to me."

"Is that what you want, Helen...roses?" The intensity of Hawk's gaze made Helen realize he was asking in earnest.

Helen shook her head. "I don't give a shucks about roses. Alls I want is a good dog, an honest man and...."

"And what?"

"A beautiful life." Helen shrugged, hoping it didn't sound silly. She glanced down at Chester who was curled blissfully at the foot of the bed. She knew he'd be fussing for his breakfast before long. "If we don't get out of this bed, we might never," she warned.

"Wait," Hawk said, unwilling to let the discussion rest. "I know where to find a good dog...maybe even an honest man. But where do you expect to find this so-called beautiful life?"

Helen hesitated, knowing the answer but reluctant to spoil the moment.

"I'm going home, Hawk."

"Home? You're going back to Todd?"

"No, I said I'm going *home*. I'm going back to Dock Watch Hollow."

"When?"

"As soon as I find the ways and means to get there. I can't possibly leave Chester behind and the buses and trains won't allow him. I was hoping I might stay here with you until then...."

"So this is just a stop on your farewell tour?" Hawk's jaw rippled as he awaited Helen's reply.

"Not exactly."

"What do you mean, *not exactly?*"

"Like I said, I was hoping for an honest man who might want to drink of that lonesome water with me."

"Lonesome water?"

"That's what hillfolk call the sweet water that springs from the land where they were borned. Everybody knows where to find their lonesome water...unless they have a mind to forget."

"I'd like to taste that lonesome water," Hawk whispered, thirsty for the goodness of Helen and the mountain spring from which it flowed. It had been years since he'd ventured far from China Beach. Now that his company of men had been disbanded, there was no longer any reason to stay put – and a powerful incentive in Helen's eyes to leave the rest of his world behind.

"I got a car, Helen. It's been holed up in the garage for a few months but it still runs." Hawk stood and stretched his limbs, enamored by the sight of Helen in his bed, awash in morning sunlight.

"Where you going?"

"I'm going to walk the dog – and then I'm going to start the car."

"What for?"

Hawk grinned at Helen's bewildered expression. "Do you want to go home or don't you?"

Helen sat upright and scrutinized Hawk's face, thinking it would be just like him to make light of her predicament. But Hawk only met her incredulous stare with a resolute gaze of his own.

"Yes, Hawk..." Helen faltered, as she realized the extent of his offering. She began to weep a bounty of tears that tasted joyful and sweet. "Please, take me home."

Hawk leaned down and kissed the trail of tears that rolled down Helen's cheeks until his mouth met hers and sealed the unspoken covenant between them. This, Hawk knew, was his lonesome water, the place where his body and soul had been reborn.

He vowed, then and there, that he would never leave nor forsake it.

Chapter 14
Semper Fi Redux

Helen was glad the odometer on Hawk's car was permanently stuck on 97,999 miles. It was almost too much, the anticipation she felt as the balding tires whirred away the hours and the terrain grew steeper and more familiar by the mile. She thought if she had to actually count the 592 miles to home, she just might die of the all-over-fidges. As it was, she desperately hoped they would make it to Dock Watch Hollow by nightfall. If they didn't, they'd have to wait until morning to call on Joan and solicit her hospitality. Not that she worried Joan wouldn't greet her with open arms; it was her *happie-pappy*, live-in lover that made her think twice. Robert was one of the local boys who went from one makeshift job to another, spending time in between on the public dole and disappearing for long stretches in the mountain woods to make moonshine for his own pleasure. Helen had done her best to warn Joan about the likes of him before taking leave for Richmond with her momma. All

Joan said was that she felt lucky to have man to help with the bills, especially since she'd lost both her parents to the cancer in the last year.

It was a particularly virulent sickness that took hold of the hillfolk, especially the ones living downstream from the slurry ponds and pillaged mountaintops that rained down their indignation in the form of toxic chemicals and coal dust that coated swing sets and rooftops and lungs, and crept into bubbling branches that assaulted livestock and people alike with liquid stealth.

"You want to stop somewhere for the night?" Hawk asked. Helen hadn't taken her eyes from the setting sun outside her window, and now, it seemed to accelerate its descent behind grand peaks coated in a stunning spring green. He wished she would say something *fisty*, something to break the tension that had thickened in the car over the course of the last 500 miles like the purple haze of a smoke grenade. He knew it would take some time for Helen to come to terms with the end of her marriage and Todd's cruel betrayal. He only hoped she didn't have regrets that she had traded a secretly homosexual husband for a battle-fatigued Vietnam vet whose sole purpose in life up till now was to kill before he was killed in the name of God and country. Hawk tapped the steering wheel impatiently. Jesus, he wished she would say anything at all!

"Helen?"

"Hmmm?"

"Sign says sixty miles to Bluefield. You think

we should stop somewhere for the night?"

"I don't know, what do you think?" Helen replied absentmindedly.

"I think it might be better to try to find your friend in broad daylight. It's been a long day, doll. Maybe a good night's rest would do us both some good."

Helen glanced at Hawk and smiled faintly. "I reckon you're right about that. Once the sun goes down it'll get dark as the devil right quick."

Hawk nodded and continued driving west on Highway 460 heading straight for coal country, a place that had begun to reveal traces of itself in Helen's voice like a lost civilization come to light after years of obfuscation and denial.

Twenty miles further down the road, he veered onto an exit ramp marked by a sign for a local budget motel. They'd have to find a way to sneak Chester into their room, Hawk thought. He imagined Helen would just as soon sleep in the car if it meant leaving Chester behind. He didn't mind. He loved the way she loved her dog. *Semper Fi,* he repeated to himself. He respected a woman – and a dog – who understood what that meant.

"Wait here with Chester," Hawk commanded. "I'll get us a room, then recon the perimeter and come back for you."

"Yes, SIR!" Helen said, offering a sharp salute. She giggled at the startled look on Hawk's face and then tilted her face upward to be kissed. The gesture surprised and delighted Hawk, who had thought of little else but Helen's kisses for the last five hundred miles.

"Don't be long," Helen said warily. "There's haints in these parts."

"There's what?"

"*Haints*…you know, ghosts…."

"Ghosts?"

"Hear that?" Helen said, putting her finger to her lips.

Hawk paused and cocked his head. "I hear the wind."

Hawk knew a few things about the wind: the distinct sound it made when it was blowing in a rainstorm, like the way it sounded just then; the way its velocity could carry a bullet a hundred yards past its intended target if a sniper wasn't careful to factor it in; how to read its precise speed and direction by analyzing the arc of the grass; and more recently, how it could carry the scent of a beautiful woman wearing jasmine perfume and make him weak in the knees faster than a grunt on the losing side of a firefight could pull the pin out of a hand grenade and pitch it across enemy lines. The wind was a force to be reckoned with, of that much he was sure. Many a good man in his company had been lost in battles that were waged amid monsoon winds and hard rains that exacerbated the chaos of war. Hawk tried to mentally block out the sound, fearing where it would lead him if he indulged it for too long.

"They're a-moaning…if you listen close, you'll hear 'em." Helen closed her eyes and leaned into the headrest of her seat, her brow line furrowed in contemplation.

Hawk paused. He sensed a sea-change in Helen – or rather, a mountain moving, for she was suddenly filled with conviction regarding what she knew, and how she knew it, without needing to hear or see proof of it, without second guessing her own instincts. He had caught glimpses of this woman before, but not the face unveiled until now. He smiled, loving what he saw.

As night began to fall, a red neon sign began to blink and point the way to the motel's office. Hawk could smell the rain coming. He glanced up and hoped the roof wasn't quite as dilapidated as it looked. Just the same, he prayed for a long, hard rain that would drown out not just the mournful cries of the ghosts who rode the wind, but the taunts of the ones that sprang from coalfields and battlefields and every dark place in between. Until then, there would be no restful slumber. Until then, there would be no peace.

***

The next morning, Helen awoke to a stream of golden sunshine seeping through the wide crack around the ramshackle doorframe. She stretched and propped herself up on her elbows, glancing around the room in search of Hawk and Chester. Finding neither, she shucked off the shabby yellow bedspread and coarse cotton sheets, wincing at the cool floorboards under her feet. She strode to the window and peeled aside the calico curtains, certain that she'd seen that same print before on one of Jane's cotton blouses. She paused, remembering Jane's parting words: *God wants you to be happy, Helen....*

Maybe it was true, she thought, because Laws a mercy, she was happy this day. It wasn't just the sight of Hawk running Chester in the parking lot and tossing a stick into the grassy patch alongside of it. Nor was it the blissful release she felt in her body that came from being thoroughly loved the night before. It was a deep happiness that infiltrated the root of her and coursed throughout her veins in the same way a tree planted on the banks of a mountain stream draws water to its leaves and bears fruit in due season. She wrapped a thin blanket around her naked body and opened the door, relishing the sunlight on her face. Then she put two fingers to her lips and whistled, the shrill, familiar sound stopping Chester in his tracks and redirecting his path on the instant. Helen laughed as he galloped toward her, his four paws splattering mud and water in every direction. Hawk glanced behind him, awestruck by the sight of Helen standing in the doorframe in a dazzling pool of light. He waved and smiled from across the parking lot. She waved back and crouched low to welcome Chester into her arms, nestling her face in his long, silky neck and drawing him closer. Hawk thought if he could freeze-frame one moment in his entire life, it would be that one. In fifty-seven years, there had been none that compared with its simplicity, its beauty, its natural goodness that bordered on the divine. Jesus, he thought. What if he'd been wrong all this time…what if God wasn't dead…what if he'd simply been blind to His presence all these bitter, lonesome years, trapped in a hell of his own making when heaven was as near as a girl and her dog?

Helen ushered Chester inside and closed the door behind him, then watched as Hawk approached her, his eyes vigilantly scanning their surroundings.

"All clear?" Helen teased.

"I just don't like surprises, that's all," Hawk said.

"You worried Todd's a-coming after us or something?" Helen tried to sound nonchalant but had to admit that she found the thought worrisome.

"I don't know, should I be?"

"I think not," Helen said. "He's way too biggity to show his face in these parts. Besides, he's got time on his side. Everybody thinks I'm in Haiti with Jane, remember?"

"And a month from now?"

"I'm sure he'll think of something that'll paint me a sorry excuse for a preacher's wife." Helen rolled her eyes and smiled half-heartedly.

Hawk stepped closer and tucked a long, wavy strand of hair neatly behind Helen's ear. "I'm sorry, Helen."

"What for?"

"For what happened to you; for the break-up of

your marriage."

"It's all right, Hawk. I think I always knew me and Todd were a blossom out of season. And all this time I thought I just wasn't woman enough." She laughed bravely and reached for Hawk's hand, squeezing it tightly. The truth was, she didn't begrudge Todd his newfound love, only the cruelty and deceit that protected it at her expense. "No sense getting down in the mulligrubs over it. Lord knows, I've lived over worse things."

"So you *are* a fighter after all," Hawk said approvingly.

"And a lover," Helen parried.

"And a lover," Hawk confirmed as he kissed her softly and set his powerful hand on the small of her back, gently steering her back inside and closing the door behind them.

It was noon by the time they set out on the road, this time without the anxiety that had dampened their spirits the first five hundred miles. It brought Helen peace and pleasure to fix her eyes on Hawk's strong, chiseled profile and the firm set of his brow as he focused on the winding road that would soon turn from asphalt to gravel and eventually to dust before ending in the narrow valley known as Dock Watch Hollow.

She didn't mind the silence that settled between them, having talked long into the night as the rain beat on the aluminum roof and eventually lulled them to sleep. At least that's what Helen thought had happened. She didn't know that Hawk had crept

out of their double bed and slept in the car, setting
the alarm on his wristwatch to wake him just before
dawn. He didn't know how long much longer he
could avoid telling Helen about his debilitating
flashbacks and twisted dreams, how many more
nights he could get away with sleeping apart from
her or not even sleeping at all. It was a double-
edged sword, knowing that the more sleep deprived
he was, the weaker and more vulnerable his mind
became to the reliving of battles fought and won, or
fought and lost, all with indiscriminate blood and
fury.

"Take a left here," Helen said as they approached an imprecise fork in the road that seemed
to signal the end of civilization.

Hawk swore as the car hit a wide, muddy divot
in the road and set them swaying in their seats.

"Love hole," Helen giggled.

"What?"

"That's what we call a love hole. You know, it
jostles you out of your seat and if you're lucky, onto
the lap of your beloved."

"I guess it's not my lucky day," Hawk muttered.

"Oh, but the day is young," Helen said, "and
I'm feeling optimistic."

Hawk averted his eyes from the road to steal a
glance at Helen's face. She was fixated on the
mountaintops that loomed overhead, their tall peaks
emphasizing their smallness in a valley that was divided straight down the middle by a wide creek
filled with swirling water.

"That's Parson's Branch," Helen said, pointing to the fast-moving stream. "And that mountain there – the one with that dark patch of green running down the middle – that's Rattlesnake Mountain. Snakes up there are thick as thieves. You mind snakes?"

Hawk thought of the cobras and little green vipers he'd encountered in the fields and jungles of Vietnam, and how quickly he'd learned they were not to be trifled with. More than once, however, he'd been forced to use his military-issue Ka-bar knife to decapitate such unwelcome intruders, not because they were a threat to any soldier minding his own business, but because he couldn't risk the possibility that their movement in the tall grass beside him would attract the attention of Viet Cong snipers who stalked him day after day with uncanny stealth and determination. After all, it was considered a particularly noble feat to exterminate an American sniper before he had a chance to fire the first shot.

"Nah, I don't mind 'em. In fact, I find them quite beautiful."

"Really? I'm ascared to death of 'em!"

Hawk laughed at Helen's round-eyed horror.

"Well, then don't go up Rattlesnake Mountain."

"I wish it were that simple," Helen grimaced. "The timber rattlers and copperheads, they're everywhere. You'd best look twice before you set down on just any old log. This isn't China Beach, you know. It can get pretty wild out here."

Hawk grinned and patted Helen's thigh. "Relax, Helen. I think I can handle it."

"There!" Helen said, gesturing to a crooked, white house in the distance. "That's Joan's house. Hurry, Hawk! I can't wait another minute to see her!"

Chester woofed at the excitement in Helen's voice, which in turn set off a telegraphic chain of barks that bounced off the sandstone walls on every side of the holler.

"Pull over here," Helen said, pointing to a thin patch of grass. Hawk had barely brought the car to a full stop before Helen pulled on the door handle and raced from the car, bounding up the rickety stairs and onto the wide front porch. She knocked sharply on the knotty pine door, which clung to the doorframe by a single hinge. A rusty horseshoe had been nailed above it and dangled precariously over Helen's head. Hawk got out of the car and leaned against the hood, folding his arms across his chest. He hoped Helen knew what she was doing; he'd come to learn that old memories were often kinder than old friends were inclined to be, especially when too much time and distance had come between them.

Hawk noticed two small faces pressed to the fractured windowpane. A moment later, the front door swung open, an event punctuated by a long, slow creak and Helen's happy squeal.

"Joan!"

"Helen? Aye God, Helen, what are you doing here!"

Hawk couldn't get a clear view of Joan, but he could tell from the inflection in her voice that she was thrilled to see Helen standing on her doorstep.

"Where's Todd? Did he come with you?"

Helen shook her head and shrugged. Hawk imagined there were tears welling up in her eyes right about now.

"Oh, honey, I figured him for an oddling from the start. I heard his daddy preaching on the radio once and he scared the bejesus out of me!"

"Where's Robbie?" Helen asked.

"Gone. Long time gone."

"Dead?"

"I wish!" Joan replied, setting off a round of girlish laughter. "So, you just gonna stand there all day?"

Helen shook her head. "I got someone I want you to meet, Joan."

"Yeah?" Joan said, poking her head past the doorframe and zeroing in on Hawk. "Ohhhhh," she cooed softly. "He's a fine looking man, Helen. A little older than I'd expect from you, but awfully fine just the same."

"I assure you he's a lively one," Helen whispered.

"What's his name?"

"Hawk."

"What?" Joan said, wrinkling her nose. "What kind of name is that?"

"It's a nickname from his days in the military. They called the snipers *Hawkeyes* and I guess it just stuck. His real name is Mickey."

"Mickey!" Joan called out, waving her long, skinny arm in the air. "Come on over here and make yourself at home!"

Hawk grinned at the gangly redhead who had the palest skin and the widest smile he'd ever seen.

"Hawk, bring along Chester, will you?"

Hawk nodded and fastened Chester's leash to his collar, then led him out of the car and up the porch stairs.

"I'm Helen's best-friend-on-the-planet, Joan. It's real nice to meet you," Joan said, sticking out her hand but clearly transfixed by Hawk's tattoos. "I take it that's a Hawk on your...neck," she finished awkwardly.

"Good eye," Hawk said, amused by Joan's sudden shyness.

"Don't let his tattoos fool you," Helen said. "He's not nearly as fierce as he looks."

"Well, that's a relief," Joan said. "We got enough half-crazed hillbillies in these Godforsaken hollers....but listen to me going on about didly. Come on inside and meet my babies."

"You got babies?" Helen said, her voice soft with awe and wonder as they stepped inside, careful to avoid the holes in the floorboards.

"Emma Louise is going on six, and Robbie Jr. just turned four last month."

Helen approached the children who had rushed to Joan's side and clutched their wooden dolls with jelly-smeared hands. She fell to one knee and smiled. Emma smiled back fearlessly but Robbie whimpered and ducked behind his mother's long, denim skirt.

"Hey there," Helen drawled, "my name is Helen and this is my friend, Hawk."

Robbie glanced up at Hawk with eyes that were brown as chestnuts and began to whimper in double time.

"Aw, you don't have to be ascared, I promise," Helen said. "In fact, I'll bet if you be real nice to Hawk he just might whittle you a brand new doll."

Hawk raised an eyebrow, surprised and touched that Helen recalled how he'd taken up whittling as a mindless diversion in the years following his discharge. He'd mentioned it just once by the fireside at China Beach, a trivial, passing remark that unbeknownst to him had flooded Helen's heart with memories of home.

"Sure I will," Hawk chimed in. "Unless you'd rather I whittle you an airplane with big fancy wings."

Robbie brightened and clapped his chubby hands. "Yeah!" he cried out in a husky little voice that made everybody laugh.

"Well, why don't we go outside and find just the right piece of wood?"

"Can I come, too?" Emma pleaded.

"Sure," Hawk said. "I don't know my way around and I wouldn't want to get lost."

"You can't get lost around here," Emma declared. "You just follow the water. It'll always take you home."

Hawk and Helen exchanged a tender glance. "That's what I hear," Hawk replied.

"Don't you make a nuisance of yourselves," Joan called out as the children, together with Chester, scampered out the door, clamoring for Hawk to follow. Once they were gone, Joan gestured to a lumpy sofa draped in a floral sheet.

"Sit down, Helen," Joan said, her tone turning solemn.

"Is something wrong, Joan? Are you mad at me for barging in on you this way?"

Helen took a moment to leisurely examine Joan's long, narrow face, noticing the sunkenness of her eyes and the dark circles that surrounded them. Her complexion was not merely pale – but ashen – and Helen began to worry that all was far from well.

"Mad? Why, I can't begin to tell you how happy I am to see you. I reckon you're truly God's answer to my prayers."

Helen nodded, terrified by the thought of what Joan might say next.

"I've been feeling poorly."

"How poorly?"

"I got the cancer, Helen."

"No…" Helen faltered.

"Doc Riley says I can count my days, I got a month left if I'm lucky."

Helen reached out and grasped Joan's hands. These were the hands that had lifted and supported her through the worst indignities a girl child could suffer, hands that lovingly stroked her bruised arms and legs and assured her that someday they would marry handsome flatlanders who would take them far away from coal dust and dirty deeds. Oh yes, she had married a handsome flatlander from Richmond all right, trading her barefoot misery for Dolce Vita heels. It had turned out to be a sorry trade indeed!

"I've been wracking my brains trying to think of what I'm going to do with my babies...I got no one to care for them. I ain't seen or heard from Robbie since before Robbie Jr. was born," Joan said, beginning to weep softly and breaking Helen's heart in the process. Tears didn't come naturally to her and the sight of them made Helen weak in the knees.

"Will you raise them up, Helen? You can live here, in this house. It's in my name and I'd just as soon will it to you, if you'll have it. You know we got a fine boundary of land, fifteen acres cleared and fifteen more that can be cut and plowed."

"Of course I will," Helen said without hesitation. "I'd be honored to raise up your babies the best way I can." Helen took a deep breath, sensing this was the reason for which she'd come, the urgency that had propelled her towards home, the ultimate counterbalance to a terrible wrong that had stolen her childhood but now allowed her to safeguard and sustain another's.

"I know you'll be a right good mother, Helen. Your own momma was just as fine a woman as they come."

"Yes, she was," Helen said wistfully, swiping

her own tears with the back of her hand.

"Aren't we just a couple of weeping willows," Joan chided. "Hey, what do you say we set on the front porch and drink till the world seems little?"

"I think that's a grand idea," Helen replied.

"I'll get the 'shine."

"Lordy, Joan, not moonshine."

"What, you gone soft on me?" Joan laughed. "I know if I want to get to the bare-naked truth about you and Hawk, I'm gonna have to unloose your lips with a little greased lightening."

"Well, maybe just a little," Helen consented. The last thing she needed was for Hawk to see her all dauncy on Appalachian moonshine. God only knew what she might let slip under its mule-kicking influence!

By the time Robbie and Emma Louise had finished showing Hawk around the homestead and gathered the finest whittling wood to be found, Joan and Helen had already toasted to a dozen memories, shared a spate of secrets, and sealed the solemnest pact between them. Hawk climbed the porch stairs and immediately noticed the half-empty bottle of amber liquor perched on the porch swing, squarely between Helen and Joan.

"Come on, chickies," Joan clucked. "Let's git inside now and give Uncle Hawk a little time alone with Aunt Helen."

Emma Louise nodded approvingly. "She's right pretty, Uncle Hawk."

"I know," Hawk replied with a wink, tousling

Emma's hair as she bolted past him and into the house at her mother's bidding.

Helen patted the empty space beside her. "Come on and sit a spell," she beckoned.

Hawk picked up the bottle of moonshine and inspected it more closely. He took a deep sniff and tossed his head backwards in disgust.

"Jesus, you're not actually drinking this stuff, are you?"

"Go on, try it. Guaranteed to wipe the expression off a man's face," she said proudly.

"That's some endorsement," Hawk replied, placing the bottle well out of Helen's reach. "So, is Joan okay with us crashing in on her like this?"

"Oh yes. She's okay. But she's not okay."

"What do you mean? Is she okay or not?"

"She's happy as can be that we're here," Helen said, nodding emphatically. "But she's dying, Hawk. She's got the cancer. Doc Riley gives her a month at the outside."

"Christ…" Hawk said. "I'm sorry, Helen."

She had to admit, this revolving door that ushered people in and out of her life with amazing speed and frequency was making her feel dizzy. Or maybe, she conceded, it was just the natural consequence of knocking back too much mountain dew. She peered at Hawk and wondered if it was only a matter of time before he'd take his leave as well.

"Just so you know…" Helen shifted so as to draw from the warmth of Hawk's body pressed to hers. "I've agreed to be Emma and Robbie's legal guardian."

Hawk stroked his chin, deep in thought. "So, I guess that means you'll be staying here in Dock Watch Hollow?"

"Yes, Joan is leaving the house and the land to me."

"And what will you do with all of this?" he asked, wondering how Helen would manage two children and a thirty-acre homestead on her own.

"I'm no stranger when it comes to working with my hands and I've got a strong back to boot," Helen said with some difficulty as her speech began to slur.

"I see," Hawk said. "So you know how to milk a cow."

"I do."

"And you know how to farm the land."

"I do."

"And you know how to cook and split wood so as to keep the children warm and properly fed?"

"Not really, but I could learn."

"Well..." Hawk lazily stretched out his arm and draped it over Helen's shoulder. "I know how to split wood."

"Do you?"

Hawk nodded. "Maybe I could be of some service to you here."

"You mean like a hired hand?"

"Not exactly."

Helen smiled slyly. "Well, you know I'm in the

market for an honest man." She hiccupped and giggled.

Hawk pushed off with his foot to set the porch swing in motion, saying nothing.

"You'd best not be leaving me now, Mickey Lightfoot," she sighed, leaning into his chest. "I'm afraid I *am* hopelessly attached to you. Heck, I'm even worse off than that...."

"How so?" Hawk asked.

"I think I love you, Hawk. In fact, I know I do."

"I love you too, Miss Hell-On-Wheels," he replied without hesitation.

"No, no. I mean I luuuuuuve you," Helen said, closing her eyes and snuggling deeper into the cradle of Hawk's arm.

He stroked her hair and held her tightly, wishing for the day when she would speak those same words sober.

"Do you luuuuuuve me, Hawk?" Helen asked.

"I do," Hawk repeated.

"You talkin' moonlight, Hawk?"

"I'm telling you the truth, Helen."

"Well, all right then," she said with a long, contented sigh, then quickly drifted off to sleep in the brief silence that followed. Joan winked and smiled as Hawk carried her into the house.

"She's gone dauncy on you, eh?"

"I'd say so."

"Put her down in my bedroom. I'll bunk with the young'uns from here on out."

Hawk nodded and walked toward the larger of

the two bedrooms which was still barely big enough to contain a double bed and a small chest of drawers.

"Hawk?"

Hawk stopped and glanced over his shoulder.

"Don't hurt her," Joan implored, her hazel eyes fixed on the delicate woman he held in his arms.

"Hurt her?" Hawk echoed. He glanced down at Helen's exquisite face, his own expression hard with conviction. "I'd lay down my life for her," he whispered.

Joan turned aside, too proud to cry in front of a stranger. She nodded her approval and set about the task of preparing a feast worthy of Helen's homecoming. She knew it might well be among the last opportunities she'd have to express the fullness of her love and gratitude before the sickness rendered her weaker than a newborn calf. She'd seen how quickly the end had come for her own mother. She made a mental note to tell Helen she wished to be buried not in the family graveyard at the north end of the property, but on the eastern face of Benedict's Mountain, where the two of them had spent hundreds of hours hunting and harvesting ginseng – less for the money than for the safe and happy haven the mountain provided to two abused and battered young women in their times of need. But there was something else she needed to tell Helen, a parting gift she wished to give the best friend she'd ever had – save Jesus, who in His great and tender mercy had brought Helen to her door and in doing so made it possible for her to die in peace.

She wiped the tears from her eyes with her apron and began to softly sing hymns of praise; hymns that she had no idea were joined to the choirs of angels who were joyfully preparing to receive her.

Chapter 15
Eveglom

"Morning, Hawk!" Joan called out toward the tree stump where she'd found Hawk sitting at the crack of dawn for the last five mornings, whittling away. "How's that airplane a-comin'?"

"It's coming." Hawk glanced up and smiled. "It looks more like a flying hot dog at the moment but it's got promise."

Joan laughed and began to gather a stack of wood in her arms. Hawk set down his knife and rushed to her assistance.

"Let me do that for you, Joan."

"I can manage," Joan protested. "I'm a self-sufficient woman."

"Is there any other kind around here?" Hawk stuffed his hands in his pockets as a means to fight the urge to take the wood from Joan's spindly arms – arms that in just five days had lost even more of their sallow flesh.

"I'm afraid not," Joan said. "Helen's bouncing

back nicely, don't you think?"

Hawk nodded, her meaning clear. Helen's transformation, or perhaps her restoration, had been nothing short of remarkable. He had never seen her more content than she was performing simple tasks that kept the farm running as proficiently as any military operation he'd ever seen. He suspected the familiar and comforting routine of life in Dock Watch Hollow was not only good for her body but also balm for her weary soul. He had to admit, life in the mountains suited him as well, even though the occasional blasting of the mountaintops in the distance set his teeth on edge and his mind on red alert.

"You don't sleep much, do you?" Joan grimaced, her disapproval clear.

"Isn't that the early worm preaching to the meadowlark?" Hawk teased.

"Yeah, but I'm dying. What's your excuse?"

"Three tours in Vietnam steals your peace of mind, I guess."

"You a believer?" Joan asked matter-of-factly, setting down her bundle of wood on the porch steps.

"What?" Hawk said, not sure he'd heard her right.

"You believe Jesus Christ is your personal God and Savior?"

Hawk sat on the step next to Joan and shrugged. "I don't know. It's hard to believe in a God who would rain down such misery on the human race…wars, natural disasters, wholesale devastation…" Hawk said, sweeping his hand toward the balding mountaintops in the distance that had been stripped of their timber and flattened into stubby plateaus by strip mining companies and their machines of mass destruction. "And then there's personal pain and suffering..." he finished, glancing tenderly at Joan's hollowed out cheeks and pale lips. He'd seen that ashy color on the lips of many a soldier gunned down in the field, their innards torn to pieces and their eyes trained on a vanishing sky.

"Should I ask for something different than what our Lord himself endured? My suffering has value...maybe not to you, and not to my young'uns just yet, but maybe...just maybe, it's useful to the Lord for His purposes."

"I wish I had your faith, Joan."

"It's yourn for the askin', Hawk."

Hawk shook his head, his skepticism showing in the arch of his brows. "You don't know the things I've done in my life."

"You don't know the things I've done in mine," Joan countered softly. "But they don't stop me from throwing myself on the throne of God's mercy. There's no hardness in His heart for a repentant sinner."

Hawk glanced toward the eastern horizon where the sun had just begun to clear the grassy plain.

"Think about what I said, Hawk." Joan slapped her knees and struggled to her feet. Hawk braced her at the waist and helped her to rise.

"Go down to the bottom of the creek on any

given Sunday and get yourself reborn," she said, gesturing toward the running stream. "Do it soon and do it right. Maybe then you can stop sneaking out of Helen's bed every night just past midnight and sleeping in the car." Joan winked, leaving Hawk to ponder her advice by the ruddy light of dawn.

***

Three weeks later, Joan was dead. Helen honored her request and buried her in a simple pine box on the Resurrection side of Benedict's Mountain on a beautiful May morning with the jonquils in full bloom. The children cried and inspected Joan's bed pillow each new day to see if the feathers inside had formed into a crown, a sign that their momma had made it into heaven. Helen indulged the lore in accordance with Joan's wishes, but only for three days, after which time she took it upon herself to make a circle out of the pillow's downy feathers in order to relieve their troubled souls. It was only upon lifting the pillow that Helen discovered the lumpy envelope that Joan had tucked beneath it. Helen surveyed the crooked letters that spelled out her name and betrayed Joan's waning strength. She broke its seal and stared inside at a bundle of hundred dollar bills bound by a red rubber band. She rifled through the stack and took a rough count, guessing there was close to four thousand dollars, maybe more. A handwritten note was stuffed alongside.

Dearest Helen. I'll bet you're bumfuzzled how a girl like me comes by this kind of cash without making love or moonshine. Truth is, this is the same money that came from all the times we went sanging on Benedict's Mountain. I never spent a dime of it. I know you wanted me to, but I couldn't. It was OUR money and I pray it's sufficient for your needs. At least it will give you a favorable start and maybe even buy you a pair of those fancy shoes you like so much. Anyhow, take care of yourself, Helen, and take care of my babies. I love you. Joan. P.S. There's more ginseng hanging in the barn to dry. Just look up.

"What's that?" Hawk asked. Helen squared her shoulders and straightened her back, determined not to appear downhearted.

"Joan left us some money," Helen replied, stuffing the envelope into the back pocket of her jeans.

"Perfect timing," Hawk replied, clutching a thin stack of envelopes. "I picked up the mail this morning – mostly bills and an official looking notice from the state." Hawk waved a thin, blue envelope that bore the stamp of the Commonwealth of Virginia.

"Go on, open it," Helen prodded.

Hawk tore open the envelope and shook his head at the news it contained.

"What is it?"

"They've approved the strip mining of Rattlesnake Mountain. They'll start blasting in late June or early July."

"Rattlesnake Mountain?"

"Says so right here, Helen."

"They'll bury us in coal dust, Hawk. Laws a mercy, we'll never get out of here alive!" Helen lamented, knowing her words were tried-and-true. "Surely there's something we can do."

"We? You mean you and me?" Hawk said dubiously, fishing another envelope out of the stack and tearing at the back of it. He grunted at the bold words printed on the bright yellow flyer inside. "Looks like a bunch of tree-huggers are staging a protest," he shrugged, then crumpled and tossed the paper aside.

"What did you do that for?"

"It's useless, Helen. It's just another version of war: man versus machine. You'll never win."

"I thought you were a fighter."

Hawk returned her droll stare.

"Come on, doll, you know how these things go."

"What I know is that we got a month, maybe two, to try."

Hawk nodded and smiled at Helen's resolve, the fire in her belly racing all the way to her eyes. "These are *ourn* mountains, Hawk. They belong to us hill and holler folk and no one has the right to destroy them. Not for timber, not for coal, and certainly not to line the pockets of biggity executives who seem to think God's good earth was made for their profit!"

Helen retrieved the flyer from the dresser where

it had landed.

"So what's your plan, Helen?"

"I'm going to call this Jack Billingsly and ask him to come for supper. I'm thinking brown-sugared ham and mashed potatoes and round of banana pudding on the side?"

"Sounds good to me," Hawk said, having quickly developed a palate for the rich Southern fare that Joan had elevated to an art form and spent almost every last minute of her dying days teaching Helen to cook, dish by dish, until she turned them out just right.

"Uh-huh. I'll bet Todd would be salivating on his shoes right about now."

Hawk bristled at the sound of Todd's name. He grunted his agreement and turned to take his leave.

"I ain't never going back to him, Hawk. You know that don't you?"

"Sure, Helen, I know that." Hawk set the rest of the mail down on the dresser and continued toward the door.

"Hawk?"

Hawk spun around, alert to the subtle change in Helen's voice.

"I woke up last night and you were gone. Where were you?"

"Sitting on the porch swing. I get a little insomnia now and then."

"Is that all? I mean, are you unhappy here?"

"Jesus, Helen," Hawk said, fleetly closing the distance between them. "Why would you say something like that? I've never been happier in my whole life."

It was true; Hawk loved the rhythm of life in Dock Watch Hollow almost as much as he loved Helen. Its tranquil routine and back-bending chores provided powerful relief from the haunting memories that for years had stalked him broad daylight and brought him to his knees. In fact, he hadn't experienced a single flashback since they arrived, which he credited as much to the growing serenity in his soul as to the absence of the sounds and smells of diesel fuel, jet engines, backfiring cars and trucks, and other subliminal triggers that punctuated urban life. Now, if only he could conquer his dreams…

"You wouldn't lie to me, would you?"

"Have I ever?" Hawk challenged.

"Uncle Hawk?" Emma's small voice drifted into the room. She stood in the doorframe with a brand new doll in her hands that Hawk had carved in two days flat.

"There's a tall, skinny fellow dressed in black outside who wants to see my parents. I told him they was dead and gone, and he said you'll do."

Hawk hastened from the room with Helen right behind him. There were only two kinds of visitors in Dock Watch Hollow – those who were friendly folk in need of food or lodging for the night – and the other kind, who were seldom up to any good.

"Can I help you?" Hawk said, as he swung the porch door wide open. The long creak of it made the stranger turn around and Hawk startled at the sight of a priest.

"Good morning!" The priest stuck out his hand, eager to make Hawk's acquaintance. "I'm from the little mission church on the hill," he said, nodding toward the eastern sky. "Jack Billingsly, pastor of The Church of the Little Flower."

"Well, isn't this a happy coincidence," Helen drawled. "We were just talking about you not five minutes ago!" Helen thrust forward the wrinkled yellow flyer. "But it didn't say you were a...you know...."

"Priest?"

Helen nodded, feeling awkward and embarrassed. She hadn't looked into the face of a priest since the day she sat behind a grainy, black screen just before her seventh birthday and confessed that she'd helped kill Maize the pig, but only at her father's bidding.

"I don't publicize it much," he replied. "Tends to make some folk suspicious, like maybe I have some kind of hidden agenda for wanting to save the mountains. But for me, it's simply about being good stewards of God's creation. That's why the strip mining of Rattlesnake Mountain has to be stopped."

"It surely is a pleasure to meet you, Father," Helen said, reaching out to grasp the hand that Hawk had left unclasped. Helen thought Hawk appeared a little flummoxed; in fact, he'd yet to speak a single word.

"Please, call me Jack." His lopsided grin and friendly dark brown eyes made him seem like an altogether ordinary fellow. If it wasn't for his clerical collar he might have been mistaken for just another flatlander passing through.

"I'm Helen. Helen Hicks, and this is – *Mickey*. Would you like to come in?" Helen gestured toward the sofa.

"It's a beautiful morning. I'd be delighted if we could just sit here on the front porch and chat for a while. I hope I'm not interrupting."

"Not at all, Father. I mean, *Jack*," Helen replied, unaccustomed to calling a priest by his first name.

"Nice hat, Mickey," Jack said, recognizing the insignia of the United States Marines Corps. "Semper Fi!" he declared and saluted. Helen thought Hawk looked about as comfortable as an earthworm in hot ashes.

"You can call me Hawk," he finally replied.

"Did you serve in 'Nam?" Jack asked. Hawk felt only people who had actually been to Vietnam had the right to call it by its short name. He narrowed his eyes and crossed his arms defensively over his chest. "Yeah. Three tours. You?"

"Chaplain to the U.S. Marines. Stationed in De Nang and Ana Hoa from '68 to '72. I flew home with the first POWs released from the Hanoi Hilton by the NVA."

Helen breathed a sigh of relief as the tension drained from Hawk's face and he offered a belated salute.

"Let me fetch a round of sweet iced tea. I'll be right back," Helen said as she ushered the children inside and busied them with a batch of colorful blocks she'd picked up from the local thrift shop the day before. By the time she returned with a pitcher in hand, Hawk and Jack were sitting on the front steps shoulder-to-shoulder, immersed in tales of honor, guts, and fallen glory. Hawk found himself strangely drawn toward Jack, who had seen first-hand the death and dismemberment of war and yet – unlike he and his comrades at China Beach – had managed to come through with his mind, body and soul intact. It was a curiosity to him that he couldn't easily dismiss. He wondered if the difference was that the good chaplain had merely witnessed the war while Hawk and his fellow leathernecks had merci-lessly perpetuated it – engaging the enemy unto mortal death.

He was sure Jack had heard thousands of deathbed confessions. He often wondered what those solders said with their dying breaths as holy oil trickled down their faces and a priest absolved them of their sins. Did they confess to violating the Sixth Commandment, or did the rules of engage-ment in times of war necessarily trump the laws of God? It was a question that had burned in his brain since the time of his first confirmed kill on Hill 55 when he was fresh out of sniper school. Not that he'd been a choir boy, by any stretch, before he was recruited by the U.S. Marines. But neither had he ever killed a man in cold blood. Gook or not, he was still a man.

Jack Billingsly tarried long into the day, sharing

with Hawk and Helen the modern history of strip mining in the mountains of Appalachia and the grassroots movement he'd founded to put a stop to the bulldozers that clear-cut the mountaintops in advance of the explosives and heavy augers that violated the earth to its core. He said their organization was over five hundred strong but that no voice was as powerful as the one that came from the hills and hollers themselves. If Helen and Hawk would take a stand and allow their farm, which stood in the shadow of Rattlesnake Mountain, to be used as a staging ground for the fight, he was sure they stood a chance of stopping – or at least slowing – the wholesale devastation that had already cut a wide path through the Cumberland and Blue Ridge Mountains and left them looking like the remnants of a modern-day apocalypse.

Helen and Hawk pledged their full support. As a gesture of thanks, Jack offered to stop by the following Saturday with a small contingent of men to help them repair their sagging roof and rebuild the side of the barn that was caving in from years of neglect.

"That's a mighty huge favor you'd be doing us," Helen said, grateful for the offer. "This is an awfully big farm to run with just the two of us."

"Don't ever forget you're a part of a larger family," Jack said. "We're all kinfolk here in God's country."

Helen smiled and nodded. "Won't you stay for dinner?"

"I'm afraid I can't. I promised to stop by John and Sally McClure's and baptize their new baby before sundown. Their farm is just a few miles past the brown picket fence and around the corner from the hundred-year oak that got split in two by a thunderbolt this past spring. You can't miss it. You should stop by and neighbor with them sometime soon."

"I'll do that," Helen said, sending Jack off with a fresh baked lemon pie and extracting his promise to return for dinner before the week was through.

"I'll walk you to your car," Hawk offered, falling into line with Jack's long stride. "I haven't seen one of these since the sixties," he marveled, running his hands over the stout hood of the yellow Volkswagen bus. "Hey, before you leave, I got something to ask you." Hawk absentmindedly tugged at his ear and fumbled for nothing in his pocket.

"Ask away."

"Helen's friend, Joan – you know, the one who just passed away?"

Jack nodded, allowing Hawk to take his time forming the question at hand. He had a feeling it had been a long time coming.

"She says I can go down to the creek bottom and get reborn. You think that's a good idea for someone like me?"

"What do you mean, *someone like you*?" he asked gently.

"Well, I got a…burden…in my soul…and in my mind."

Jack nodded sagely. He had seen that kind of torment before in the eyes of many a man come home from a bloody and mind-boggling war.

"Were you baptized a Catholic?"

Hawk nodded.

"Well, you can go down to that creek bottom and get yourself soaked to the skin. It won't do you any harm. But I'm pretty darn sure the first one took. You're already a child of God, Hawk, and nothing can change that. But insofar as your burden..." Jack continued. "Well, that's what confession's for. It truly is good for the soul."

Hawk shifted his feet in the dust and thrust both hands into his pockets.

"You want me to hear your confession, Hawk?"

"Here? Now?"

"Why not?" Jack answered, lifting his hands up high. "We're already standing in God's greatest cathedral."

Hawk nodded, the movement of his head barely perceptible but the movement in his heart causing Jack's to soar with joy.

"All right then, let's do this," Hawk said gruffly. "You want me to kneel?" he asked.

"Nah..." Jack said, throwing his arm around Hawk's shoulder and setting his sights on the sunlit field. "Let's just walk."

***

"Hawk, I almost took you for lost!" Helen said

as she heard the screen door open and Hawk's footsteps drawing near. Helen was hard at work constructing a blackberry pie from a jar of preserves she'd found in the corner of the pantry. She was having a devil of a time getting the pie crust formed to the right consistency and squeezed her eyes shut, trying to recall Joan's rapid-fire instructions that she'd rattled off like the dying woman she was.

"I know where to find my lonesome water," Hawk replied, sidling up to Helen and wrapping his arms around her waif-like waist. "You ought to think about eating some of those pies you've been churning out lately. You're working too hard and getting too thin." Helen leaned into Hawk's chest and sighed, glad for the moment's rest.

"Come and watch the sun set over the mountains with me," Hawk implored.

"Can't you see I'm in the middle of making a blackberry pie?"

"Surely you can spare five minutes."

Helen glanced up from the mash of dough and flour that was spread over the countertop. Hawk's eyes were bright with expectation and she nodded her consent. He leaned down and swept her off her feet, carrying her out the door and setting her down atop the split-rail fence. "I've never seen anything like it," he said, feeling awestruck.

"Oh that," Helen said, looking into the western sky that was tinted a dark, sapphire blue. "We call that eveglom. Every once in a while the night sky is so clear and the setting sun so strong that the two collide and make for a whole 'nother realm in between. That's eveglom," she repeated as a glowing twilight streaked across the sky and descended over them.

"Helen?"

"Hmmm?" Helen's nose was lightly dusted with flour and her cheeks were streaked with blackberry preserves. She looked like a fierce kitchen warrior and Hawk tried not to laugh. Helen was sensitive about her fledgling cooking skills; he didn't want to discourage her.

"What are you grinning at?"

"You're so beautiful, Helen."

"You just like that I'm a-cooking right good for you, now don't you?"

"Doesn't hurt," Hawk admitted. "But that's not what makes you so beautiful."

Helen's heart quickened at the gleam in Hawk's eyes, a gleam that lit a fire in her body and her soul and made her forget all about blackberry pies.

"I've been getting a few things off my chest today," he said. "And in the spirit of a good confession, I just want to tell you that I love you, Helen...that I love everything about you, right down to your fisty soul. And that I'm so grateful you never gave up on the man you had the eyes to see in me. Thank you for showing me a better way...for making me a better man."

"Maybe I just had the good sense to see past the battle scars," Helen said softly. "You left yourself for dead after the war, Mickey Lightfoot, but I assure you, your heart is alive and well and forever one with mine." Helen placed Hawk's hand in the center of her chest, just like she did that day at China Beach when she'd first professed the desires of her heart. She paused and stopped short of telling him just how long she'd loved him. Someday soon, she would tell him.

"Did you say forever?"

"Forever," Helen replied.

Hawk turned his face aside before Helen caught sight of the tears in his eyes. He hadn't cried since he was twelve and he wasn't about to start now!

"Where are the children?"

"Down by the chicken coop with Chester. He's been having a grand old time antagonizing the rooster." Helen grinned at the thought.

"Does that mean we can steal a few minutes to ourselves?"

"I'm making a pie," Helen said coolly.

Hawk sighed and leaned back against the fence-post, gazing into the gloaming.

"Race ya!" Helen blurted. She giggled as she hopped off the fence and scurried toward the porch, her bare feet kicking up a trail of dust.

Hawk laughed and hurried after her, then loved her with a lightness of being that made every touch more thrilling, every breath more inspiring, every taste of lonesome water sweeter than he ever dreamed possible.

"Hawk?"

"Yeah, doll?"

"I've always loved you," Helen whispered, as she floated down from the peak of ecstasy he'd conceived with his bare hands. There was no longer any reason to fear or deny it, Helen realized, Hawk's own profession of love emboldening her heart and making it impossible to hold back any longer. As soon as she said it, she knew she'd given roots and wings to the truth – a truth she felt had resided in her almost from the beginning of time, as though she had somehow mysteriously known and loved him all of her life.

Hawk closed his eyes and offered a prayer of thanks for the words he'd longed to hear since the first day he saw Helen kicking her fancy high heels against the stage at St. Paul's. Suddenly, it no longer felt odd to pray in such a way; it was as though someone had flipped a switch that energized his spirit and sent a healing current throughout his entire being. He leaned down and kissed Helen deeply, hoping to breathe into her soul the supernatural joy he felt in his own. Afterward, she sighed contentedly and muttered something about blackberry pie, then drifted off to sleep in Hawk's arms. Had Chester and the children not clamored into the house she might have slept long into the night. Helen startled at the sound and leaped from their bed, wrapping a thin cotton robe around her.

"Aunt Helen's a-coming!" she called out through the bedroom door. "Go on and wash up. It's past your bedtime!"

Later that same night, Hawk crept into bed beside Helen and stayed there until sunlight streaked through the windowpane, coaxing them into a brand new day. He smiled at the sight of Helen's long, brown hair tumbling over his chest as she nestled closer and uttered a small complaint at the crow of the rooster announcing the break of dawn.

"Good morning," she said sleepily.

"Good morning, doll," Hawk replied, stroking the strong arch of her cheekbone and gently shushing her back to sleep. He felt well rested and profoundly grateful for having slept soundly – dreamlessly – throughout the night, for the privilege of waking up to Helen in his arms, and for the peace in his heart that surpassed all understanding.

Yes, it was a very good morning, indeed.

Chapter 16

Lost & Found

Helen's budding prowess in the kitchen came in handy that summer as their fields were sown, and new barns were built, and the roof was fixed with the help of Jack and his company of saints who worked overtime to make sure that the farm was ready for the camera crews, activists, and others who would soon descend upon their land in the hope of saving Rattlesnake Mountain. For her part, Helen fed them all with large, flat pans of golden cornbread and country fried chicken that was fresh from the field. She took pride in her country cooking, in the satisfaction that came from nourishing her new friends and family with honest fare that warmed their hearts and stuck to their ribs as the pleasant days of June rolled into a mid-summer swelter.

On the tenth day of July, despite their concerted efforts, the yellow bulldozers began their ascent up the side of the mountain, clearing the tangles of laurel and ivy and every tall, living thing that stood in their path. A few intrepid souls braved the wrath of rattlesnakes and man to lay themselves down on the path of progress. That usually brought the bulldozers to a grinding halt for a day or two – one for the actual protest and one for the media coverage that followed. But after awhile, the television crews from the city lost interest and the ravishment of the land continued with only sporadic protests from weekend environmentalists and the occasional rattlesnake shaken from its nest.

"Well…we fought the good fight," Jack said a few weeks later as the bulldozers began their trek down the mountain, their work all but done. Helen, Hawk and Jack stared up at the mountain's majestic peak as dusky-dark settled over it and the song of the whippoorwill began. Long black seams of coal were now fully exposed and made the mountain look like a seven-layer cake. Come morning, the blasting would begin and shake the sides of the mountain until it yielded its treasure to mercenary hands and minds that cared nothing for its natural splendor.

"Isn't there anything else we can do?" Helen said, clutching Hawk's hand for comfort.

"We can always pray for a miracle," Jack answered. He smiled wanly, clearly exhausted by the fight. "I'd best be going. Thanks for dinner, Helen. It was magnificent, as usual."

"You flatter me, Jack." Helen replied, forcing herself to smile back.

"See you tomorrow?" Hawk asked, hopeful that

the mining of Rattlesnake Mountain wouldn't keep his best friend from dropping by unannounced to share in the working of the farm and the attendant conversation that ranged from the mindless to the wildly profound.

"See you tomorrow," Jack replied with a wave of his hand. Helen and Hawk watched forlornly as his yellow bus rolled out of sight, disappearing into the deep blue mist.

"C'mon, Hawk, let's set on the porch and drink till the world seems little."

"I have a better idea," Hawk replied. "Let's put the kids to bed and make love until it disappears."

"Oh, I like that idea," Helen said.

And that's what they did, long into the night until at last they fell into a blissful slumber. But when the morning sun came up, their sleep was shattered by an earth-shaking rumble that made Emma Louise and Robbie cry, and Chester yelp at the foot of the bed.

"Bastards!" Hawk cursed, bolting upright.

Helen gathered the children who had rushed to her arms and shushed their plaintive cries. "It's nothing but the mining company tearing into the mountain. It won't hurt us," she said, tears welling in her eyes at the sound of her own lie.

"Where you going, Hawk?" Helen asked as Hawk zipped his jeans and pulled a black tee shirt over his head.

"I'm going out to the barn to check on the animals. Then I'll secure the perimeters and have a sneak and peek. I won't have those sons of bitches infiltrating our farm."

Helen cocked her head, confused by his reply and frightened by the glint of his combat knife. She hadn't heard him lapse into military jargon since before their arrival in Dock Watch Hollow.

"The animals are fine, Hawk. We'll all be fine. Please, stay with me."

Hawk hesitated, then shook his head forcefully as another blast rocked the fragile foundation of their house. "I won't be long," he said, his expression softening at the sight of Helen's distress.

"Promise? You'll come back right soon?"

"God willing..." Hawk said, coaxing Helen's participation.

"And the creek don't rise," Helen finished softly, placated by the love in his eyes.

Hawk nodded and walked away satisfied. She heard the screen door shudder behind him, then watched from the window as he strode toward the barn at the edge of the field, his shoulders broad and square, his entire being as mighty and resolute as the once-unmovable mountain that was now crumbling in their midst. She longed to stand watch over him, but the insistent cries of Emma and Robbie diverted her attention. She settled them down and then set about making a hot breakfast of scrambled eggs and buttermilk biscuits. She tried not to flinch every time the house shook as the explosions came fast and furious. The children looked to her for reassurance and she did her best to smile and make a game of it all.

"Wheeee!" she cried out gleefully, "that was a BIG one!"

After awhile, Emma caught on and began to play along while Robbie teetered on the edge of indecision. It was all Helen could do to keep her mind off the clock as the hour turned and at last the blasts seemed to come at longer intervals until they suddenly stopped all together.

She startled as Chester woofed and jumped off the sofa.

"Helen?"

Helen ran to the front door to see Jack standing on the porch, excitedly waving a stack of papers.

"What is it, Jack?" she said, stepping outside.

"They've issued an injunction against the coal company!"

"What does that mean?" Helen said, encouraged by the smile on his face. It looked like good news. Lord, she hoped it was good news! She wished Hawk was there to receive it with her.

"The courts have stopped the work on Rattlesnake Mountain." Jack laughed and shook his fist, clearly attributing the victory to God. "They finally approved our motion to stop the mining until the OSM can study the impact on our streams and drinking water. Not only that," he continued excitedly, "the courts agree that removing three peaks from Rattlesnake Mountain will destroy over four square miles of habitat occupied by the endangered Northern Flying Squirrel, as well as impact seventeen other species of wildlife and native fauna in direct violation of the Endangered Species Act." Jack pointed to the rows of black ink on the page. "It's all right here!" he said, gesturing gleefully to the ream of paper he held in his hands.

"Well, God bless those odd little squirrels," Helen said, growing giddy at the news. "Jack, go and find Hawk, will you? He's out there in the field somewhere. Tell him to come home. I've got breakfast waiting for y'all."

"Sure, Helen. Come on, Chester," he beckoned with a whistle. "Come with me!"

Helen grinned at the sight of Chester frolicking alongside the preacher, then went back into the house and set the table. She had made the biscuits extra large and fluffy, knowing Hawk preferred them that way. She winced at the memory of how her earlier attempts had produced dense, unsavory specimens that Hawk joked would've won the war if the Viet Cong were forced to carry them in their rucksacks. Now, they were perfect: golden brown and light as sunshine. She knew he would approve and confirm it with a tender kiss.

"Helen."

She hadn't heard Jack come through the front door.

"Come quickly!"

Helen threw down the plate of biscuits and ran after Jack into the open field. She followed him into the tall grass at the furthest boundary of the property and sank to her knees at the sight of

Hawk lying motionless on his belly in a combat-crawl, right next to a beheaded rattlesnake that had likely descended in a fury from the mountain. There were multiple bloody fang holes in his left hand and his Ka-bar knife was still clenched in his right. Instinctively, she threw herself over him, wanting to protect him from further harm.

"He's gone, Helen," Jack said. "He's already gone. Come, child," he said softy, extending his hand.

"Call an ambulance, Jack," Helen cried, refusing to believe him. "I ain't a-leaving him here all alone. Please, get us some help."

Helen turned Hawk onto his back and flinched at the emptiness in his eyes. They were still just as blue as the summer sky above them; she lingered in them, wishing she could fly into them and disappear like the whippoorwill at the break of day. Too soon, Jack stooped beside her and gently drew down his eyelids, an act of dignity and kindness he had visited on thousands of soldiers throughout the years.

Helen watched in horror as a small fleet of police cars and an ambulance rolled into view, their red and blue lights flashing with unnecessary urgency. She allowed Jack to shepherd her back to the house only after the local coroner declared Hawk officially dead and loaded his body onto a rickety steel gurney.

"Where are they taking him?" Helen asked, flinching as the back doors to the ambulance slammed shut.

"To the local funeral home where they'll prepare him for burial at one of the National Cemeteries. It may take a few days to verify his eligibility. It's his right as a veteran, Helen," Jack explained gently.

"Don't I get a say in the matter?" Helen began to weep. "After all, he's my family."

"I'll do my best to get him back to you."

Helen nodded, stifling her cries so as not to alarm the children. She made them lunch, then dinner, then gave them a bath and put them to bed. It wasn't until the house grew dark and silent that Helen unleashed the fury she'd held back for far too long. She buried her face in Hawk's pillow and railed against God and the universe until she didn't have the strength to lift her fist again. Then she cried long into the night, the muffled sobs wracking her body until she thought surely it would break. But when the sun came up, she made the children a hot breakfast of oatmeal and bacon, and explained in a small but courageous voice that Uncle Hawk had gone on ahead to be with their momma and see to her well being.

"But what about us, Aunt Helen?" Emma Louise asked. "Who's gonna take care of us?"

"We'll take care of each other," Helen replied. "You're a strong mountain girl, just like me. We can take care of ourselves, you hear?"

Emma Louise nodded and wiped a diminutive tear from her eye. A few moments later, Helen heard the sound of a procession of cars rolling up the gravel drive. She ran outside to see Jack's yellow bus, followed by a black hearse and several other cars trailing behind it.

Jack climbed out of the bus and wrapped his arms around Helen.

"Where do you want us to lay him down?" he whispered.

Helen pointed toward the east. "Let's lay him on the hill there, facing the day of Resurrection, of course."

Jack nodded and waved his entourage from their cars; men in their Sunday best who came with shovels in hand, and women who followed with billowing bouquets of summer's finest flowers. She smiled in gratitude and sorrow at the sight, wishing she had enough food on hand to nourish their kind and merciful souls. Just the same, she managed to whip up a ham and cornpone repast that gave rise to plaintive fiddling and storytelling that lasted long into dusky-dark.

By the time the last respects had been paid, it was nearing eveglom. One by one, Helen thanked the men and women who had done Hawk that final and eternal kindness until at last, just she and Jack were left to ponder the mound of dark earth and flowers.

"I have his personal effects in the car," Jack said. "His jewelry, his dog tags, the contents of his wallet and such. I assume you want them."

"Of course," Helen said as they departed from the graveside and strolled arm-in-arm toward the house. When they reached the driveway, he gestured for Helen to wait for him on the porch. He returned a moment later with a zippered, plastic bag that held precious few items. He handed it to Helen, turned to leave, and then hesitated.

"Do you want me to stay?"

"Yes," she said, drawing a deep breath. "Just awhile longer, if you don't mind. It eases my burden to have you here, Jack." She reached into the bag and pulled out a yellowed piece of paper that had been folded several times over. "What do you suppose this is?"

"It's a copy of his DD214."

"His what?"

"It's his certificate of discharge from the military. Vets carry it to prove they've been honorably discharged from active duty and that they're eligible for benefits. It lists his name, rank, and serial number, his tours of duty, that kind of thing."

Helen nodded in understanding, carefully unfolding the paper which had turned brittle over time. She held it up to the porch light, trying to discern the faded ink. Then she put her hand to her mouth and slowly sank to the ground.

"What is it, Helen?"

Helen stared at the paper in her hands and laughed. It was a hard, bitter sound.

"His name wasn't Mickey Lightfoot," she finally said.

"I know, I read the coroner's report. You mean you never knew his real name, Helen?"

She shook her head, feeling foolish. "But I know this name, just as well as I know my own: *Michael L. McMahon, rank E5. MIA. June 15, 1968*," she recited from memory. "I just never knew what the 'L' stood for...Lightfoot, of course. Says so right here." Helen waved the yellowed paper, then doubled over and began to rock in silent pain and disbelief. Jack stooped beside her and draped his arm around her shoulder.

"I'm not sure I understand, Helen."

"You will, I promise. But for now, I just need you to watch the children for a spell. I got somewhere to go."

"Let's put the kids in the car and I'll take you," he bargained.

"All right," Helen conceded, grateful for protection from any haints she might encounter along the way.

"I'll get the car."

"Bring a shovel, too," Helen instructed, then went inside to retrieve Emma and Robbie from their beds. She tenderly laid Emma down on the back seat and then went back for Robbie, allowing him to sleep on her shoulder as they got underway.

She issued a series of rapid-fire directions over bridges and washes and open fields that comprised the shortest distance between two points. It was less than a mile, but in the dark of night it seemed like nothing short of eternity between one part of the holler and another. She avoided looking toward the hillside and the abandoned aluminum trailer that had once been her home and was now reduced to a heap of scrap metal.

"Stop here," Helen said, handing over Robbie as soon as the bus came to a halt. "Shine the headlights on me." She grabbed the shovel from behind the back seat and strode toward the inky silhouette of a weeping willow arching beneath a starlit sky. She thrust the shovel into the ground, twisted its handle in a forceful half-circle, then knelt down in the dirt, pulling back layers of grass and soil with her fingers. She cursed as she came up empty, then repeated the process several inches to the left.

It was on her third try that she reached down into the dirt and retrieved the silver bracelet that had been buried there for nearly ten years. It didn't look any worse for the wear, the blocky, black letters stamped into the metal band still as crisp as the day her mother had first shown it to her and invited her to pray each day for that poor soldier's deliverance. Now it was Helen's bittersweet honor to wear it in remembrance of her beloved, Michael Lightfoot McMahon, who had been lost – then found – twice in one lifetime. Jack would have argued it was actually three times, counting his return to the heart of God. She tenderly traced the imprint of his name with her fingertip, recalling the many hours she and her mother had spent praying for his return. It was no wonder she felt that she had known and loved him from the start, the eyes of her soul recognizing him as the answer to her prayers. She slipped the bracelet on her wrist and stood beneath the willow tree, peering into the gaping hole below. She shuffled the dirt with her feet and tamped it down for good measure, then returned to Jack's car with a thankful nod.

"You found what you were looking for?"

She thrust her wrist toward Jack, who inspected the bracelet closely.

"No wonder you were the one he called his lonesome water."

"He told you that?" she said with a sentimental smile.

"Yes, he did. I think he always felt there was something deeply and beautifully familiar about you; that there was some kind of supernatural bond between you...like you were soul mates."

"Heap of good it does now."

"Don't you believe in eternal life, Helen?"

"I don't know what I believe anymore."

"Then I'll tell you what I believe. I believe that the spirits of our loved ones are always present to us. And someday, maybe even someday soon, God will heal your broken heart with some kind of sign that Hawk is among the company of angels and saints that surrounds us each and every day. That you don't acknowledge them doesn't mean they don't exist. Open the eyes of your heart, Helen. The saints of God are everywhere...in the city, in the country, even right here in Dock Watch Hollow...."

"Saint Hawk?" Helen asked incredulously.

"Why not?"

"And what would he be the patron saint of...

maybe people suffering from post-traumatic stress disorder?"

"I think St. Dymphna's got that covered," Jack replied.

"Well, what then?" Helen asked, strangely comforted by their capricious conversation.

"Well, I'd say maybe he'd be a good patron saint of lonesome water."

"You mean showing people where to find it?"

"Or helping them to remember."

Helen paused, recalling how Hawk had always made her feel right proud to be a girl from the coalfields, a strong, independent woman with a worthy heritage. "I think that would be a fittin' honor," she finally replied.

Jack nodded and smiled. Helen smiled back.

"I'd like to go home now, Jack."

She gathered Robbie from Jack's shoulder and pressed his tiny head to her chest. She had a family to raise and a farm to keep. She didn't know how she was going to do it, but by grace and by God, she knew she would!

Chapter 17
A Better Way

"Aunt Helen?"

Helen wiped her dough-crusted hands on her apron and strode toward the front door. She was desperately trying to make sure she had enough dough for all the pies she was intending to make in advance of the huckleberry harvest. Pies for the McClures, who lived in the holler around the bend; pies for Jack and the poor families in his parish on whose behalf he begged for simple luxuries like pickled beets and fresh baked pie; pies for the roadside farmer's market where she could earn an extra eight dollars for each one sold to flatlanders who were passing through, lured by what seemed like exotic Appalachian fare. Now if only Emma Louise would quit interrupting her!

"What is it now, Emma?" Helen called out, sure to keep her voice soft and low. Emma Louise was a sensitive girl, and Helen worked hard to strike a balance between raising her up to be a soulful child while making sure she had the grit of a true Appalachian. She knew that Joan would have wanted it that way. She'd had a knack for making the people around her feel special without coddling them in the process. That was what Helen tried to do with Emma and Robbie Jr., though she knew she often fell short of the mark, hugging them too much when they cried and spoiling them with kisses in the morning sun. She was certain Hawk would've made darn sure neither one of them grew up sissified – yet she also knew that had he lived to raise them with her, he would've treated them like his very own, with the most diligent and tenderhearted care.

He'd already been five weeks cold in the grave; it was hard to believe how quickly the landscape had changed since then. It seemed that everything green was quickly turning purple or gold or red, ripe with late summer fruit or leafy with vegetation begging to be picked and pickled or pied before the land grew brown and lazy once more and the early snows came to put it to rest. She didn't know how she was going to get to it all, along with feeding and caring for a barn full of livestock. Most days she didn't think about the whole of it, just the one thing before her, trusting the rest to keep for another day. Come moonrise, she fell into bed dog tired, almost too tired to mourn the empty space beside her, but never tired enough to keep her imagination from seeing Hawk lying beside her, his keen blue eyes urging her to remain faithful to the charge.

"Look, Aunt Helen, there's a big fancy car a-comin' up the road! See it there?" She clapped her little hands together and squealed with excitement.

Helen stared at the sight of a long black limousine grinding up the dirt road, churning up the dust and bobbing in and out love holes with a clumsiness that betrayed its elegant stretch.

"Well that just doesn't make a speck of sense, now does it, Emma?"

Helen couldn't recall ever having seen a limousine within a hundred miles of Dock Watch Hollow. She thought them a citified wonder that most poor hillfolk would give their right arm to ride in, even just as far as to the market and back!

"What the devil and Tom Walker!" Helen exclaimed as the limousine veered in her direction, lumbering up the driveway until it stopped ten feet from the porch where she stood. She untied her apron and tossed it on the swing, then put her hand to her brow to deflect the glare that bounced off the shiny black panels and made it even harder to see through the darkly tinted windows.

The smooth hum of the engine ceased. Helen took Emma's hand, thankful that Robbie Jr. was down for a nap. And where, she wondered, was that dog of hers when she needed him? Probably still a-chasing that wily rooster down by the barn!

She felt her breath stutter in her chest as the rear door swung open and a pair of familiar brown sandals touched the ground.

"Frankie?" Helen cried out, afraid she was seeing

a haint.

"Helen!" I shouted gleefully. I thought she would run to greet me but she stood frozen in wonder and awe as yet another pair of sandaled feet emerged from the back seat of the limousine. She struggled for a moment to recall the time and circumstances that matched the smiling, apple-cheeked face.

"Tess? Is that you?"

"Hello, Helen," she answered shyly.

"Lordy, who else is in there?" Helen called out in a voice that resonated with disbelief.

"Just me," Dorothy said, maneuvering her tall, willowy body through the doorframe and standing tall in a ray of golden sunlight.

"Now exactly how is it that y'all managed to get to Dock Watch Hollow in a stretch limousine?" Helen began to laugh at the sight of us saints from the city covered in dust and wonder at the spectacle of Rattlesnake Mountain's majestic peak.

"It's an embarrassment, that's all I can say about it," Dorothy said gruffly.

"C'mon Dorothy, don't be that way. It was a gift, remember?" Tess said softly.

"A gift?" Helen echoed as she began to descend the porch stairs with Emma's hand held fast to hers.

"Yes, from Joseph," Tess volunteered.

"Joseph?" Helen repeated.

"He owns a cab company in the city. When he heard the three of us were looking for a way to get to Dock Watch Hollow he offered to lend us a driver and a cab. Only he didn't have any cabs to spare, so he sent us down in one of his limousines instead," Tess explained. "He says he's a friend of yours, Helen, is that true?"

"Yes," Helen said, recalling Joseph's paternal care and kindness. "It's true."

"He said he would have liked to come himself but he had another commitment. He sends his blessings and says he might even join us sometime soon. I hear he's a pretty handy fellow to have around."

"I don't understand," Helen said, stepping closer yet clearly wary of our intentions. She wanted to reach out and hug us. Or maybe pinch us. But she didn't.

"Why are you here?" she finally said after a long, thoughtful pause.

"We're here to help you run the farm, Helen. Dorothy's got a lot of experience with that kind of thing and Tess – well, she's got a really green thumb when it comes to cultivating all kinds of plants, especially roses. And as for me," I said, throwing out my arms to each side, "I can assure you I'm the most joyful beggar you'll ever meet. I think I can help you rustle up whatever it is you'll need to care for your family…as well as the children of want who live in these hills and hollers."

"You mean you want to turn this into a community farm of some sort?"

"Yes," Dorothy chimed in. "That's a good way of putting it. Imagine the possibilities, Helen. We could feed and care for more people than each of us could ever do alone. Maybe some people would come here for prayer and refuge, some would come for food, others might come for a sense of family. But all of them would come to work. This is a fine plot of land, Helen, and I'm sure you could use the extra hands."

Helen stared at the three of us, shaking her head in disbelief as Emma tugged on the hem of her shirt, awaiting an introduction. "How did you even know where to find me? Or what I needed just when I needed it most?"

"Word travels fast on the street," I said. "It's no secret what happened between you and your husband."

"And we just want to say how sorry we are for your loss," Tess interjected.

"You mean Todd?"

"No, we mean Hawk."

Helen's lips trembled at the sound of his name. I could see the confusion in her face as she pondered how we could've possibly known about the sorrows that had come to pass. I wanted to tell her that what happened to Hawk was a cautionary tale as old as time: that the Prince of Darkness is constantly on the prowl, eager to sink his teeth into souls who belong to the Supreme Enemy, who is God. But Hawk had died forgiven and redeemed. It was a conversion that took all of us by surprise, myself chief among doubters. But my Master continues, in this day and time, to reveal the depths of His divine mercy, which exceeds His justice toward those who seek Him with a contrite heart. Instead, I merely echoed the wisdom of the apostle, Paul. "Our true citizenship is in Heaven, Helen. Surely you believe that Hawk's spirit lives on."

"I want to believe that, Frankie." At Jack's bidding, she had opened her heart to the possibility that someday she would receive a sign that the veil between the citizens of heaven and earth was as thin as the iridescent wings of the katynippers whose dying numbers announced the end of summer was near. Their fleeting yet intense existence reminded her of Hawk's valiant life – and death – even more so than the glorious raptors streaking across the sky on lofty currents of rapidly cooling air. Surely God had too much imagination to simply send a red-tailed hawk to comfort and console her! And so she continued to wait and watch and wonder when – and if – that day of holy reckoning would come.

"So what do you think of our proposal, Helen?" Tess asked at Dorothy's nudging.

"Well, I think it's awfully ambitious, don't you?"

"Then let's take it one task at a time," I suggested. "How can we help you?"

"Well, I *was* just making some huckleberry pies," Helen said, no longer interested in answers to the great unknowns before her. She glanced down at the silver bracelet on her wrist, a sure reminder that there were some things in life that were simply meant to be gift and mystery. In fact, she never questioned our appearance on her doorstep again, choosing in the days and months and years that followed to make each of us – and all those who would come after us – feel useful on the farm, in the kitchen, or in the work of prayer, each in his or her own beautiful way.

It was a mere seven months after our arrival that my Master called me home once more. With a final kiss of peace on Helen's cheek, I departed from this earth singing psalms of thanks and praise, just as I have done time and again for the past several hundred years in times and places of the Lord's own choosing.

Helen laid my mortal body to rest next to Hawk's. She thought it was fitting that the two men she loved most, both of whom had entered her heart through the portal of St. Paul's Soup Kitchen, should be buried side by side. The next morning, just after sunrise, she laid a fresh batch of yellow daffodils on my grave, then meandered along the banks of Parson's Branch till it bottomed out in a pool of tranquil water that was reedy and brown.

She was surprised by the sight of a tow-haired boy about the age of twelve perched on the edge of a wide flat rock. He clutched a fishing pole made out of poplar in his hands and dangled his bare feet in the shimmering water, his gaze fixed on a piece of cork bobbing on the surface. She called out to him as she approached.

"Fish biting today?"

"No ma'am, not yet. I've never fished this hole, but I'll get the hang of it yet."

"What's on the end of your line?" Helen asked.

"Earthworm."

"Catfish around here like bread. And hot dogs," Helen volunteered.

"Really?"

"Really." Helen laughed at his surprise.

"Maybe I'll try that next time. Thank you, ma'am."

"My name is Helen."

"I'm Gunner Brown."

"Nice to meet you, Gunner," Helen replied. "I live in the holler just around the creek bend and over the second hill. I got a couple of young'uns who like to fish. Maybe we could meet up sometime. I'll bring the hot dogs."

"Sure," Gunner said. Helen suspected he was merely being polite.

"Heck, I'll bet you'll have already caught a golly-whopper by then."

"Maybe," he shrugged. "But I'd take it kindly if you'd show me a better way."

Helen smiled, convinced of his sincerity. "If you want, we'll come on Saturday morning round about this time. Will you be here?"

Gunner set down his fishing pole and turned toward Helen, his piercing blue eyes filled with morning sunlight that bounced off the water.

"God willing, Miss Helen..." he said, allowing the sentence to dangle like a strand of pearls. She waited for him to continue, but he didn't. He merely picked up his fishing pole and went back to

wiggling his toes in the cool, life-giving waters of spring.

"...and the creek don't rise..." Helen finished as the eternal refrain of Hawk's love and fidelity echoed within and soothed her soul. Gunner's wide grin expressed his satisfaction. She lingered in the moment, intrigued by both the sign and the vague familiarity of the one who had revealed it. I prayed she might yet learn to trust the eyes of faith.

She never did see Gunner Brown again; after awhile she stopped looking for him, taking him for just another come-by-chance child who was at the mercy of his momma's deep poverty and shame. She didn't have time to lament the loss. God knows, there were a dozen more like him back at the farm to love and nourish each day with fattened calves and fresh, green peas and lonesome water that flowed from cool mountain springs, passing over lips and into hearts and seeping into proud, Appalachian souls where it could never be forgotten.

And if for a time it seemed as though it was...well, there was a certain someone Helen knew she could patronize for help, someone who was as near as the beating of her own heart and the new life inside her that was soon to be born and baptized with those same lonesome waters. She smiled at the thought and then set her mind to fixing a fresh batch of buttermilk biscuits, as sweet and golden as the Appalachian sunlight on her face.

May your love draw down upon you the mercy of the Lord, and may He let you see that within your soul a saint is sleeping. I shall ask Him to make you so open and supple that you will be able to understand and do what He wants you to do. Your life is nothing; it is not even your own. Each time you say "I'd like to do this or that," you wound Christ, robbing Him of what is His. You have to put to death everything within you except the desire to love God. This is not at all hard to do. It is enough to have confidence and to thank the little Jesus for all the potentialities he has placed within you. You are called to holiness, like me, like everyone. Don't forget.

— Jacques Fesch

Printed in the United States
210531BV00001B/3/P

9 781432 711047